TRAIL OF
Deception

OTHER TITLES BY AMANDA MCKINNEY

On the Edge Series

Buried Deception

Steele Shadows Series

Cabin 1 (Steele Shadows Security)

Cabin 2 (Steele Shadows Security)

Cabin 3 (Steele Shadows Security)

Phoenix (Steele Shadows Rising)

Jagger (Steele Shadows Investigations)

Ryder (Steele Shadows Investigations)

Her Mercenary (Steele Shadows Mercenaries)

Road Series

Rattlesnake Road

Redemption Road

Broken Ridge Series

The Viper

TRAIL OF
Deception

On the Edge Series, Book 2

AMANDA
MCKINNEY

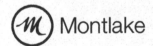

Published by Montlake, Seattle

www.apub.com

Amazon, the Amazon logo, and Montlake are trademarks of Amazon.com, Inc., or its affiliates.

ISBN-13: 9781662500589 (paperback)
ISBN-13: 9781662500602 (digital)

Cover design by Caroline Teagle Johnson
Cover image: © Nestor Rodan / ArcAngel; © Cavan Images / Getty;
© Leslie Taylor / Stocksy United

Printed in the United States of America

For Mama

Chapter One

I dipped my finger into the slit in her skin. Dragged and swirled it around the soft, cushiony layer of fat.

Once I was certain the tip of my finger was saturated, I examined the color. Her blood was a dark rust, the vibrancy of the red muted by the growing darkness, by the haze of fog that was beginning to settle within the woods. Around her, around me.

The smell hit me like a drug. That distinct sweet, metallic scent, bolstered by the fragrance of the longleaf pines crowding the thicket where I'd chosen to create my next masterpiece.

There's nothing else like the scent of blood. Nothing. No drug, no amount of alcohol, no memory, can deliver an instant rush like that of a bleeding human.

In training, I had learned that blood is one of the most stimulating olfactory cues in the human body. Our automatic response to it is buried deep in our subconscious. The cue taps into our survival instinct, something that lives deep within our genetic makeup, originating from primal times when fighting for mere existence was done by fists and swords, not test tubes and artificial intelligence.

For better or worse, I believe that I connect with those primal times more than most people do. It's something special. A gift I've been given. One that I was only just beginning to enjoy.

Inhaling deeply, I closed my eyes and tapped into my inner artist, cataloging the feelings and emotions swimming through my body. Excitement, delight, pride, arousal. I took in the sounds around me. The winter wind howling through the trees, their barren branches ticking against each other. The tap, tap, tap of a woodpecker somewhere nearby, searching for sustenance in the frigid temperatures. I zeroed in on the feeling of the tiny droplets of fog slowly saturating my pores.

Then I focused inward, aware of my beating heart, the feel of the blood pumping through it, pulsing through my veins. I allowed each sensation to filter into my consciousness and form the vision of what would become my next piece of art.

Once centered, I began.

There, in the middle of the woods and under the cover of nature, I painted her naked body, bleeding brushstrokes over her pale skin.

Carefully, I dragged the tip of the knife vertically along her arms and legs, severing one artery after another, watching the blood pop to the surface and slowly seep down soft folds of skin, creating a new path for me to paint, to explore.

Her blood was different, I realized as it began to cover my hands and arms. Darker. I'd never seen blood so dark. Why? Why was she different? Slowly, I rubbed the slick blood between my fingertips, studying the essence of my latest kill.

Excited now, I refocused on the canvas. Slowly, the lines of blood blended to form shapes, an interpretation of my innermost thoughts in physical form.

This application of art never ceases to amaze me. The transformation of paint to canvas to creation. A journey of each element coming together to tell a story, one that most of the time, only a few understand. It's a narrative that highlights our strengths and weaknesses, the paths that we've walked, the ebbs and flows of life. All right there in the painting.

Right there on her body.

Of those lucky enough to see this particular creation of art, each would have a completely different interpretation of it. Isn't that an interesting thought? This, the beauty of art. Everyone's interpretation is different.

Me? My views are a bit unusual; I know this. Then again, I am unusual.

For example, when you think of blood, you probably think of pain and suffering. Of death. Or, depending on how you've allowed your experiences to shape your perspective, perhaps blood reminds you of life. A baby being brought into the world. An essential courier of oxygen and nutrients to our organs that allows us to thrive.

Regardless of your interpretation, one meaning is shared across all cultures. The color red is potent. The symbolism and interpretation of the color are potent.

Red is violence, anger, aggression: potent.

Red is love and physical passion: potent.

Red is the color of life beating through our veins: potent.

It's the color of war, of courage: potent.

For me, however, it's about power. It's the ability to control the most coveted thing on the planet—human life. The ability to take it away, or to revive it.

She was my fourth victim. My fourth sacrifice. And what a masterpiece she was.

I looked up at the waning light. I could smell the snow on the air.

Yes, something was coming. A storm was brewing. I could feel it in my bones.

One that the small town of Skull Hollow would never see coming.

Chapter Two

Jo

I kicked my boots up onto my desk and leaned back in the oversize black leather chair I'd received from Sweden the day before. An authentic, ergonomic Scandinavian office chair, tailor-made to fit my body. An extravagant purchase, but considering my job as the only psychiatrist at the Dragonfly Clinic has kept me behind my desk 90 percent of the time, I decided it was worth it. My bank account, on the other hand, had a very different opinion.

I took a sip of coffee.

My mind was blank, failing to interpret the collage of images I'd spent hours strategically tacking onto my office wall. As if someone had simply pulled the plug, like the forgotten Zoltar machine left on a vacant, littered lot long after the carnival had packed up and moved on.

That was me. A flurry of ideas, thoughts, plans, and then *bam*. The inevitable mental block that stops them all.

My eyes stung from focusing for so long. Frustration brewed.

Would my patients have a similar reaction to taking this test?

Chewing on my lower lip, I stared at the ten inkblot cards tacked on the wall. The Rorschach test, a dated and controversial psychological test that analyzed a patient's interpretation of seemingly random patterns of ink.

I'd become fascinated with it.

Mindlessly, I sipped again, then slid the mug onto my desk, sending a stack of papers teetering off the side and fluttering to the floor.

Ignoring the whisper of an urge to pick them up, I lifted the cigarillo from the ashtray and, while studying the pictures, gently rolled the tip against the crystal ashtray. *Tap, tap, tap.* The ashes floated to the bottom like tiny feathers on the wind. Another mindless behavior I could do in my sleep.

I took a deep drag, allowing the thick vanilla-flavored smoke to roll around my mouth. Then, craning my neck like a turtle emerging from its shell, I leaned back in the chair and blew the stream of smoke out the window I'd cracked open.

It was a bitterly cold, dark, and gloomy day.

Heavy cloud cover blanketed the winter sky. Big billowing clouds had rolled in, bringing with them an undercurrent of tension that I could feel in each of my clients. They were wired and restless.

According to the weatherman, the small southern town of Skull Hollow was in for one of the worst ice storms in decades. Temperatures had fallen well below normal, sending the citizens into a flurry of activity, preparing for what was surely the end of times.

Freezing weather was uncommon in this part of the state, ice even rarer.

Skull Hollow was nothing more than a dot, a blip in the vast, untamed wilderness in the Piney Woods of Southeast Texas. Known for its diverse landscape, the region was home to nine different ecosystems, including longleaf pine forests, cypress-lined bayous, rolling hills, and murky wetlands. Tourists from all across the country flocked to the area year round. Most were nature lovers, but some, however, sought the adventures of the dark side of the forest. A very dark side that included bears, black panthers, wolves, alligators, and hundreds of ghost stories and creepy legends sure to keep you up for days.

I imagined the dark, ominous atmosphere of that day in particular attracted an unsavory type of tourist.

It did feel like something was coming, I thought as I stared out the window at the rolling terrain of tall loblolly pines, their branches sagging as if weeping from the cold. The usually vibrant, lively forest appeared bleak and lonely. Haunting almost.

I settled back, refocusing on the images on the wall.

I need to give it a rest, I thought as my vision blurred and the edges of the ink began to merge as one, creating an entirely new set of images.

Odd, I thought, how fluid the brain is in its interpretations.

What did *I* see? What did *I* feel?

Stressed. That's what I felt.

Edgy. Distracted. An unwelcome state that had become more and more common over the last few years.

I looked down at the small space underneath my desk. Then I glanced at the office door, confirming it was tightly closed.

My chair creaked as I lowered my boots to the floor and pushed back. I bent at the waist, reaching for the small safe hidden in the shadows. As if having a mind of their own, my fingertips found the small dial that served as the lock.

My pulse started to increase.

Then the office door flew open.

Startled, I surged upward, slamming my head on the underside of my desk.

"*Christ*, Jo, it smells like a strip club in here. And what are you doing with a window open? It's, like, forty below zero outside."

Rubbing the knot already forming at the crown of my head, I righted myself in my seat. "Good to see you, too, Mia. It's thirty-five degrees, and I can't close the window if you want it smelling any less than a stripper joint."

"Well, it's *freezing* in here."

"Pick one. Cold or stinky?"

Mia, the clinic's psychologist, rolled her eyes. (A trait common in the profession, I've come to realize.) "I want you to throw away your cigars."

"Ain't happening, sweetheart. And I told you, I don't inhale."

"Right. Then why do it?"

"What's with the mood?"

Mia launched a pair of keys into the air before sinking like deadweight into the chair opposite my desk. She was . . . styled oddly. Her long brown hair was pulled into a frizzed ponytail. A pair of tortoiseshell glasses sat a bit crookedly on her nose. Her usual tailored suit had been replaced by a ridiculously baggy sweater adorned with a crocheted kitten missing one button for an eye and some sort of yoga pants that were supposed to pass for skinny jeans.

I glanced at the clock, realizing I hadn't seen her all day. It was just past three in the afternoon. Had Mia just gotten in?

"I just found those in the refrigerator," she said with more attitude than I was comfortable with.

I looked at the keys she'd just tossed at me, now in my palm. They were mine.

"Huh. In the fridge, you said?" I shrugged, then tossed them onto the floor, next to my purse. "Better than the microwave like last week, right?"

Mia didn't laugh. She'd gotten used to my disorganized, absent-minded ways, but that didn't mean she accepted them. Apparently, my partner in crime was still upset that *I* was responsible for almost burning the place down when *she* had heated up her Lean Cuisine without noticing the keys inside.

"I thought you were going to put one of those digital tracker thingies on them," she said, dramatically running her hand over the top of her head as if it took every ounce of energy she had to even speak to me.

7

"I did get one of those thingies, but I kept forgetting to charge the batteries in it." I regarded the mess that was my best friend. "But I'm going to go out on a limb here and say that my occasional absentmindedness isn't what's got you in this vile mood?"

Mia sighed. "No. I'm sorry. I spent the last twenty-four hours with my head in the toilet." She groaned, scrubbing her hands over her face—which was a bit green, come to think of it.

Shit.

I promptly stomped out the tip of my cigarillo, grabbed the box fan from the corner, clicked it on high, and blew the smoke out the window.

Why was it so damn hard for me to remember that my best friend was pregnant? Oh yeah—because babies were as foreign a concept to me as the diamond ring that had recently shown up on her left hand.

Mia went on, and as I knew what was meant to be my role at that moment, I sat quietly and listened.

This, by the way, was a new thing in our friendship. Before Mia met Easton Crew, the handsome CEO of the LYNX Group, she'd been a locked box. Mia Frost had been an absolute pro at keeping her emotions tucked deep inside and rarely spoke about anything personal—a defense mechanism I understood far too well. But since tumbling madly in love with Easton, Mia had become a wonder of taxicab confessions. Constantly talking about this and that, her likes, her dislikes, her *feelings*.

I was completely flummoxed by this new woman. I didn't understand her. How was it that the simple act of falling in love could change someone so much?

Or was it the pregnancy, perhaps? A combination of both?

Regardless, this drastic personality shift fascinated me. People spent thousands of dollars on therapy to accomplish what Easton Crew had done with only three little words.

Love. Was it really that powerful?

I forced my focus back on the vomit story.

"Does this explain the sweater?" I asked, frowning at the disfigured kitten that would surely visit me in my nightmares.

Mia sniffed, nodding. "I haven't done laundry in days. Everything else has puke on it. My grandma knitted this for me in the eighth grade."

"Your grandmother knitted in the eighth grade?"

"No, I was in the eighth grade when she gave it to me. And the worst part about it all is that Easton won't leave me alone. He's constantly by my side, doing this, doing that, asking—*my God*, the *questions*. And he's so damn busy—he should leave me alone and deal with work."

Understanding, I nodded.

The LYNX Group, a prestigious tactical-tracking company, had recently been catapulted to success after signing a contract with the United States government to train select soldiers in the specialty of combat tracking. A lost art form in a world driven by technology, according to Mia's fiancé. The company was in talks to expand its responsibilities to work alongside federal agents, something that was apparently giving Easton Crew and his business partner, Beckett Stolle, quite the headache.

"Isn't that how it's supposed to be?" I asked. "Isn't he *not* supposed to leave you alone right now? Isn't the man supposed to hold your hand through this incredible journey of the creation of life?"

Mia narrowed her eyes. "You read a pamphlet, didn't you?"

I lifted the folded paper, front and center on my desk, that I'd taken with me from my last OB-GYN checkup. The pamphlet was one of many free educational materials the clinic offered. Its theme, understanding a woman's emotional journey through pregnancy. I thought it might help me relate to my "new" best friend.

"Anyway," she snapped, as if I'd been the one to interrupt her, "yes, Easton is supposed to hold my hand through this journey, but not when I'm literally vomiting my guts into the toilet. No man needs to see that."

"Every man needs to see that," I said with a wink. "Just like every man needs to buy a box of tampons at the store, walk five minutes in six-inch stilettos, wrestle their way into a pair of Spanx, and squeeze a living, breathing human out of their body."

Mia released a long, exasperated, antacid-laced exhale as she sank deeper into the leather chair—and that was when she noticed, for the first time, the collage of pictures that covered my office wall.

She gaped at the wall. "What the hell is *all* that?"

I cleared my throat and swallowed the sudden flutter of insecurity. "Inkblot tests."

"Yeah, I know. I'm familiar with the Rorschach inkblot test. I'm curious why you have them posted all over your office like a psych ward." She looked at me, frowning. "Do you have an appointment with a schizophrenic or something?"

"No, that was last week."

"Okay then, talk. What is this about? And by the way, your mother would kill you."

I cringed, my gaze darting across the tiny thumbtack holes that now speckled the wall.

Mia was right. My newly divorced, now-has-more-money-than-she-knows-what-to-do-with mother would have a heart attack if she saw the desecration of the office she had spent hours designing and had paid someone else to renovate.

When we'd purchased the building to open our first mental health clinic, four years earlier, we'd hired my mother to renovate. In under six months, Melinda Bellerose had turned the weathered barn Mia had purchased into a stunning two-story sanctuary with exposed beams, gleaming hardwood floors, and floor-to-ceiling windows that flooded the space with natural light. Worthy of a feature in *Architectural Digest*, according to the headline of the local news story that ran on it.

Intrigued now, Mia sat up straight in the chair and scanned the room, looking over her shoulder. Then her head snapped back toward me like the exorcist, her finger pointing to the back of my office.

"What the hell is *that*?"

"Well, Mia, those are called easels, and next to them are paint-brushes, and that's paint, and—"

"Stop, smartass. I can't." Mia jabbed her palms against her eyes and sank back into the chair. "I'm just gonna need you to go ahead and talk, Jo."

I took a deep breath, and after a brief moment of hesitation, allowed Mia to enter into my twisted thoughts.

The ones that had kept me awake for the last three months.

Chapter Three

Jo

"You said you're familiar with the Rorschach inkblot test, right?" I said to Mia.

"Yes, from what I remember from school, yes."

"Well then, allow me to give you a refresher."

Mia rolled her hand with a flourish. "Refresh away."

"The inkblot test consists of ten cards with ambiguous ink patterns. Some are black or gray. Others contain applications of color. The test taker is asked to provide their perceptions on each card—basically, what they see when they look at the card. The results are recorded and then examined to look for patterns of thought disorders, like schizophrenia, depression, psychosis, anxiety, and, on the flip side, elevated levels of intelligence."

I stood, a sudden rush of energy tingling through me, and walked to the cards on the wall.

"But that's not all—and this is where my interest comes in. The results can also help tap into past trauma in the test taker's life. One that he or she might not even realize is a ruling factor in every single decision they've made in their life." I spun around. "How fucking powerful is that?"

"Pretty fucking powerful."

I wasn't sure if Mia's response was genuine or if she was simply placating me.

Regardless, I continued, gesturing to a card on the wall. "What do you see here? On this card?"

Mia regarded the inkblot closely. "I see two people fighting, kind of like sumo-wrestling stuff. I see blood and chaos—and quite frankly, it makes me a little uncomfortable. God, you're weird, Jo."

"Exactly—but not about the weird part. So you, Mia Frost, are interpreting this ambiguous, innocent little smear of ink as anger. Why? Because *you're* angry. Why? Because you spent the last twenty-four hours vomiting up your guts and realizing your body now exists only to serve as a vessel to grow another human being."

"I think you need therapy, Jo."

"You're probably right." I returned my focus to the card. "So, when *I* look at this card, I don't see two people fighting. I see something totally different. I see two people in a meditative position, their palms pressed together in front of their hearts, their heads bowed. Peaceful. I see peace in this image."

"So, the total opposite of me—maybe I'm the one who needs therapy."

"Maybe, maybe not, but your perception is by far the most common. There are a lot of angry people walking around in this world; trust me on that. Most people say this image looks like two animals fighting. My point is, these little inkblots can reveal a great deal about you."

"Okay, so I'm angry, and you've laced your cigar with something." I winked.

Mia gestured to the canvases and easels in the back of the room. "This doesn't explain the art shop behind me."

I walked to the back of my office. "Well, okay . . . so . . ."

I hesitated, realizing I was nervous. Shy to reveal the idea I felt so passionate about to my best friend. And what did that say about me?

"Spit it out, Jo," she said.

"Well, I figure if the interpretation of staring at an inkblot can reveal so much about a patient, think of how much can be revealed by simply handing the patient a paintbrush, a block of colors, and a canvas and seeing what they come up with."

"I hate to break it to you, sweetheart, but that's called art therapy, and it's already done in pretty much every country in the entire world."

"But not here. Not here at the Dragonfly Clinic."

Mia arched a brow. "Good point."

"Right? I think we should add both inkblot testing and art therapy into our diagnostic procedures. I've read a ton of articles about it and taken a few online classes, and I've also contacted someone about getting my state certification. I think it'll be fun and interesting. Fresh, you know? I'd like to set it up as a medical study of sorts for myself—maybe publish it when I'm done."

As Mia stared at me with an unreadable expression, I felt my heart stutter.

Finally, she said, "I love it. I think it's an awesome idea."

I exhaled. "Good, because I've already expensed the paint supplies."

Mia laughed. "This doesn't surprise me." Then her smile dropped, and her face turned green. Her cheeks began to expand.

I frowned. "Mia? Are you—"

She shot out of the chair and lunged toward the bathroom. Responding in kind, I rushed after her, gathering her hair as she threw herself over the toilet and retched.

And retched.

And retched.

Bile rose to the back of my throat, and sweat began to bead on my forehead.

I'd never been good with vomit. Who is?

I closed my eyes, willing my now-churning stomach to calm, when suddenly, by me—

14

"Oh . . . my . . ." Luna Raimi froze midstride into the bathroom.

Peeking through one eye, I feigned a smile.

"Gawd." Luna covered her nose and mouth with the paisley-print shawl that draped over her shoulders. A pair of faded boyfriend jeans and flip-flops—despite the frigid temperatures—completed her usual hippie, earth-child look.

Luna was the Dragonfly Clinic's newest hire. Specializing in cognitive behavioral therapy, she embraced the unconventional therapeutic methods that the clinic had quickly become known for, integrating exposure therapy into her work plan. Luna was the yin to my leather-wearing, cigar-smoking yang, known for her relaxed demeanor, her boho-chic style, and her closet full of shawls and caftans.

Breathing through my mouth, I said, "Luna, come on in."

Mia groaned, then gagged again.

Scrunching her face in disgust, Luna took a reluctant step farther into the bathroom. It was then that I noticed her puffy eyes and flushed cheeks. She looked like she'd just woken up from a cat nap, or, more likely, had just emerged from her afternoon meditation.

Luna dropped her hand from her mouth and smoothed back her long blonde hair, taking a moment to gather her inner badassery.

"Have a seat," I said. "Actually, no, why don't you grab that strand of hair that's falling into Mia's face?"

Luna shot me a look of pure horror.

I jerked my chin toward the strand of hair that Mia was now gumming like a fish gasping for air.

Using two fingertips, Luna plucked the hair off Mia's pale face, dropping it like a ticking bomb on the top of her head. "Mia," she whispered loudly. "Do you want me to get you some Pepto or something?"

Mia lifted her head slightly. "Pepto doesn't help morning sickness, you idiot."

Luna looked at me, shrugging helplessly.

"Stella!" I yelled out the door. "We need some peppermint tea up here, stat."

"Stop yelling," Mia grumbled.

"Sorry."

"Uh . . ." Luna looked at me. "I came up here to ask if you wanted me to reschedule Mrs. Morris's appointment for you."

"What appointment?"

"The one you missed at noon today. When you didn't show, she wandered up to my office. Thanks for that, by the way."

"Jo," Mia snapped. "This is the third appointment you've forgotten or been late for in the last few weeks."

I cringed. I'd taken my lunch to the local library, where I'd immersed myself in books about Hermann Rorschach, the Swiss psychiatrist and founder of the inkblot test—and lost track of time, apparently.

"Sorry. I'll call her before I leave today to reschedule."

Ⅾ

Five minutes later, my postage-stamp-size bathroom was packed with the three most important women in my life, who had become like family to me.

I was seated next to Mia on the bathroom floor, opposite the toilet. Luna hovered above us, fanning Mia with the latest edition of *Parenting* magazine. (I would have gone with *Vogue*.) Stella, our office manager, perched on the sink, her long curly red hair matching her silky red slacks. She was an explosion of color against the muted beige of the bathroom and the dreary afternoon.

Stella had news. "I just heard they've officially declared that girl a missing person."

"What girl?" Luna asked.

"Aria Ledger."

"The autistic girl," I said, which was what the media had uncouthly labeled her as if her diagnosis was her complete identity.

"What are you talking about?" Mia asked, lifting her head from between her knees.

"Aria Ledger," I said, "age seventeen, reported missing four hours ago. I got an alert on my phone about it."

"I thought they couldn't officially declare someone a missing person until they'd been MIA for twenty-four hours."

"Rules are different when that person has a significant mental disorder."

"What?" Mia frowned. "I hadn't heard . . ."

"Because you've spent the day with your head in the toilet."

Stella continued, reciting the latest news of Skull Hollow with the polish and enthusiasm of a seasoned journalist. "Aria's mother, Jamie Ledger, says Aria stayed home from school today because she wasn't feeling well and spent the morning doing schoolwork and listening to music. When Aria didn't come out of her room for hours, Mom went to check on her. Aria was gone, as was Mom's car—Aria doesn't have her own car. Mom called the cops, and considering the girl's medical condition, they sent out an alert immediately."

"So, Aria took her mom's car without asking?"

"Allegedly, yes."

"And hasn't been seen or heard from since?"

"Right. According to Charlene at the Sunrise Café—oh my gawd, she cut her hair, by the way, you've got to see it—tips began flooding the station the moment the alert was sent out. Two people—one local, one tourist—mentioned seeing Jamie's car, a gunmetal-gray SUV, parked at Camper's Hollow around midday."

"It is there now?"

"Nope."

"Camper's Hollow?" Luna frowned. "That campground off County Road 49? The one that's supposed to be haunted?"

"Haunted? Why am I so out of the loop here?" Mia asked, her frown deepening.

"Yeah. A long time ago, Camper's Hollow was a gathering site for a satanic cult or something. They'd meet there to perform some sort of ritual under full moons. Rumor is, one night, they all became possessed, sat in a circle, and shot each other in the head, execution style, one by one, until the last guy shot himself. You guys ever heard of Old Man Marshall?"

Mia, clearly not impressed with the rumors—or the spreading of them, perhaps—rolled her eyes. "Oh, come on, Stella."

"Who's Old Man Marshall?" I asked.

"He's been a widower for, like, ever. Big hunter. Stays at the campground every year during deer-hunting season. Anyway, he said he sees them every now and again."

"Sees who?"

"The cult, their spirits. Supposedly, they'll come out on a full moon and circle your tent, begin humming some weird shit, and then gunshots echo in the distance. And then they're gone."

"What happened to Marshall's wife?" I asked, questioning the validity of the old hunter.

"Got run over by a logging truck."

"Oh my *Gawd.*" Mia rolled her eyes again. "Can we please—"

"Would be interesting to know if Aria has any interest in ghost stories, folklore, local legends," I said, thinking out loud.

"Is autism her only condition?" Luna asked.

"Yes, but apparently, she has significant symptoms."

I looked out the small bathroom window at the cold gray landscape beyond it. "Are there a lot of people camping right now?"

"Doubt it. On account of the weather."

"It's supposed to freeze tonight," Mia said.

Stella nodded. "I know. That's why they've organized a search and rescue op. They're hoping to find Aria before nightfall, or worst-case scenario, before the ice storm hits in a few days." She looked at her watch. "The search is starting right about now."

Mia blinked, fully alert now and a little less green around her mouth. "Wait a second—that's right. I got a text from Easton about thirty minutes ago saying that he and his team got called out to a job. Said he'd be late getting home. This must be it—LYNX must have been called in to help search for her."

"The storm is supposed to be bad," Luna said. "Several rounds of sleet starting tomorrow, I think, then two or three inches of ice on top of it—all in a few days."

Stella nodded. "Yeah—don't even try to go to the grocery store. Milk, bread, toilet paper, everything is gone."

"Did Aria have a boyfriend?" Luna asked, reading my thoughts.

Stella shook her head. "Not that I've heard. Not many friends either."

"Due to her autism?" I asked. "Social interaction challenges?"

Stella shrugged.

"Well . . ." Mia shuddered. "I hope they find her before the ice hits."

The room fell silent for a moment. The sudden unease was palpable.

As usual, it was Luna who broke the silence and said what every one of us was thinking.

"Did you hear that guy officially got a name?"

"You mean the serial killer who attacks random young women, slices them to shreds with a hunting knife, and then paints them in their own blood?"

"Yep—that's the one. The media has officially dubbed him the Pollock Butcher."

My stomach plummeted.

"Pollock Butcher? Why?" Mia asked.

"Jackson Pollock," I said, the room falling silent at the sudden change of my tone. "He was an American painter. I read about him recently while researching art therapy, actually."

"I've heard of him. What kind of art?"

"Abstract art, but he's most known for using something called a drip technique on his paintings. It's the process of splattering or dripping paint all over a canvas, creating a total mess of interlacing and overlapping color. It's chaos personified. Makes me itch just looking at them."

"I'm familiar with that," Luna said. "It was all the rage for a while. But he didn't just drip or splatter the paint, there was a process to it, right? He'd use different strokes or speeds to splatter the paint, creating different kinds of paintings."

"And this is why they named the serial killer the Pollock Butcher. Because this is what he does to his victims . . . paints them in this way," Mia said, connecting the dots.

"Right," I said. "Except with blood. *Their* blood. He paints a pattern of waves over their torsos with their blood. Each pattern is similar but different."

It was a story that had quickly gained national headlines due to the brutal, grotesque manner of the slayings. The Pollock Butcher's first victim was found in a nature park in Houston, Texas, last April. A young, single mother had taken her baby for a walk. The baby was found crying in the stroller under a shade tree. The mother was found twenty yards away, her torso flayed open like the underbelly of a fish, her skin streaked in intricate patterns of her own blood.

A month later, the Butcher's second victim was found in a heavily wooded nature reserve in Waco. This victim was sliced open along the wrists and ankles with long, straight slices tracing the veins, and one down the center of her jugular. The woman was painted in the same manner, left to rot in a ditch.

The latest victim was found six months ago off a desolate county road in Tyler, Texas. Long, thin, gaping wounds like the others, except the killer had sliced open this one's scalp from front to back, like zebra stripes.

In each case, the medical report noted a single stab wound to the back of the neck on the victim. The working assumption was that this was how the Butcher made his initial attack. From behind, shocking and immobilizing his victims before dragging them into the nearby woods, where he would then strip them of their clothing and meticulously slice open their bodies. Each autopsy report noted that the women were still alive when he began cutting them. The reports also indicated that a tool or some sort of blunt object—possibly a paintbrush—had been inserted into the wounds, dipping into and stirring them like they were paint cans.

The women weren't raped or tortured before or after their deaths. No vaginal or anal penetration of any kind occurred. The killer left no DNA on their bodies. No one reported seeing the women before they were killed, nor was any unusual or odd behavior by the victims beforehand mentioned by friends or family. No security cameras or CCTV cameras recorded a suspicious person or a recurring mystery vehicle at any of the murder scenes.

There was also no commonality to the appearance of the women, and because of that, there was no way to determine victim typology, therefore, no way to build a psychological profile of the suspect or to protect women who fit the typology. All three victims had differing heights, weights, hair color, and ethnicities. The women's clothes were never found. Their cars, purses, wallets, and other belongings were untouched.

The slayings appeared to be random, the killer not interested in money or sex, just painting the women.

The combination of the lack of leads, absence of evidence, and macabre mystery had made for a harrowing, nightmarish tale that had quickly gripped the nation.

We looked around the room at each other, again thinking the same thing: had missing-person Aria Ledger, one of Skull Hollow's citizens, fallen prey to the Pollock Butcher?

Was the Butcher here? Now?

Luna shuddered, shook her head, and raised her palms as if to push the bad energy away. "Enough about that." She turned to Mia. "Mia, do you need us to stay with you tonight until Easton gets back? Make you soup, maybe?"

"No—God, *no*. All I want is to be left alone, something Easton doesn't seem to understand."

As Luna, Stella, and Mia fell into conversation about the idiosyncrasies of the male psyche—or lack thereof—I turned to the wall outside the bathroom, to the ten inkblot cards that covered it.

I paused on the one I'd questioned Mia about. And for the first time, I didn't see two people meditating. I didn't see peace.

For the first time, I saw blood.

Pain.

Death.

Rage.

Chapter Four

Beckett

I glanced up at the sky as I walked down a dusty footpath blanketed by brown pine needles.

Billowing, ominous gray clouds crowded overhead, unmoving, as if here to stay. On cue, a blast of cold air whipped past me, cutting through the fleece pullover I'd grabbed on the way out of the office. The forest moved around me, leaves and twigs falling to my feet.

Fucking cold. I wasn't a fan of the cold.

A torn piece of yellow "Do Not Cross" tape flapped wildly in a nearby bush, a crude warning of what lay just beyond its withered branches.

I checked my watch—4:07 p.m., yet it looked like dusk. Not ideal for a search and rescue mission. Nor was my mood, for that matter.

I inhaled, popped my neck from side to side.

I was late. I didn't do late well.

The trail took a turn, the woods opened up, and I stepped onto Camper's Hollow campground.

Lights were being erected around the command post that the LYNX Group had already established in the center of the grounds. A sign of the long night to come.

Scattered around the LYNX service truck were at least a dozen volunteers, a few police officers, and a group of wayward teens who had been drawn to the commotion like moths to a flame.

My jaw clenched.

Why the hell hadn't anyone run them off? There was no telling what potential tracks the kids, reveling in the excitement of what might or might not involve a dead body, were destroying as they buzzed around in the woods.

Bundled in heavy coats, scarves, and insulated overalls, the volunteers huddled in circles, bouncing from foot to foot to ward off the cold, coffee cups gripped in gloved hands. Loud, uncomfortable, excited voices buzzed like white noise in the frigid air.

Thankfully, the campground was vacant of tourists. According to the manager, they'd packed up early and gone home the moment the temperature dropped below fifty degrees.

The sour scent of cigarette smoke carried on the wind from a duo of cowboys huddled under a pine tree.

I held my breath as I passed. I couldn't stand cigarettes, the smell, the weakness of the person addicted to the buzz of the nicotine. I had no patience for weakness—or the chaos that was quickly overtaking the woods. What was usually a calm, low-key campground was now a flurry of activity.

Of all the groups that populated the campgrounds, one drew my attention immediately.

A group of local firefighters stood in a line off to the side of everyone else, like soldiers awaiting orders. Their faces were hard, their jaws tight with annoyance. They were unimpressed at the shit show in front of them. I couldn't blame them.

In contrast to the stoicism of his comrades, one man stood out from the rest. The missing girl's stepfather, Fire Chief Cyrus Ledger, paced back and forth like a caged animal, his face flushed and wild with adrenaline.

A few yards away stood his wife, Aria's mother, bundled in mismatched outerwear, a thick scarf, and a fuzzy beanie. She was a mess, sobbing into a tissue—reddened with either blood or lipstick, I couldn't tell. I assumed the latter.

I spotted Easton immediately, huddled in the corner of the grounds with Sheriff Andrew McNamara, likely reviewing the search plan. Next to him stood Dane Stratton, the LYNX Group's newest hire, an imposing and rather prickly presence that I'd responded positively to during his first interview. No small talk, no bullshit, all action. My kind of guy. In no time at all, it had become apparent that Dane had one hell of an analytical mind, and therefore, Easton was training him on operational planning.

Alek Romanov, grandson of a former Russian mob boss, stood off to the side, readying the packs that the volunteers would carry during the search. He'd taken his place in the shadows, alone, as he preferred. Good thing, too, because no one came within a ten-foot radius of the guy. Alek was almost as feared around town as the latest COVID variant.

There was no mistaking the men of LYNX from everyone else. It wasn't just the matching uniforms of khaki tactical pants and navy pull-overs adorned with the LYNX logo—the face of a panther—but also the commanding, calm-but-deadly presence of each man. We'd been trained to operate in this way. We were known as silent professionals, as it was called in the military. A soldier who had honed the ability to control his emotions as easily as delivering a single fatal blow to the head.

I was proud of my company, of the men we'd hired. I trusted them and no one else.

Especially on this mission.

A young, freckle-faced kid jogged up and thrusted the sign-in sheet at me. I slapped it out of his hand and kept walking.

There wasn't much else that I despised more than rules and red tape. And that was exactly why Easton Crew was the CEO of our company, and I'd accepted the title of the COO—despite my aversion to labels. In Easton's words, I had as much grace as a grizzly bear in a fish market. I didn't much disagree with this, other than the fish part. I hate fish.

Bottom line, I knew how to get things done, and ten times out of ten, it wasn't standing around and talking about how to do it.

Easton spotted me, lifted his chin in greeting, then jerked it to the group of firefighters standing along the tree line. I nodded and picked up my pace, my role now officially identified: I'd handle the people, and Easton would handle the analysis. That was why we made such a good team.

Missing-person cases contain two equally important elements: statistics and behavior.

Statistics provide probabilities of where the subject might be located and a general overview of the case. This strategic phase—what Easton was doing at the moment—includes a detailed investigation, determination of search areas and segments, development of the action plan, and assignment selection and briefings, otherwise known as my hell.

Easton is the statistics guy.

The behavioral element, on the other hand, relies on experience and instinct.

I'm the behavior guy.

My motto is "Know your enemy," or in this case, your victim.

Understanding your victim's motives and habits allows for greater tactical advantage. When you know these seemingly small details, you can apply them to your mission by hand selecting specific areas to search. This saves time, lending itself to a more targeted, fast-moving operation. And more often than not, *this* is the make-or-break in a life-and-death scenario.

But this isn't where the mission ends. There is still a major phase to be completed: the extraction of the victim. Once your victim is found, understanding their personality and behavior is key in a smooth extraction. I need to know things like:

Does the missing person have a history of dementia? Mental illness? Substance or drug abuse? Criminal behaviors? Has the victim ever been suicidal? If so, the search expert—me—must know how to handle these scenarios once contact is made.

One thing I'd learned in many years in both special ops and search and rescue was that the mental state of your target was directly linked to the success of the extraction—and nine times out of ten, this mental state would surprise you.

You see, when a "normal" person finds themselves in extraordinary circumstances, an entirely new part of themselves is revealed. This is known as our survival instinct. This comes in many forms, but one common thread is volatility. There is nothing to throw you off center more than staring death in the face. It is my job, the rescue expert, to understand my target and react accordingly.

"Beckett." Alek met me in the center of the campground. "Nice of you to show up."

"Fuck you."

Alek and Easton both knew my entire afternoon had been monopolized by an impromptu meeting with the head of the FLETC—the Federal Law Enforcement Training Centers. Herald Powell had requested to speak to me personally after one of my former military teammates had recommended the LYNX Group for off-site training. I was reluctant to take the call—you know, the whole grizzly-in-a-fish-market thing—but sucked it up and handled the suit.

Alek grinned. "I'm just messing with you. How did the meeting go?"

"Let's just say we're going to need to hire more staff."

"No kidding? So, good, huh? They're thinking about working with us?"

"Yeah, they requested to see a draft contract."

"Holy—Easton is going to shit."

"Easton is going to get much richer. Read me in," I said, refocusing on the matter at hand. "I don't like how quickly the temperature is going to drop tonight."

"Agreed."

I listened intently as Alek gave me the latest updates on a mission I knew very little about. The first of what would be many surprises to come.

Chapter Five

Beckett

"So, to be clear," I said, "no one here has actually seen Aria Ledger, correct? Just her mom's SUV?"

"Right. One camper said they saw a gunmetal-gray SUV driving by, and the other saw it was parked over by that tree." Alek gestured to a massive oak towering in the distance with no cars under it.

"It's not there now."

"Nope. Found it at an alternate parking lot for the campgrounds, about a klick north."

"Hang on. So, she parked there under that oak tree first, then for some reason, moved her car?"

"Appears that way."

"Odd. What time was it seen?"

"Around 10:00 a.m.—six hours ago."

I frowned, already not liking this case. "When she changed parking spots, did she go anywhere else?"

"No."

"Did you check the tracks to confirm?"

"Yep. Studied them myself. Eighteen-inch wheels, Hankook Kinergy GT tires. The tracks go from over there to the next lot over, straight there. That's it."

"I wonder why she moved her car . . ."

"Not the focus right now. The focus is finding her."

I nodded. "How old is she? Sixteen?"

"Seventeen. Height, five nine. Weight, one hundred fifty pounds."

"Tell me about her autism."

"According to the medical report provided, Aria Ledger was diagnosed at age three, after her parents sought treatment for what they thought were developmental delays."

"Is she verbal?"

Alek shook his head. "According to the mom, most of the time, no. She can speak, just chooses not to. Best you're going to get is one- or two-word answers. But she understands everything you say."

"Does she use sign language?"

"No."

"When was her last communication?"

"Parents haven't seen or heard from her since she went up to her room to listen to music this morning. And when the mom noticed the car was gone, she freaked."

"Is Aria allowed to drive?"

"No. But she knows how to."

"How?"

"Cyrus taught her. Wanted to ensure she knew how so that in case of a random emergency, his daughter wouldn't be totally inept."

I saw Cyrus Ledger distancing himself from the other firemen, growing more and more impatient.

"What was her mental state before she took off?" I asked.

"Good question. The mother said she'd been abnormally agitated. Wasn't sure if it was due to her period, or PNS—"

"It's PMS, you moron."

29

Alek shrugged. Understanding the ebbs and flows of a woman's emotional psyche wasn't exactly his area of expertise. "Anyway, Mom said Aria seemed off, abnormally vexed about something—her words exactly."

"Any boyfriends?"

"Stepdad doesn't allow it."

"Step? Cyrus isn't her real dad?"

"Right—and before you ask, we already tracked her father. Dead. Died of a heart attack seven years ago."

Considering eight out of ten missing people are abducted by someone they know, I was sure it was the first place the police looked.

"Aria's last name is Ledger, right? Cyrus's last name."

Alek nodded. "Mom changed it when she changed her last name."

I refocused on the details that mattered at that moment. "Gait?"

"She walks pigeon-toed, according to the report."

I looked down at the withered grass spearing up from the soil, picturing how Aria's tracks might be different from someone with a normal gait. The searchers would need to know this. They would need to know what to look for, the differences in the tracks.

"Cell phone?" I asked.

"Was left in her room. Mom said she uses it rarely. So, no, there is no sort of tracking device on her."

"Anything unusual with her car?"

"Nope. Locked, and nothing appears to be out of sorts inside. Definitely no signs of struggle or anyone breaking in."

"So, by all accounts, Aria stole her mom's car and decided to go hang out at Camper's Hollow." I glanced at the wayward teenagers who Easton had now quarantined under a tree. "Did you talk to the kids?"

"Easton did. Say they didn't see her, and don't know her, for that matter. They're a few years younger."

"What were they doing out here?"

Alek shrugged. "Drinking, smoking pot, waiting around for the full moon to rise."

My brow arched. "Do people still come out here for that?"

"Oh yeah. Kids wanting to see the ghosts from the so-called cult."

I glanced up at the darkening sky, trying to recall when the next full moon was. Soon, I thought, and something twisted in my stomach. "Has Easton established a path of highest probability?"

"He and Dane are working on that now."

"All right, well, while he's working on that, you can tell him I'm going to the Lookout Point at Sherman's Cove, about seven miles out."

"Why there? And, dude—I really think you should wait on his official orders. You know how he gets when you just go off without telling anyone."

"He also knows how I get while standing around waiting for orders."

Alek shook his head. "Fine. I'll tell him. Why Sherman's Cove?"

"Three reasons. One, 95 percent of all autistic missing persons are found within a nine-mile radius from the point last seen. Two, 45 percent of autistic missing persons are found huddled around some sort of structure. And three, over half of autistic children are also drawn to water, the reflection of it, the movement. Sherman's Cove." I ticked off each point on my fingertips. "Seven miles out, check; structure, check; water, check. Seems pretty damn obvious to me, so that's where I'm headed while everybody else stands around with their balls in their hands. Tell Easton."

"Isn't this what got you kicked out of the military? For doing whatever you wanted?"

"I got kicked out of the military for punching my commanding officer in the face."

Just then, an argument broke out among the group of firefighters.

"The stepdad's about to internally combust," Alek said. "I've told him Easton's going as fast as he can to gather everything and create the search grid. Dude's just gotta calm the fuck down."

"Not gonna happen. I'll handle it."

I left Alek to his packs and made my way across the clearing to the group of firefighters now huddled around Cyrus Ledger, trying to calm him.

The men turned as I approached, squaring their shoulders, sizing me up in the way that men do in emergency situations where everyone wants to be the leader, the hero.

I extended my hand to the only man in the group who I knew well enough to acknowledge first. Thomas Wangler, a tough-talking cowboy I'd beaten at a game of scorpion shots at Jolene's bar a month earlier.

So I'm told, anyway.

"Beckett." We shook hands.

"I don't understand what the hell we're waiting on," Cyrus Ledger interrupted, red faced and barrel chested. The large scar that ran down his jawline and neck shimmered under the Klieg lights. Deep black circles shaded puffy, bloodshot eyes. His short brown hair was mussed, his coveralls wrinkled and dirty, suggesting he'd pulled them off the closet floor hours earlier. In summary, the man looked the worse for wear.

This surprised me.

I'd never met Cyrus Ledger but had seen him around town a time or two. The man, late thirties, was always well put together and carried a swagger in his step that suggested he was fully aware of his good looks. Cyrus was known in Skull Hollow as being a bit of a ladies' man despite the three-year marriage to his wife, Jamie Ledger. I assumed his appeal had more to do with his status than his appearance, considering the massive burn scar that resembled hardened melted skin. He had been dubbed a small-town hero after saving three children, ages ten months, five, and seven, from a burning mobile home, almost getting himself killed in the process. He was willing to sacrifice himself, he'd said from the confines of his hospital bed. Men cheered; women swooned (proving the old cliché is true: women love a man with battle wounds). Since that day, rumor was Cyrus Ledger had yet to pay for a single meal at the Sunrise Café.

"Are we getting ready to get this goddamn show on the road?" Cyrus barked, a bit of spittle escaping his lips.

"Yep," I said, extending my hand. "I'm Beckett Stolle, and you and I are going to head out right now."

Cyrus raised his brows in surprise and shook my hand.

"Everyone else," I said, glancing at the other firemen, "is going to have to wait until their coordinates are announced."

Cyrus said something to his buddies, then met me at the edge of the woods.

"Before we get started," I said as I shrugged into my pack, "do you mind if I ask you a few questions?"

"You can ask me anything you want as long as we start searching these goddamn woods for my daughter."

Daughter. Not stepdaughter. He was close to her, emotionally, and I assumed this explained his volatile state.

"I understand from the incident report that Aria has been upset over the last few days. Any reason why?"

Cyrus shook his head, his jaw clenching in annoyance. Or was it anger?

"No, I don't know—and to be totally honest with you, Jamie, my wife, keeps telling people that. I don't know why. I didn't think Aria was any more agitated than she usually is. It's normal for her to get very emotional about things. I didn't notice it any more than usual. And Jamie keeps telling people that as if it's some clue to this whole thing. It's not. That's how Aria is."

"Emotional?"

"Yeah. It has to do with her condition . . . according to the doctor, anyway."

"What kind of emotional? Sad?"

"No . . . well, kind of. Irritated, tense. Easily annoyed, short tempered—you know, normal teenage-girl stuff."

Except Aria wasn't a normal teenage girl.

"I understand Aria was listening to music in her room this morning, correct?"

"Yes." Cyrus nodded. "It's a new habit she's picked up. She'll just sit on her bedroom floor and listen to music for hours." He shrugged, a nonverbal way to say he didn't understand it. I got the impression that Cyrus might not understand very much about his stepdaughter.

"What kind of music does she listen to?"

The corner of his lip twitched, and a spark of pride crossed his face. "Garth Brooks."

I grinned. "No kidding?"

"Yep. He did a special on TV not long ago, a concert at Notre Dame. She watched it and has listened to him ever since. Can't say I mind it."

"Nope, definitely nothing wrong with a little Garth Brooks."

Cyrus looked down, but not before I noticed his flash of emotion. Sadness, worry, fear, the weight of every parent's nightmare coming true.

I smacked him on the back. "Let's go find your cowgirl, shall we?"

He nodded, sniffing back the emotion.

Easton's voice boomed over the speaker, addressing the volunteers as Cyrus and I stepped into the woods.

"As you know from the incident report we handed out as you arrived, Aria Ledger has a specific medical condition to consider. She's autistic. You need to be aware of general behaviors associated with her condition and how they might affect the search.

"One: It is a possibility that Aria might be evasive. She might run when she sees you. Announce yourself immediately before proceeding.

"Two: Aria is almost fully nonverbal, although she can hear and understand everything you're saying to her. Be sure to focus just as much on your nonverbal cues as what is coming out of your mouth.

"Three: As is common with most autistic people, Aria can't accurately assess danger—meaning she has no real fears and therefore makes poor and unusual choices. Examples here could be that she attempted to cross a river or even a dead tree stretching over a ravine. Look for these high-probability areas that you would assume someone would naturally know to stay away from.

"Four: Aria has an undersensitivity to pain, according to her medical report.

"And lastly, per her mother, Aria struggles emotionally and is easily irritated and angered. Be cognizant of this and aware that these emotions, coupled with the mental state of being lost, could lead to unexpected reactions, such as aggression."

Chapter Six

Beckett

The noise and commotion of the campground was replaced by creaking trees, chirping insects, bellowing bullfrogs, and a canopy of singing birds overhead. Dusk was the loudest time of day in the Big Thicket, the rare time when both diurnal and nocturnal creatures mingled together as one.

Except there was no dusk that day, no slanted spears of light shining through the trees. No pink clouds and deepening blue overhead.

No, that day there was nothing but the fading presence of light, a slowly diminishing bleak gray growing darker by the minute. The temperatures were also dropping with the light.

There was no time to waste in the search for Aria Ledger.

"So—"

Cyrus immediately cut me off. "Yeah, I know. We're looking for tracks, bent grass, broken twigs—I know. We went through similar tracking training at the academy, along with wilderness survival skills, the works. You don't need to give me the rundown."

"I wasn't about to give you the rundown. I was about to tell you where I want you to go."

He looked at me.

"We're going to split up," I said. "I want to find your daughter before nightfall. You have a headlamp?"

"No."

I stopped and slipped out of my pack. Cyrus impatiently paced next to me as I retrieved the extra headlamp I'd thrown in at the last minute.

"You need to put this on and turn it on before you think you need it. You'd be surprised—"

"I will when it gets dark."

I cocked a brow. "Fine. Turn around."

Cyrus shot me a look before turning.

I zipped open his pack and shoved in the headlamp, taking note of the mess inside. A bag of chips, a canteen of water, tissues—most used—an extra sweatshirt and gloves, a first aid kit, a handheld GPS. I counted three knives and the butt of a pistol, none of which were uncommon for a first responder to carry. The small silver flask hidden behind the bug spray was, however, uncommon. A key chain tumbled out of the pack as I attempted to zip it back up.

"Jesus, dude." Cyrus turned around, annoyed.

I plucked the mess of keys from the grass. Over a dozen old and new keys were secured around a handful of rings that included a fireman's helmet; a Dallas Cowboys Super Bowl key chain; another one with a triangle engraved on it; and perhaps the most surprising, an ichthus, a symbol otherwise known as the Jesus fish.

Cyrus Ledger was a religious man? That surprised me. Although, if anything could bring someone to Christ, I'd imagine coming face to face with death in a burning mobile home would do the trick. I thought of his wife, wondering if she were religious as well.

I handed him the keys. Instead of replacing them in his pack, he stuffed them into his pocket.

"Can we get going again?"

"There's a bridge," I said as we began again through the woods. "An old wooden bridge that weaves through the swamps on the east side of Sherman's Cove. Do you know where I'm talking about?"

"Yes."

"Good. I want you to search there first. There are multiple spots to hide underneath it, and there are a lot of shade trees that grow over it. Lots of natural shelter. Based on what I know from similar searches, we would consider this a high probability for someone with autism to go."

Cyrus nodded, a bit of life sparking in his eyes. Hope.

"Where will you search?" he asked.

"I'm heading to Lookout Point at Sherman's Cove. With you searching the bridge on the east side and me going there directly, we'll cover a lot of high-probability areas—just you and me."

"Good. Sounds good."

"Meet back at command in exactly ninety minutes."

We both looked at our watches. Then Cyrus locked eyes with me for a moment, asking for a sign of reassurance that we would find his stepdaughter. I nodded back. *Yes, we will,* because somehow, I knew neither of us were going to leave these woods without her.

Cyrus split to the left while I slipped on my headlamp and pressed forward, weaving through the tall loblolly pines, searching the ground for tracks, cataloging everything around me.

The wind picked up, sweeping through the treetops and sending dead leaves and debris swirling around my feet. I didn't like this. Wind was almost as damaging as rain when it came to finding tracks laid by a missing person.

The air was sharp, bitter cold, and smelled like snow.

An armadillo scurried through the prairie grass, causing a flock of sandpipers to flee their hiding spots and settle onto the branches overhead.

I clicked on my headlamp.

I imagined how an autistic mind would interpret the thriving eco-system around me. Delight at the flashes of movement, the cacophony of sound, the rainbow of colors, the sporadic spotting of fauna. She would be drawn deeper into the thriving atmosphere, transfixed by the sensory explosion of light, sound, touch, and emotion.

One mile passed, two, three. Not a single sign of Aria Ledger.

The sky was growing darker, the light nothing more than a dim illumination in the woods. It would be completely dark in under thirty minutes.

I was resigned to searching only within the small pool of light shining from my headlamp. With daylight no longer a guiding factor, I slowed, allowing my instinct to guide me as I neared the swamps.

A cottonmouth snake caught my attention, its long brown body weaving through the green duckweed that blanketed the surface of the stagnant black water. Its tail flicked as it disappeared into the base of a cypress tree spearing up from the murky swamp.

Scanning the wet, packed mud, I slowly walked the shoreline, stopping several times to examine overturned mud and random animal tracks. Still, no sign of a human.

I pushed deeper into the swampland, wading through streams and creeks, following the damp, musty scent of the shoreline of Skull Lake. The trees thinned, the terrain leveled out to nothing more than a mixture of rocks and weeds leading to the shoreline.

I paused and closed my eyes, sensing the air around me, feeling it as I opened my palm and held my hand out in front of me.

I listened, stilled myself. I walked a few steps, then took another deep breath.

My eyes opened and locked on the deep water of Skull Lake. Whitecaps rippled across the black water. There was no reflection of light, no sunlight to dance on the surface. Just black and cold. I imagined a young woman would be very scared in this part of the woods.

Keeping my head down, my focus on finding tracks, I followed the shoreline, yet still found nothing.

I pressed on until eventually a rocky outcrop came into view. Beyond it, the small dilapidated wooden structure that locals referred to as Lookout Point. It was nothing more than an old shack that served as a place for wayward hikers to take shelter during the rain or a resting place for those seeking refuge from the blazing summer sun. A structure out in the middle of nowhere, beckoning curiosity.

A crow called out, flying off its perch on a nearby branch and dipping down in front of me. I watched it soar across the water as I stepped through the tall grass.

"Aria!" I called out as I neared Lookout Point.

I called her name again and again, but I received no response.

My hand itched to reach for my gun as I approached the small wooden structure.

"Aria!" I called her name one more time before stepping inside.

The torchlight from my headlamp swept across the small space. The single-room structure was vacant. Piles of dead leaves gathered in the corners. Spiderwebs stretched from one side of the ceiling to the other. Old, faded graffiti colored the walls. A few cigarette butts. A few beer bottles. A few roaches.

No sign that anyone had been there recently.

Frowning, I looked around. Where the hell was she?

Just then, the air around me stilled. The skin on the back of my neck tingled. The instinct I'd been trained to never ignore suddenly surged to life. My hand slipped to the pistol on my belt, hidden underneath my pullover.

With my senses on high alert, I stepped out of the structure and froze, taking in everything around me. An angry blast of wind blew leaves across my boots. I followed the leaves, watched them tumble over the rocks.

My gaze landed on a pile of stones. A tiny tower of six stones, each stacked perfectly on top of the other. Almost invisible to anyone not looking for it. I surveyed the area around the formation before approaching, so as not to destroy any tracks.

I knelt down and studied the stones, each hand selected to fit perfectly on top of each other, as if marking the spot. Settling back on my haunches, I looked around. A thicket of pine trees just past the shoreline pulled my attention.

I stood.

"Aria!" I called her name again, now focusing on the thicket.

I crossed the shore, stepped into the prairie grass, and gently called her name one more time before ducking into the deep shadows of the trees.

A pink scarf lay tangled in a thorn bush, the long tassels on the ends whipping in the wind.

I felt her presence before I saw her.

Slowly, I turned, my torchlight sweeping the ground until it locked on a pair of wild bloodshot eyes staring back at me.

Aria Ledger was seated on the ground, leaning against a tree, her knees pulled up to her chest, her arms wrapped around her legs. Her clothes were dirty, wet, and soiled, her long blonde hair tangled and speckled with leaves and twigs. Her jeans were torn, and an angry red scrape ran down her pale cheek.

Her entire body trembled.

I quickly lowered the light from my headlamp, pointing it downward. Staying rooted in place about five feet from her, I relaxed my stance, relaxed my face, calmed my voice.

"Aria, my name is Beckett Stolle. I'm here to take you home if that's okay with you?"

Aria said nothing, just continued to tremble—frozen, it seemed—her bulging eyes locked on mine. I'll never forget it. That look. Her eyes. Wild. Feral.

"Aria, there are a lot of people that are very worried about you," I said softly. "Your stepfather and your mother, they would love for you to come home. I know they're very excited to see you. May I take you home?"

Again, nothing.

I scanned her body for sign of any injury that was perhaps preventing her from moving. I didn't see any. "Okay, well then, if you don't mind, I'd like to sit down here with you."

Still, nothing.

Very slowly, I backed up, keeping my eyes on hers, and lowered myself to the ground. I leaned against a tree, and we stared at each other for a long minute.

Casually, I picked up a twig, rolled it between my fingertips, then tossed it aside. I ran my fingers along the forest floor. Picked up a clump of dirt, let it run through my fingers. Each slow, deliberate movement pulling her attention and beginning to decrease the intensity of her shudders.

I began humming slowly, gradually getting louder and louder.

Aria's eyes began to soften, to return to the present moment. Her focus was now tuned completely into me.

"Blame it all on my roots," I drawled softly. "I showed up in boots . . ."

Color began to filter back into her cheeks. Her shoulders relaxed.

I sang the entire Garth Brooks song, sitting there in the middle of the woods with nothing but the dying light of my headlamp shining onto a nearby tree. Eventually, I let the song trail off.

Aria was a completely different person now. Calm. Centered, almost oddly emotionless compared to her manic demeanor when I first approached.

I smiled. "Ready to head on back now?"

Her gaze shifted over my shoulder. Slowly, she lifted her long, thin arm, uncurled her index finger, and limply pointed to something behind me in the darkness.

My hand went to my gun, my weight shifting to my toes as I slowly looked over my shoulder.

No more than three feet from me lay a naked woman, sprawled on the forest floor, sliced to shreds, and painted in her own blood.

Chapter Seven

Beckett

A frigid cold settled into the woods, a stinging physical discomfort that added to an already chilling atmosphere. Klieg lights had been taken from command, driven by four-wheelers to Lookout Point, and erected around the body. Blinding fluorescent torches cut through the blackness, shining down on the macabre scene before us.

Dressed in a hazmat suit and blue gloves, the county coroner hovered over the body, conducting her initial inspection. Under the harsh light, both her white suit and the bloodless gray body seemed to glow, emanating a kind of ethereal light that suggested God himself was about to swoop down and carry them both to heaven.

Because heaven was the only place the woman, who was identified as Marissa Currie, deserved to go after what had been done to her. It was an absolutely horrific scene.

Long honey-blonde hair spun from her head, intertwining in the leaves and grass where Marissa's body had been so carelessly dumped. Her eyes were open, a milky opaque staring up at the winter sky, her jaw slack as if she'd died in midscream. Bloated black ants swarmed her body, dipping in and out of her mouth. Long, narrow slices ran up Marissa's arms and legs where her killer had used a knife to shred her from head to toe. And on her torso, an abstract painting of rust-colored waves, each line meticulously placed, one on top of the other.

Except it wasn't paint; it was her blood. Wave after bloody wave, her body the canvas for a madman. A pattern we had all seen before.

A tent had been assembled at the shoreline of Skull Lake to allow for both warmth and privacy for interviews. Lookout Point was now officially a crime scene, crawling with first responders and what remained of the volunteer search team, many of whom had already snapped photos and spread the gossip.

Alek had shown up shortly after I'd radioed that I'd found Aria Ledger, and also, a dead body—presumed to be Marissa Currie. Easton and Dane remained at the command post, receiving and recording information and, most importantly, preparing a barrier for the media vans that had already shown up.

Aria's stepfather, Cyrus, and her mother, Jamie, had been ushered with her into the tent, where they were being questioned by one of the first responding officers. Aria sat stoically in a plastic chair, covered in thermal blankets, and was flanked by Jamie and Cyrus like soldiers guarding the queen.

Jamie was a complete basket case, a trembling incoherent mess of sobs and questions, trying to console her daughter who, strangely enough, didn't appear to need it.

Aria wasn't talking, not even in her usual one- or two-word responses. Instead, her eyes were fixed on me.

Despite all the commotion, questioning, and examinations, Aria remained focused on me—*only me.* The teenager watched my every move, where I went, who I spoke with. Her gaze never left me, not once—something that had not gone unnoticed by not only her father, Cyrus, but also Sheriff McNamara.

It was odd, to say the least, and quite frankly, made me a bit uncomfortable.

I walked up to Alek, who was in deep conversation with Sergeant Rosa, a short, stocky Latina woman who was known for her gentle hand and her precision marksmanship. Rosa held the record for both the most hours volunteered at the local food pantry and for the most bull's-eyes in the annual Targets for Tots, a fundraiser for the county children's shelter.

She nodded when I walked up, her face pale despite the freezing temperature, and her lips a bit green. I couldn't blame her.

The conversation halted, and we stared at the carnage on the ground.

"Marissa Currie," Rosa said quietly. "Thirty-four years old. Team leader for the third shift at the chicken plant. A Skull Hollow native. I recognized her immediately."

"Is her identity officially confirmed?" I asked.

Rosa shook her head. "No. They called her father to come for an official identification. But I'm sure of it. I know everyone in this town. It's her."

"Who's her dad?"

"They call him Old Man Marshall. A navy veteran, a bit of a recluse now. Used to serve pancakes at Sunday breakfast at the church when I was a little girl. I'm shocked he's still alive, to be honest." Rosa shook her head, staring down at the body. "God, I just saw her last week at the coffee shop . . . too young. Much too young."

We fell silent, watching the medical examiner use small silver tweezers to pluck a sample from one of the many gaping wounds on Marissa's body. In decades running special ops for the military, I'd never seen anything like this.

The fourth now, of its kind.

"He's here," Rosa whispered, her voice chilling. "In Skull Hollow. The Pollock Butcher. It's him."

"Has McNamara informed the FBI?" I asked.

"I'm sure he has. If not, he will. The Butcher is officially their case now. Some guy named Martin Lance is running the show. New to the job, so I hear."

After victim number three had been found in Tyler, Texas, sliced open and painted in her own blood, it became unquestionably evident that the Houston and Waco killings were linked. The investigation was begrudgingly handed over to the Feds, as was procedure when dealing with serial killers. It was always a sticky situation when the FBI took over a case from local authorities, an ongoing pissing match between two authorities who believed they should take the lead in the investigation.

Rosa tore herself away from the body. "I need to go check on Stripes."

"Stripes?"

"Yeah." Rosa jerked her head toward a young officer hovering under a tree a few feet from a pile of vomit. "It's his first dead body. He's fresh from the academy. Excuse me."

We watched Rosa weave through the crowd, into the darkness.

Alek nodded toward the tent. "How are interviews going?"

"Not sure." I looked over my shoulder, meeting Aria's stare once again.

"What did you say to her—to Aria?" he asked incredulously. "When you found her?"

"Just that I was there to get her to safety."

"She won't quit staring at you. It's weird."

It was weird.

"McNamara questioned her," Alek said, lowering his voice.

"Did she speak?"

"No."

I glanced over my shoulder once again. Of all the times to speak, this was it. *Speak. Defend yourself.*

"Do you think she could've done it?"

46

"Do I think Aria could have kidnapped or lured Marissa Currie to the middle of the woods, sliced her open, painted her torso, then froze like a statue next to her dead body?"

"The case report says she has aggression issues."

"So do you. So do I."

"Point taken."

While the thought that a teenage girl would be capable of such a savage act seemed inconceivable, I knew from experience to never assume one thing or another. And there was something about this case that was piquing every instinct I had.

"She's got the size and weight on her," Alek said. "Not sure about the wherewithal. But physically, Aria could've done it."

"I searched for the murder weapon—the knife—already. Before you guys even showed up. There was no knife on Aria, and there's no knife within ten klicks of this area. Trust me."

"Doesn't mean she couldn't have tossed it and come back."

We looked to the black mass that was Skull Lake.

"Wonder what's hiding in that lake," Alek said.

"I'd bet my life savings a knife."

Alek nodded, then continued theorizing. "The medical examiner guesses the body hasn't been dead for more than six hours. About the same time Aria went missing."

"Listen, if Aria did it, there's no way there won't be traces of Marissa's blood on her body somewhere. Under her nails, whatever. On her clothes, on her shoes, in her hair. Whoever did this played in the victim's blood like damn watercolors at a preschool. If Aria did this, we'll know within twenty-four hours."

"*If* the stepdad lets them do a full medical examination on her. God, he's intense."

"So is the mom," I said, glancing back at Jamie Ledger, now chewing her fingernails to the quick. There was something about her that intrigued me. I wanted to know more about her, the family.

"If Aria did it, then she's the Pollock Butcher, which, yeah, doesn't seem to fit. I'll admit that. But if Aria didn't do it, then maybe she saw whoever did. Hell, maybe she saw it happen."

"If that's the case, then Aria Ledger might be the only person on Earth who could identify the Pollock Butcher."

Aria and I locked gazes once again.

"Dude, seriously," Alek said, watching her watching me. "She will *not* stop staring at you. What did you say to her?"

I stared back, my mind racing.

The question wasn't what I'd said to her. The question was, What was it that she was trying to tell me?

Chapter Eight

I wasn't always like this. In fact, I was quite normal once.

Though, I know now, the signs were there.

I was nine years old the first time I imagined killing someone. My father, to be exact. I imagined skinning him alive. I think it's interesting to note here that the act of the actual death—ending a human life—was never my central focus. It was always about what I would do to the body, dead or alive. Or all the things I could do, I should say.

I've always been a practical man. Focus on the job at hand and how to do that job quickly and efficiently. No emotions, no theorizing, no spending hours considering this and that. It was the act of skinning that I was interested in. The methodology. I became immersed in it. Researching, watching videos of how to skin a fish. A very delicate process, the articles said. I needed to practice, I told myself.

And then one day, I did it.

After stealing a fishing pole and a handful of my father's knives from his shop in the garage, I skipped school and sneaked down to the river. Alone, under the scorching southern sun, just me, the rushing water, and the woods.

It wasn't long before I was spending every waking minute that I wasn't in school at the river. I learned patience there. I felt the thrill of slamming a rock into the beady eyes of a wriggling, panicked fish, gasping for air.

I made a table of sorts—a workbench—out of logs and a long, flat rock. There, I taught myself the most efficient way to flay a fish.

Hold the tail end, make a small incision between the flesh and skin, carefully separate the skin from the flesh. Pin down the skin, and then make a smooth, sawing motion—slowly. While keeping the knife level, slowly peel away the skin. Use long, fluid cuts so as not to tear the flesh.

I learned there are two keys to success when skinning a fish: patience and choosing the correct knife. You must have both for a successful flay.

I learned a lot that year. About myself, about the wilderness, about survival. I felt one with myself, alone in the woods. Like, for the first time, I was my own person. A boy, coming of age. Learning to be a man. Someone more than just so-and-so's kid in the sixth grade.

That year, I caught and flayed close to a hundred fish.

"He's got a hobby," my mom said, pleased I'd found something productive to do with my time. All-American. Her little boy. She bought me the best fishing poles and tackle box in town.

Yes, I did have a hobby.

Soon after, this urge to skin my father turned into somewhat of an obsession. Dreaming of all the vile things I could do to a human body became full-blown fantasies.

I began putting faces to these fantasies.

My teacher, Ms. Miller, an annoyingly homely, bland woman with psoriasis who seemed one bad day from swallowing the barrel of a gun. My crush, Annie Wilkerson, who didn't even know I existed. Her boyfriend, the all-star football player and full-time douchebag, Nick Bowen. Courtney, the brunette who sat in front of me in class who constantly popped her gum. God, I couldn't stand her. Oh, and the lunch lady, the one who takes your money. Jabba Jenkins, the kids called her—a rudimentary combination of her last name with Jabba the Hutt. She was grotesquely overweight, rolls and rolls of skin that would surely take hours to peel from her body.

Looking back, this was when, a psychologist might say, things became dangerous. That my thought patterns went far beyond what a normal, curious boy fantasized about. I didn't know this at the time, of course. Just that I had a secret, one that, although I clung to it with bloody fingernails, seemed to be screaming to get out of me.

Have you ever noticed that it seems like the most "important" people always have secrets?

These lucky people are always a topic of conversation, of questions. Of rigorous speculation. They live fun, exciting lives that stretch far beyond the four walls of their perfect little homes.

Why? Because they're bigger than anything four walls could contain. They're special, chosen for exciting, thrilling lives. Lives that were so different from my own.

Until the fantasies.

It felt fun to have a secret, made me feel like one of those important people. Like I was doing something exciting, out of the norm of the boring, mundane life I'd been thrown into.

Finally, I was the one doing something wrong. I was the one with a secret.

You see, Ms. Miller, Annie, Nick, gum popper, and Jabba Jenkins had absolutely no idea the fate that awaited them—in my mind, anyway. They each went about their days in ignorant, bored bliss, totally unaware that I'd built a step-by-step plan for how to kill them and mutilate their bodies.

It wasn't until I painted the silhouette of a dead body in art class that I realized that I wasn't normal. The art teacher—I'll never forget her face when she saw my painting. It jarred me, really. She was scared of me. I remember my stomach sinking, nerves rolling up my body in one big flush of heat. I was embarrassed. My parents had been called as a courtesy. "Hey, your kid might be crazy. Might want to keep an eye on him."

That was a bad night.

But it was nothing compared to what I would go through so many years later.

Chapter Nine

Beckett

Jolene's bar was packed to the gills, a line of tourists waiting anxiously outside, bundled in long puffer coats, braving the unseasonably cold night.

It was Scorpion Night, an infamous once-monthly occasion that drew thrill seekers from the tricounty area. The evening's festivities centered around a game of shots, including a venomous scorpion and an on-site medic. It was one of the rare occasions when tourists and locals mingled.

On this night, the town drunks would meet under the dim lighting of the old stone building that had once served as the Skull Hollow courthouse before the renovation of the town's square. The steepled gray building looked more like a traditional Catholic church than a small-town watering hole. Somewhat ironic, I mused.

Steep, cracked steps led up to an arched entryway with thick, aged wooden doors that opened up to the large barroom. Old road signs and flickering neon beer signs lined the stone walls. Booths and tables crowded a hardwood floor scarred by years of abuse by cowboy boots and dropped pint glasses.

There was a poolroom in the back, with a consistent waiting list to play.

Upstairs housed the owner, Jolene Axelrod, a sixty-two-year-old widow with sleeves of tattoos and long gray hair she wore in thick dreadlocks. Her partner of fourteen years, a woman named April something or other, I can't remember her last name, shared the apartment. April was the yin to Jolene's yang—a short, petite, soft-spoken conservative woman.

Typically, Jolene's was the kind of place where the overworked and underpaid went to forget, leaving their troubles at the door. But there was something different about this night. An uncomfortable energy that vibrated through the crowd, driven by a mixture of anticipation of the impending winter storm and the anxiety fueled by the gossip that one of their own had been slain the day before. It had been just over twenty-four hours since I'd found Aria Ledger sitting next to Marissa Currie's dead body in the woods, and already, the gossip had reached the four corners of Texas.

The ill-placed excitement was palpable in this small town. It put me on edge the second I walked through the thick wooden door that read ENTER AT YOUR OWN RISK.

I saw her instantly.

Jo Bellerose was seated on a barstool at the end of the bar, her usual seat on the rare occasion she visited Jolene's. Also as usual, she drank alone, a Corona with two limes, and had a metaphorical *Fuck you* sign stamped on her forehead.

I'll never forget the first time I saw her. There was no question in my mind that she was a taken woman. Women who looked like that were never single, snatched up by either a Tom Brady type or an old man with money. There was no in-between.

And then I found out I was wrong. Jo was single. Yet I could never bring myself to approach her. Instead, I'd watch her from a distance, studying her, soaking in the smoldering, enigmatic energy that rolled off her in waves.

I'd asked about her here and there, inconspicuously, careful to hide the interest that, quite honestly, baffled me. I learned that Jo was a thirty-four-year-old doctor, a psychiatrist with the local mental health clinic. She had moved to Skull Hollow from Houston four years earlier, drove a truck, and was rumored to own a motorcycle. I had become even more intrigued, and I wasn't proud to admit, a bit intimidated. *Doctor* Bellerose.

(Sidenote: Why did I love so much that she was a doctor? Why could I imagine calling her *Dr. Bellerose* while licking my way up her naked body as her nails ran down my back? But I digress.)

The dark, edgy, withdrawn woman quickly gained a reputation in Skull Hollow, where the hair color of choice was bleach and the median age for saying *I do* was twenty-two. The men called her demure; the women called her a snob. Some called her a bitch, depending on how much strawberry wine they'd consumed. Yet somehow these whispers didn't appear to affect the newcomer.

To most, Jo emanated a kind of staunch independence, a brick wall of emotion.

To me, she screamed insecurity. Secrets. Pain.

From that day forward, every time I opened the door to Jolene's bar, my gaze immediately went to the stool at the end of the bar, hoping Jo would be there.

This night, she was.

Her silky black hair lay in loose waves down her back. She wore a black leather jacket and skintight skinny jeans, but instead of her usual black combat boots, the staggeringly stunning Jo Bellerose wore a pair of sky-high, red-soled, patent-leather heels.

My pulse kicked. God, a woman in heels. My kryptonite.

"Beck," a familiar voice hollered out over the buzz of the crowd.

Tearing my gaze away from *Dr. Bellerose*, I wove through the motley crew of buttoned-up cowboys, drunk rednecks, and blonde Southern belles. Due to the weather, the crowd was a mess of misplaced fashion, most wearing thick winter coats and scarves that had been pulled from mothballs hours earlier. Others still sporting the tags.

My crew stood out like a sore thumb, seated around a four top hidden in the shadows, next to a fireplace with a small crackling fire. It was the first time I'd seen a fire lit in the fireplace.

Easton jerked his chin toward an unoccupied chair against the wall. I dragged it over as Alek slid a bottle of water across the table.

Next to him sat Dane, who, based on his wet T-shirt and gray sweatpants, had come straight from the gym. Loren, former National Guard turned office manager of the LYNX Group, sat at the head of the table, her short platinum-blonde hair spiked to razor-sharp points.

"How was the range?" Easton asked as I straddled the chair.

I took a quick sip of water. "Good."

"Everything ready for tomorrow?"

"As ready as it will be at this point."

I'd spent the day preparing for the arrival of a group of marines who'd been assigned to complete the LYNX man-tracking course in preparation for an assignment in Guadalajara. After that, I'd spent the remaining hours of daylight unwinding with a few rounds of target shooting.

"Anyway, these jarheads can hang out in town a little longer and help us find whoever the hell slashed open Marissa Currie and painted her in her own blood." Loren shuddered. "I get the chills every time I think about it."

Easton glanced at his phone. "Yeah, me too. I'm giving Mia five more minutes and then heading back to the house to be with her."

"Five minutes to do what?" I asked.

"Be alone." He shook his head. "She told me to leave . . . *literally* told me to leave her alone—my stubborn, independent woman who won't accept help."

"Easton, no offense," Loren said, "but I wouldn't want a man around me while I spent the evening sitting with my ass on a toilet and my head in a trash can."

A chorus of disgusted groans rippled across the table.

Dane hurled a napkin at her. "Gross, L."

Loren laughed. "You guys have no idea what a woman's body goes through—especially during pregnancy."

"I don't want to know."

"Well, I do," Easton said indignantly. "And to your point, I don't like her being alone if the Pollock Butcher has decided to make Skull Hollow his next home." He checked his watch again.

As expected, every man, woman, and child in Skull Hollow had already solved the Marissa Currie case, blaming her murder on the infamous Pollock Butcher, and therefore, cursing the Feds for not finding him sooner and damning them if it happened to anyone else.

Everyone was on edge, and I couldn't blame Easton for being overprotective of his fiancée.

It had only been a year since Mia had found herself in a dangerous situation with a savage madman. Easton had saved her life, put a ring on her finger, and with a baby on the way, was knee deep in beginning a new phase of his life.

He was different now. A softer man, less hard and calloused. It was interesting and a bit uncomfortable to watch, if I'm being honest. I didn't understand how a woman could so greatly change a man who I thought I knew better than myself.

I admit, I didn't know much about love, but seeing how it affected my best friend validated every thought I'd ever had about the subject—I had zero interest in it. Zero interest in allowing that kind of instability into my life. In my opinion, a man is nothing if he doesn't know who he is—and apparently, the only thing powerful enough to shake that up? A woman.

No, thanks.

"I heard she was cheating on her boyfriend," Loren said, topping off her pint.

"Who?" I asked.

"Marissa Currie—the woman whose body you just found."

"No, I mean who is her boyfriend?"

"Guy named Grady Humphries. I know him. Works construction. Been arrested, like, five times."

"Arrested for what?"

"Drunk driving, drugs, a few public intoxes. Overall, a bad guy."

"Bad enough to kill her for cheating on him?"

Loren shrugged.

"Bad enough to be the Pollock Butcher?" Easton asked.

Dane shook his head. "It's not him. The Feds already interviewed him—the boyfriend was the first place they looked. Grady Humphries has an ironclad alibi for the night she was murdered."

"Who?"

"Not sure."

"How do you know this?" I asked.

"I saw one of the Feds who's in town working the case at the gym. Struck up a conversation."

"Does this Fed know who Marissa was cheating on Grady with?"

Dane shrugged. "Don't think so. And unfortunately, she's no longer available for consultation on the subject."

"What about her friends?" I asked. "Someone has to know who she was stepping out on Grady with. Don't girlfriends tell each other everything?"

Loren shook her head and muttered something unintelligible under her breath, but I definitely caught the word *idiot*.

"What about Marissa's car, cell phone, purse?"

"Gone, gone, gone."

"No trace?"

"Not a single one."

I scratched my chin. "What do we know about her specifically?"

"She was dating Grady Humphries . . . doesn't that say enough?" Easton said.

"I know she parties," Loren said. "And someone said they saw her with Leif Ellis just a few days ago."

"Leif Ellis?" Alek asked.

"Yeah, you probably know him as the Medicine Man. That's what the locals call him. Long gray hair he wears in a ponytail, sleeves of tattoos." Loren leaned back in her chair. "He's an old biker—retired, I should say. Used to run with a Hells Angels type of group, traveled all over the US. Now, he makes chairs for the furniture store down the street. Works at the diner as a cook every now and then when they need him . . . come to think of it, I think he's worked just about everywhere in Skull Hollow."

"A biker turned carpenter?"

"Yeah, the story goes that he got into some hefty gambling debt with his biker buddies. Ended up leaving the group and cleaning up his act."

"Why do they call him the Medicine Man?"

"He deals drugs on the side."

Alek laughed. "Way to clean up his act."

"Pot and what he calls *clean* pills are his specialty, nothing else. It's the worst-kept secret around here. I think he considers himself a modern-day Robin Hood. Stealing medicine and giving it to the poor. People like him; he's a bit of a free spirit and has helped a lot of the elderly community get medicine they can't afford."

Loren chuckled.

"He's kind of a funny guy, actually. Plays bongos outside the courthouse on Sunday mornings . . . not really sure why . . . no one asks him to."

"Weird." I sat back, my mind racing. "So, our victim, Marissa Currie, cheats on her good-for-nothing boyfriend, Grady Humphries, and was also seen recently with Leif Ellis. Could he be who she was cheating with?"

"I strongly doubt it," Loren said, sipping her beer. "Leif is almost double her age. He's kind of like the stoners' unofficial dad. And he definitely wouldn't slice a woman up." She frowned, turning her pint glass around in her fingertips. "It's gotta be Grady. His alibi has to be lying. He's got the motive and the criminal record."

I shook my head. "No. It's not him."

"Why are you so sure?"

"Let's think about this for a second. A guy catches his woman cheating, drags her into the woods, slices her open, and paints her body. It doesn't fit. Grady's kill would have been emotional, vindictive, vengeful. Not delicate strokes of paint on a canvas."

Easton nodded. "I agree. Beck's right. Grady's got the motive, but the MO doesn't fit. And assuming the Pollock Butcher is the one who killed her, why would Grady kill all these other women in the same way? The Butcher's first victim was in Houston, the second in Waco, then Tyler, now here. Why? Why those locations? Why here? Why now? Why Marissa?"

The table fell silent for a moment. I glanced at the end of the bar, at Jo, who was now interested in something on her phone. What, I wondered. Was she texting someone? A guy?

"How is the autistic girl? The girl who was found next to Marissa's body?" Loren asked, pulling me from my totally irrelevant—and somewhat insensitive, considering the topic—thoughts.

"Last I heard, Aria was home recovering," Easton said. "Mia is going to reach out to the family, I think. Offer free therapy if they're interested. She freaked out when I told her about it—was on the phone with her friend when I left."

"You know the two fastest ways to spread gossip, right?" Dane asked.

"What's that?"

"Telephone and tell-a-woman."

Loren rolled her eyes.

I grinned, then returned to the subject. "Did they do a medical exam on Aria?"

"Not sure."

Loren frowned, shaking her head. "God, how long had she sat there with Marissa's dead body? And why?"

"McNamara still considers Aria a suspect," Alek said.

"She said she didn't do it, right?"

"Right—well, nonverbally. According to Rosa, Aria spoke very little during the interviews. Based on her responses of yes or no, the story Rosa gathered is that Aria sneaked out, drove her mom's car to the campground—it's unclear why—parked, and went for a walk. She got lost, and when she stumbled upon a dead body, was too scared to go back through the woods to her car. That's it. End of story."

"Did Aria say why she sneaked out in the first place? And why for a random hike in the woods?"

"Nope."

"What about why she moved her car? She parked it at the main parking lot of the campgrounds but then moved it a few yards away at some point. Why? That's weird, right?"

Loren shook her head. "This is too weird. Nothing feels like it's adding up."

"Why don't you go talk to her?" Alek asked me.

"Why me?"

"There's something there, dude—with you, with her. That girl wouldn't stop staring at you last night. It was creepy."

I shifted in my seat, suddenly uncomfortable. I'd come to the bar to attempt to forget, to erase the image of Aria's wild eyes locked on mine. To try to stop thinking, dissecting, wondering what the hell she was trying to tell me.

Alek nodded. "If I were you, Beck, I'd press. I'd request to talk to her."

"This is a federal investigation now," I said. "You want me to go over to the Ledger house, knock on the door, and say, 'Hey, your daughter wouldn't stop staring at me. Mind if I ask her why?'" Now solidly annoyed, I drained my water.

"Yeah, that's exactly what I think you should do."

"I need another drink." I pushed out of the chair. "Be right back."

I felt the entire table staring at me as I walked away. I didn't care.

The crowd had tripled since I'd walked in. The band was setting up on the small stage in the back of the room, and the shot glasses were being lined up. The scorpions had been brought out from the back, their cages placed next to the shot glasses.

Men were lined up at the bar, signing waivers to participate in a reckless contest to prove their masculinity.

The noise was a dull roar, the energy palpable. A bloodthirsty lust for the thrill of tempting fate. An insatiable desire that I, unfortunately, knew all too well.

I was very familiar with how the addiction to an adrenaline rush, the all-consuming throb of stimulation, can completely devour you. Deftly pulling you into its clutches until, soon, you identify with it. Soon, you believe there's no going back.

This is the birth of evil. The inability to tame our deepest cravings, our darkest desires.

I saw this lack of self-control in prisoner camps overseas, in the brothels, within sex-trafficking and organ-harvesting operations. I saw it in the daily lives of the cartels and terrorist organizations. Whether the stimulation be greed, lust, or power, most people are entirely over-taken by it.

Tonight, it was the rush of tempting fate with a (supposedly) ven-omous scorpion. What happens after that rush dulls? Will they move on to tempting someone else's?

Yet there I was, a willing witness to it. And there was April, the bar-tender for the night, making triple what she made on a regular Saturday night, feeding the crowd's desperation for that thrill.

Whose fault? I wondered. Mine and hers, just as much as everyone else's, for enabling it?

The crowd parted. My focus turned again to Jo Bellerose—and the two cowboys stumbling toward her. Slobbering drunk, elbowing each other, grinning like dogs. Both red-faced, chubby-cheeked hillbillies with matching *Mom* tattoos.

A white-hot rush of protectiveness flew over me. This reaction was understandable, as I'd like to think most men would rise to protect a woman from a pair of inebriated asswipes.

What surprised me, however, was the *possessiveness* that accom-panied this protectiveness. This emotion made no sense whatsoever because Jo Bellerose wasn't only *not* mine to protect, but I was also pretty sure she didn't even know my name.

Or, quite possibly, that I existed at all.

The portlier of the two stumbled on the ridiculously awkward approach, his bloated beer belly knocking into Jo's stool.

She didn't move, didn't speak, didn't take her gaze off the television on the wall. But I saw her stiffen. From head to toe, her body tightened, and this slight show of fear ignited the fire already pumping through my veins.

Drunk cowboy number two circled her chair, settling in on the other side, the men flanking her now.

My stride increased, but it wasn't until I saw one's fat tattooed arm wrap around the back of her chair that I began officially shoving my way through the crowd—which was already taking notice of the action at the end of the bar.

"Excuse me, ma'am, that's my seat," I said to the back of Jo's head as I approached her, dwarfed by the drunk assholes.

Her eyes met mine in the mirrored back wall. A spark bounced between us.

The two men looked at me, frowned, then looked at the chair that Jo was occupying—the one that clearly was *not* mine—then back at me. A moment of silence ticked by as they gave me the once-over. Jo, on the other hand, continued to sip her beer, attempting to portray a calm, controlled, aloof demeanor.

I looked at the men. "This is my seat," I said again.

"The seat or what's on it?" one of the drunks asked.

"Both."

Again, our eyes met in the mirror. Her brow cocked, just slightly.

Port Gut snorted, then drawled in a thick Southern accent, "I believe you're mistaken."

"And I believe you have had one PBR too many."

By this time, April, the bartender for the evening, had made her way over, assessing the situation that was quickly pulling attention across her barroom.

"He's right," April said, wiping her hands on a towel. "I just tapped out the keg." She reached under the counter, pulled two bottles of water from the cooler, and handed them to the men. "Two for the road, gentlemen."

Her message was clear—get the hell out.

Ignoring the water, Port Gut glowered at me, his pride slowly beginning to feel the blow.

"Time for you to get going." I jerked my chin toward the door, shifted my weight.

Port Gut then saw the gun holstered on my hip. His gaze darted to his buddy, and in an unspoken—and very quick—agreement, the men tucked tail and disappeared into the night.

Crisis adverted, the barroom returned to its self-absorbed state of loud, drunken laughter and gossip.

April dipped her chin in appreciation. "Thanks, Becks. What can I get you?"

"Tomato juice."

"Want some vodka in it?"

"No. Hot sauce."

April's lips twitched with amusement.

"And a lime," I said.

The bartender chuckled and shook her head. "I'll see what I can do."

"Thank you."

I watched April disappear into the cooler, then focused on the woman who was now staring at me.

"I didn't realize this was your seat," she said in the sultriest voice I'd ever heard in my life.

"Yes, ma'am, it is. Name's Beckett Stolle. My name is on the back."

A sparkle of intrigue flashed in her eyes. "Is it?"

"Yes, ma'am. Written right there on the back."

She stared at me a moment, assessing me, assessing this unexpected banter between us, or sensing the spark, perhaps.

Jo set her beer on the bar and stood from the chair. I glimpsed the slim waist as she slowly circled the stool and the long, lean legs and curvy ass that almost made me forget my own name. She smelled like the field that surrounded the shooting range, early in the morning when the flowers were just beginning to bloom.

Bending at the waist, she found my name carved into the back of the seat.

"It's true," April said, returning with a tall glass of tomato juice. "Jolene and I named Beckett honorary defendant of that stool in 2018 when he single-handedly dismantled a barroom brawl that sent three people to the hospital, three to jail, and this very stool through that window right over there." April nodded to a window next to the fireplace, where Easton, Alek, and Dane were grinning at me from their table.

Refocusing on April, I said with a wink, "I couldn't have done it without the stool."

Jo smirked.

April nodded. "We named the stool after him and gave him free drinks for life."

On cue, I sipped the juice, spicy enough to make my eyes water. Just the way I liked it.

"Well," Jo said, "please forgive me for taking this seat, one that is so unworthy of an ass like mine."

And with that, Dr. Bellerose grabbed her beer, turned, and strolled out the back exit.

I continued to stare at the door long after she'd slipped through it, analyzing the last few minutes of my life and the buzz of . . . *something* that had settled into my veins.

Who was this woman? Why did she captivate me so much?

And why the hell wasn't she interested in me like I was in her?

Hard to get? Yes.

And that made Jo Bellerose exactly my type.

I picked up my tomato juice and made my way to the back exit, to the woman I decided right then and there, I was going to take home.

Feeling a rush of excitement, I stepped out the back door and into a blast of icy air tinged with the sweet, spicy scent of cigar smoke.

Chapter Ten

Beckett

She smoked.

Jesus, Mary, and Joseph, my dream woman smoked. How could this be?

Fantasy: officially shattered.

Detailed plans of rolling around in my sheets later: gone.

Jo leaned against the stone building, her face concealed by shadows, her silhouette outlined by the streetlight in the distance. She held a cell phone in one hand and a long, thin cigarillo in the other.

The door slapped closed behind me, the loud music and laughter fading to nothing more than a low hum of energy. The night was quiet, peaceful, and I realized how much I preferred this stillness to the party inside.

Intermittent beams of moonlight shot down through the breaks in the cloud cover above. A full moon was coming. I thought of the legend of the cult and how it was rumored the spirits came out during full moons. Coincidence?

Turning her face to me, Jo took a long pull off the cigarillo, the ember briefly illuminating her face in a warm golden glow.

My stomach dipped.

Her eyes were hypnotic, dark, almond shaped with chocolate irises that seemed to penetrate my soul. The woman was even more beautiful up close.

And just like that, fantasy: officially reignited. (Despite the cigarillo.)

She blew out a long stream of smoke. "Does this spot belong to you too?"

"Not yet."

Her lips twitched, barely visible under the almost full moon. Another spark of that sexy banter that seemed to come so easily to us.

I tossed the keys she'd left on the bar top into the air. She caught the chain with the speed and reflexes of a cat, then frowned down at them as if wondering where they'd come from.

"They're yours," I said. "You left them on the bar."

"Ah." She slipped the keys into her coat pocket, unfazed by this potentially evening-ruining mistake. "Thanks."

"Am I interrupting?"

"No."

"Well, maybe I should be. It's not safe for a woman to hang out alone behind a bar in the middle of the night."

"It's not safe for a man to approach this woman, considering she has a six-inch switchblade hidden in her back pocket."

"Ah, be still, my heart." I winked. "You'd better be careful not to get caught with that, considering a body was just found sliced to shreds. Won't be long until you're questioned by the Feds or Sheriff McNamara."

Jo looked away. "I knew her, you know."

My brow arched. "Marissa Currie?"

"Yes. She came to the clinic last year."

"So, you've already heard what happened, I guess."

"Yes, you can't walk anywhere around here without hearing the words Pollock Butcher."

"Yet you came out tonight, to the bar, alone."

"You're really hung up on this, aren't you?"

"I am."

"Well, I appreciate the chivalrous nature, but the second I heard about it, I—I . . ."

Needed a drink? Needed to get away for a bit? What?

I watched her closely, picking up on nerves. Or was it sadness?

I also noticed Jo hadn't taken another drag off her cigarillo since we'd begun talking, and that she was holding it away from me. Embarrassed? Ashamed?

"Were you and Marissa close?" I asked, pressing.

"No. No, she came to the clinic about a job, not for therapy."

Not the answer I was expecting. "For what job?"

"We were thinking about adding a part-time assistant position."

"Did you hire her?"

"No."

"Why not?"

"She had a record, drunk driving."

"Birds of a feather," I muttered, recalling what I knew about Grady Humphries. "Do you know her boyfriend?"

"Nope. Just her."

"I'm sorry."

"Why?"

"It's hard to lose someone you know."

When Jo didn't respond, I frowned. "Isn't it?"

"I only met her twice. Both were interviews, at the clinic."

"I figured you would have pulled out her deepest, darkest secrets during those interviews, in the vein of your profession, of course."

"Your figurin' is incorrect," she mockingly drawled.

I smirked. "Enlighten me, then."

"People come to me for pills, not advice."

I noticed an edge to her tone, one that suggested this wasn't the first time she'd had to make that distinction. I made a mental note: Jo was defensive of her choice in occupation. Why?

"I have no doubt your job is a lot more than prescribing drugs. It must be a heavy load to carry."

"Why?"

"Because of the line between treatment and addiction. It's very thin."

"True, but I can't afford to think of that line when I know that over 90 percent of homicides are committed by people with significant mental illness."

"Meaning the thin line is irrelevant in those scenarios."

"Exactly. Pick your poison. Medicate and risk getting addicted, or don't medicate and risk not only potentially hurting yourself but also hurting others."

"Here's hoping people pick medication, then."

"Exactly."

"I hear your clinic is doing really well."

She sighed, then looked down.

"What?"

"It is. We've gotten extremely busy. I've missed some appointments, been late recently."

She laughed, then shook her head as if it were ridiculous to be sharing this with a total stranger.

"Anyway . . ." She flicked the top of the cigar, sending ashes tumbling to the ground. "I don't only prescribe pills, you know."

"No?"

"No." She threw down the cigar and delicately stomped it out with her sexy red shoe. "Flick on the outside light."

I frowned, looking over my shoulder at the dark stone wall.

"Go on," she said. "It's just inside the door. Flip it on."

I did as I was told, and a dim orange light illuminated the small stoop. "You come out here a lot, don't you?"

Ignoring my question, Jo picked up her beer and proceeded to empty the contents onto the concrete block in front of us, splashing booze and lime juice all over my boots.

She peeked up from under her lashes, gauging my reaction. Testing me, seeing if this big, tall country boy would squeal and jump away.

This woman.

"Okay." She stepped back—pleased with my nonreaction, I think— and set the empty bottle on the HVAC unit. "What do you see?"

Jo gestured to the fizzing puddle at my feet.

"A wasted four dollars and twenty-five cents."

"No, I mean, what do you see in the puddle?"

"You mean, like, a picture?"

"Yeah, don't overthink it, just—what do you see?"

I studied the liquid that was slowly converging, bubbling, gathering in small rivulets between the cracks in the cement. "I see Godzilla. Circa 1954."

I expected a laugh. Didn't get one.

"I see a phoenix," she said, laser focused on the puddle. "Rising from the ashes, if you will."

"Excuse me while I call Spielberg. Godzilla versus phoenix-rising-from-the-ashes would be an instant blockbuster."

Again, no laugh. It was a rare occasion that my wit went unappreciated by a woman.

Hard to get, indeed.

Jo continued. "See here?"

She squatted down in front of the puddle, and I followed suit.

"These are the wings." She trailed the silhouette of the phoenix with her finger, explaining to me exactly what she saw. And sure enough, slowly, the picture of the bird emerging victoriously with outstretched wings came into focus.

Jo looked up at me and smiled, a childlike excitement on her face. "Cool, isn't it?"

I couldn't fight smiling back. There was passion here, raw and real. Suddenly, I wanted to know more. Not just about the puddle but everything about this woman.

"Okay, sold. Tell me what you're doing here."

"It's called apophenia," she said. "Technically, it is an error in perception. The tendency to interpret random patterns in things as something meaningful. Like seeing the face of Jesus in the foam of your morning latte."

"Or a phoenix rising from the ashes in a splatter of beer."

"Or Godzilla, if you've got the maturity of a five-year-old."

I smirked. "I'm familiar with this—apophenia, you call it? I've heard of it. It's the ability to spot and recognize patterns."

"Exactly."

"It's rooted in the evolution of human survival."

"Yes."

Her eyes twinkled in interest, and just like that, I was seeing a completely new side of Jo Bellerose, a passionate, lively, radiant fire that drew me like a moth to a flame. A side of her that I assumed wasn't widely available for public consumption. I felt like she was letting me into her mysterious little world, and I liked it. A lot.

"Exactly," she said. "You're a human-tracking expert, right? In the marines before you joined LYNX. Your entire life is searching for and interpreting signs, right?"

"Ah—you know who I am."

"Mia told me. I know you're partners with her fiancé at the LYNX Group. I've seen you around."

"Now I feel a little better about you allowing me to get so close to you right now."

"Let it go. I can handle myself. The knife, remember? Anyway, what were you saying about human evolution?"

"In the marines, we called it man tracking. Interpreting the signs, apophenia, whatever. It's man tracking to us. Tracking the enemy or the reverse—covering your tracks so the enemy can't track you. Similar to what I do now in search and rescue, the foundation is the same."

"Interesting," she said, now eyeing me like a specimen in a test tube.

Note to self: the way to this woman's heart is intellectual stimulation—*dammit*—but challenge accepted, nonetheless.

Jo continued, completely riveted. "Apophenia is ingrained in your instincts, then. The military has made it that way."

"I wouldn't say that. The military merely taught us how to home in on these instincts. Pattern recognition—as you call it—in its earliest form is nothing more than a human survival skill. It was essential for our ancestors in recognizing both food and predators. Like when you see ripples of water in a swamp. Is it safe to float through? Or is it an alligator about to flip you over and bite your head off? Or a man with a gun to your head. Does his cool, calm demeanor suggest he's all talk, no action? Or does the sweat on his brow suggest he's a man on the edge and is about to blow your brains out? Your reaction to reading these signs correctly is literally the difference between life or death. Survival is all about reading the signs."

"But when this survival skill, as you call it, becomes uncontrollable, it's a sign of mental illness. And this is where I come in. Example," she said, "schizophrenia happens when the interpretation of random patterns or things runs wild. Like, when you believe you're hearing voices telling you to do things. To kill someone, to shoot up a school, set the house on fire. To—" She stopped suddenly. "Sorry, this is probably boring to you."

"Quite the contrary." I stood and offered my hand.

She hesitated but then slid her hand into mine, her cheeks flushing as she rose.

"Jo," I said before I could stop myself, "would you like to—"

My hand was dropped like a ticking bomb.

"I need to go." With that, she turned on her heel.

Uh, what the hell just happened?

I cleared my throat. "You've got a ride home?" I asked to her backside.

"I've only had one beer over an hour and a half."

"As usual, then."

She stopped, turned. "If you've seen me here before, why haven't you kicked me off your fancy stool before tonight?"

"I kinda like the thought of you keeping it warm for me."

She laughed, turned, and over her shoulder said, "You know, your reputation precedes you, Beckett Stolle."

"Yeah? What kind of reputation is that?"

"Short tempered, loose cannon—you don't think things through."

"Is that why you sneaked out here? Afraid I'd go HAM on someone else in the bar if they tried to talk to you?"

"No, it's why I cut you off right before you were about to ask me on a date."

A grin slid across my face. "Keep an eye on those keys, Dr. Bellerose."

"Yes, sir."

I watched her hips lift into the newest, shiniest, most expensive red Chevy in the lot.

A woman in a truck.

God help me.

Chapter Eleven

Jo

My house was lit up like an airport, a beacon of fluorescent light through a pitch-dark forest.

I shook my head. Even my mother's presence was loud. Obnoxious and unapologetic. *"I'm here, I'm here, I have so much going on, look at me! Look at me!"*

I took in my home as I drove up the driveway, the three-bedroom, four-bath house I'd designed from scratch. Well, that's not entirely true. Let me explain. Using the Cullen house from the movie *Twilight* as inspiration, I'd designed a modern glass, stone, and pine house with sharp, slanted, clean lines of about half the size. I'd taken care to preserve the surrounding trees, as my goal had been to make the structure blend into the landscape as much as possible. It was simple, small, and everything I wanted—exactly the way I wanted it.

The inside, however, was a different story. It was exactly the way *she* wanted it.

I sighed, watching the black garage door slide open, willing it to jam and never reach the top. It did, however, open fully, announcing my arrival like a quartet of French horns.

I rolled into the garage, turned off the engine, grabbed my purse, my briefcase, and looked at the clock—10:14 p.m.

Sighing, I pushed out of the truck, slammed the door, and crossed the garage with the enthusiasm of a prisoner dragging a ball and chain. My lip lifted into a snarl as I passed the neon-orange Mustang parked in the first bay, otherwise known as *my* spot.

Not this week. Not when my mother was in town.

I walked into *my* house, into a suffocating mixture of the heat of a blazing furnace and the smell of burned granola something and Chanel N°5.

"Josephine, welcome home!" Her voice was like nails on a chalkboard.

Wearing a pink apron that matched the ribbon in her shoulder-length blonde hair, my mother, Melinda Bellerose, shot out of the kitchen like a cartoon character. Seriously, like a cartoon character, with zero wrinkles and skin as even toned as a slab of Sheetrock and smooth as a baby's ass.

She was wearing a white tennis skirt, pleated to perfection, a white long-sleeved cashmere sweater—and another sweater draped over her shoulders, in case you didn't catch the first round of expensive cashmere.

I feel the need to insert here that I don't have a tennis court. Nor is there a tennis court within a twenty-mile radius of my house. There's no country club in Skull Hollow. No racquets, no balls, no tanned twenty-something ball boys. Lastly, I'm pretty sure my mother has never set foot on a tennis court in her life. Alas, there she was, Maria Sharapova—plus about thirty years—in all her glory, in my house.

"Josephine," Melinda said, her faux-lashed gaze dropping to my high heels. "Pumps? In this weather?"

"Don't worry," I said, making a show of lifting my heel. "They're Louboutins."

"Thank God." Melinda wrinkled her nose, then leaned in for an unnecessary whisper. "Do people around here even know what Louboutins are?"

I bit my tongue as I hung my Balenciaga purse on the hook. "It's late, Mom. Didn't the doctor tell you that you needed to get more sleep?"

"Can't sleep. Learning to cook." Melinda bounced back into the kitchen. "I decided to try a new powerball recipe."

Powerballs. Otherwise known as small pressed balls of organic oats, organic honey, organic flax seed, and organic protein powder shipped from Florence, Italy.

I kicked out of the "pumps" and padded into the kitchen, then froze as the living room came into view. "What the—*Mom.*"

"What?" She feigned surprise.

"You completely rearranged my kitchen—*and* my living room."

"Oh yeah . . . I'm also learning feng shui."

Inhaling, I closed my eyes. *One, two, three . . .*

My father walked out on my mother four years ago, leaving her four million dollars in cash, multiple properties around the world equal to at least three times that, and a bruised ego the size of the implants she'd had shoved into her chest.

You see, my fifty-one-year-old mother had spent her entire life perfecting the role of homemaker since marrying my dad at eighteen. His leaving her had spun her into a midlife crisis that involved experimenting with every hobby known to man, including interior design, gardening, knitting, ballroom dancing, a brief stint in fencing—though I'm 99 percent sure this was solely due to the tall, dark, and handsome instructor—and finally, baking. Now, feng shui . . . and tennis?

Don't get me wrong. I love my mother. She's fantastic, the picture of human perfection.

Problem was, my mother had spent my childhood trying to force me into those perfect size six-and-a-half footsteps. So, naturally, as is common with today's self-indulged, disgruntled youth, I did the opposite. I died my hair black, got a tattoo, filled my closet with combat boots and leather jackets, and purchased my first motorcycle at age eighteen. I drove a truck, smoked cigars, ate microwavable pancakes for breakfast, and learned to shotgun a beer while balancing a venomous scorpion on the tip of my finger.

The only thing my mother and I had in common was an appreciation for designer duds. I was confident that we'd have absolutely nothing to talk about if not for this shared interest.

I slammed my fists on my hips. "Mom, can you please go feng shui all over someone else's house?"

"Oh, *mi amour.*" She walked over, grabbed my cheeks, and kissed my lips. "You are my only daughter."

"I'm your only kid."

"Exactly. Who else am I to annoy?"

Shaking my head, I made my way to the fridge—which had also been rearranged and restocked with the entire vegetable section from Whole Foods.

I grabbed a bottle of water and slammed the door. We eyed each other as I sipped. My pulse rate picked up.

Damn this woman and her power over me. Why do I care so much what she thinks of me? Why do I let her get under my skin?

"How's the Dragonfly Clinic?" she asked, breaking the silence.

"Good—great, actually."

"You still like what you do?"

"Yes, Mom, I still love being a psychiatrist and will never understand how I have the only parent on the planet who isn't proud of their daughter becoming a doctor."

"I never said that," she said, and I snorted. "I just don't like the thought of you getting so close to . . ."

"To *what*, Mom?" I said, and she narrowed her eyes. "People who need *help?*"

"People with mental illness, addiction problems—"

"Mom." I threw my hand into the air. "I am not having this conversation with you again."

"I just worry about you. You're all alone out here."

"Okay, that's it." I slammed down my water bottle. "That's where this is going, isn't it?"

My mom popped a powerball into her mouth, comfortably settling into a fight we'd had a dozen times since I'd moved to Skull Hollow.

"It's not that you're worried about me; it's that you're worried that I'm not married. That I don't have a man to make sure all these, quote, *crazies* who I treat don't come and get me. You're upset that I don't have three kids, a golden retriever, and a white picket fence."

"Jo—"

"*No*, Mom—*listen*. I'm so sick of this. Being single isn't a life sentence."

"No," she said with a steely expression. "It's a brick wall."

"What?"

Melinda took a small tentative step forward. "Baby, you have locked yourself behind a wall of false security. A massive wall you've spent your life building so you don't get hurt."

"Mom—"

Melinda held up her diamond-studded hand. "No, Josephine. Listen. This wall has become your safe place for far too long. The problem is, if you don't step out from behind it once in a while, you're going to stifle the woman you *could* become. We change, Jo. Women grow and mature; it's part of what makes the human experience so beautiful. Allow it to happen."

"Mom, I don't need to try fourteen different hobbies to, quote, *find* myself."

"Don't you?" She cocked a perfectly sculpted brow. "You'd be surprised, my baby Jo, what you learn about yourself if you try something new every now and again."

I grabbed my water. "Thanks for the Ted Talk. I'm going to bed."

"Go, dear. You look tired. I'm going to perfect this powerball recipe. It's so damn close to winning me the Summer Hill Bake-Off this spring."

Because that was what mattered the most to my mother. Winning Bake-Offs.

I awkwardly maneuvered around my newly rearranged living room, clipping my knee on an end table. Fury blew through my veins.

"Good night, my only child," Melinda called out in a singsong voice from the kitchen.

"Night, Mom," I said between gritted teeth and took the stairs two at a time. "And no more feng shui."

"You'll see the change. I guarantee it! Be open to receive the positive energy!"

I strode into my room, slammed the door, and blew out a long—albeit overly dramatic—exhale. I flipped on the light and quickly turned down the dimmer. A muted glow washed over the room.

My gaze landed on the inkblot cards scattered across the bed, the nightstand, the massive black-and-gray rug that ran over the hardwood floors.

I thought of Mia's comment about my office. *"It looks like a psych ward in here."*

Fitting . . . was it?

A whisper of icy air slid over my arms, and I realized I'd forgotten to close the window after sneaking a few puffs from my cigar before telling Melinda that I was, quote, going back to the office to get some work done—a.k.a. going to the bar to escape my mother who had overstayed her just-going-to-swing-by-for-the-weekend visit by six days.

Six.

I did a quick scan of my room, ensuring nothing had been moved or taken, this feeling of paranoia pulling me back to my childhood days, when my mother would help herself to anything I owned. Nothing was mine, my own. A psychologist would probably say this was the reason for my love of designer labels. Of nice things. I valued material *things* because I'd never had any for myself.

Or was it that having these things made me feel more like I fit in with the family that had made me feel as though I didn't belong? An interesting thought.

After moving to Skull Hollow, the older, more confident MD-me had told Melinda she was welcome to visit anytime as long as she didn't set one foot into my bedroom. That was the line in the sand.

Everything was exactly the way I wanted it. This was *my* space, my sanctuary.

I'd spent two months' salary on a king-size bed with a deep-rust velvet finish and the charcoal-gray bamboo bedding. This statement piece was centered against the back wall, which I'd covered in a sheet of matte-black leather. A white leather chaise sat in the corner, popping against the long velvet curtains. The room was simple, monochrome, and super sleek.

Black, white, gray, and rust. The antifeminine.

My mother despised every inch of it but thus far had upheld her end of the bargain.

I sank onto the side of my bed and stared at the wall . . . and thought of *him*.

Yes, I was very familiar with Beckett Stolle. I knew his type very well. In fact, the partners of "his type" made up at least a third of my clientele at the Dragonfly Clinic.

Beckett Stolle was the kind of man who thought of women as objects, as things to collect and use until the thrill was no longer there. In which case, the women would be tossed aside and replaced with a new group of idiots. The ruggedly handsome, charming type that looked like a real-life G. I. Joe. A jarhead with a short temper and a God complex.

He also had eyes the color of whiskey, blond hair mussed to perfection, an unruly five o'clock shadow that suggested he didn't know—or, perhaps, care—how beautiful of a man he was. The kind with plump lips that quirked into a cocky smile that made women drop to their knees. The kind with thick, ropy forearms that I could imagine lifting me off the floor and tossing me onto the bed, seconds before smothering me with that superhero chest.

When was the last time I'd had sex?

When was the last time I'd allowed myself to be taken by a man?

Keyword: *man*. A man like Beckett Stolle who does what he wants, how he wants to do it, and when he wants to do it.

When was the last time I felt that tingle between my legs like I had when Beckett grabbed my hand and pulled me off the ground?

When was the last time I'd had a real crush?

I looked from one inkblot card to another, mindlessly analyzing the patterns, the chaos, the confusion of the splatters.

Recognizing it in myself.

Chaos, confusion.

Patterns . . .

Habits.

A sudden blast of Swizz Beatz vibrated from the kitchen speakers below, the loud bass rattling the windows.

Rap music? Since when did Melinda Bellerose begin listening to *rap*? Who *was* my mother?

I surged off the bed and began pacing. She would be up all night, which meant *I* would be up all night.

I couldn't. I had a busy day tomorrow. I had to sleep. I had to calm the hell down.

I walked to the bed, dropped to my knees, lowered myself onto my stomach, and retrieved the small locked safe I kept under the nightstand.

I noticed my hands were trembling as I keyed in the code and slipped off the lock.

After a quick glance over my shoulder, I pulled open the small steel door. A rush of heat spread over my skin as I looked at the little orange prescription bottles with their bright white lids.

I sat back, pulling my legs into a crisscross. One by one, I pulled each bottle from the safe, lining them up in a perfect row in front of me.

I stared at them.

Minutes ticked by.

I closed my eyes, then inhaled, exhaled. My thoughts began to fade, and my body began to relax.

With steady hands now, I mindlessly picked up the first bottle, read the description and the name printed on the sticker. Not that I needed to; I had the words, names, and numbers on every single bottle memorized by heart.

Inhale, exhale.

I rolled the bottle over in my palm.

I blinked. The prescription was expired.

I picked up the next bottle—also expired.

"What?" I whispered, frantically picking up the next, and the next. All expired.

Shit.

I surged off the floor, grabbed my cell phone, and dialed without thinking. How had I been so careless?

I began pacing, pivoting with each new ring.

No answer.

I looked at the name blinking on the screen to ensure I'd dialed correctly:

Leif Ellis

I dialed again, and again—and again.

Again, no answer.

Chapter Twelve

Jo

I continued pacing, tapping my phone on my chin wondering where Leif was.

I dialed one last time. No answer.

"*Dammit*, Leif."

I threw my phone on the bed and walked to the window. Frowning, I watched my mother's Mustang slowly reverse out of the driveway. Her headlights were off.

I looked at the clock—10:45 p.m.—then back at the car that was obviously attempting to sneak out of the driveway. "What the . . ."

I turned around, looked at my closed door.

Swizz Beatz was now rapping something about hating the game. She'd left the music going and had turned up the volume.

I watched the car slowly pull onto the dirt road that ran in front of my house. Two seconds later, the headlights clicked on.

"Oh *hell* no."

I spun around, then slipped into my boots and my oversize red puffer jacket that hung to my knees.

What the hell was Melinda Bellerose up to?

After grabbing my cell phone, I sprinted downstairs. The lights and television were on. Her purse and her cell phone were gone. Definitely a covert op.

My mind raced as I yanked open the garage door, jumped into my truck, and pulled out of the driveway. Where the hell was my mother going in the middle of the night? Where was she *sneaking* off to?

I sped down the narrow dirt road. Finally, the glow of two red taillights twinkled in the distance. I slowed, clicked off my headlights. Two could play this game.

My eyes took a minute to adjust to the dark night. If not for knowing this road by heart, I'd probably already be in a ditch.

My palms grew sweaty as I followed the little red lights.

Never once did I question what I was doing. Something in my gut was screaming at me, an instinct that I wouldn't ignore.

Melinda pulled onto the two-lane highway. I hung back a minute, then continued the pursuit. The roads were eerily vacant.

Skull Hollow's citizens were home, tucked warmly into their beds, dreaming of better days and better things. The thick cloud cover had separated into what looked like a million different clouds crowded together, illuminated by the full moon behind them.

The Mustang slowed. A turn signal pulsed in the darkness, and then the car disappeared.

"What the—where is she going? The *lake?*"

I slowly pressed the gas, then turned onto the county road that led to Skull Lake. My back wheels spun on a sheet of black ice, jolting the cab and sending my heart into my throat.

Where the hell was my mother going?

I searched my memory for anyone I, or she, knew who lived out this way, but came up with no one. I couldn't think of a single reason Melinda would be sneaking around Skull Lake.

Nerves bubbled in my stomach the deeper into the woods I drove.

The road became narrower, winding through miles and miles of crowded trees. Because of the remote location, I distanced myself from the Mustang to ensure I stayed out of sight.

The tree canopy grew thick overhead, blocking the dim moonlight I was using to navigate.

"Screw it." I turned on my headlights.

A pair of white-tailed deer leaped out of the tree line, their brown coats flashing in my headlights, missing my bumper by less than five feet. I slammed on the brakes, skidding on the icy gravel.

I punched the steering wheel, an explosion of emotions finally bubbling over.

Why does she do this to me? Why is it always about her?

Why do I feel like I need to take care of her?

"*Dammit*, Mom!"

I hit the gas, no longer caring if I was discovered. I was ready to confront her.

But it was too late.

I'd allowed for too much distance between us, and she was gone. But gone *where*?

Clicking my headlights on high, I slowly scanned the woods as I drove. I wasn't particularly familiar with the area—it wasn't like my inbox was overflowing with invites to lakeside barbecues—but familiar enough to know that this was the main dirt road that led to the lake. Surely there were others, but I didn't know them, which meant there was no way my mother knew them.

What was she doing?

Minutes passed.

I rolled down the window, listening as I drove. The woods seemed to close in around my truck—thick, gnarled brush pushing its way onto the dirt road. The trees grew like a tunnel overhead.

Fear began to mix with the nerves.

It was then that I realized I was nearing Lookout Point, the location where Marissa Currie's body had been found.

A knot formed in my throat, and suddenly, I wanted the hell out of there.

Screw my mom. She's a grown woman. She can take care of herself.

I pulled into a small overgrown driveway that led to what remained of an old lake house that had been burned down decades earlier. Only locals knew about this spot.

My hand lingered on the shifter. Instead of clicking into reverse, I settled into park.

I turned off the lights, curiosity getting the better of me.

Seconds passed to minutes. Ten minutes. Fifteen.

Where is she?

A loud *pop* echoed through the woods.

I startled, straightening in my seat, staring into the woods ahead.

Another *crack*. It sounded like twigs popping under someone's footsteps.

I took a quick inventory of myself and my situation. The truck was locked, the engine was off, the lights were off. For all intents and purposes, I was hidden.

My heart started to race as I stared terrified into the woods.

A silhouette passed by, not ten feet from the hood of my truck.

My pulse skyrocketed. I held my breath, frozen in place until the silhouette moved out of view.

Mom?

Was it her? What the *hell was she doing?*

After grabbing my phone and then the can of mace from the glove box, I quietly climbed out of the truck.

A biting, cold wind overturned the dead leaves at my feet and whipped through the treetops, creating a loud, static white noise. Good for sleuthing, bad for being able to hear anyone creeping up on *me*.

After zipping up my jacket, I quickly found the footpath that led into the woods. It was a trail the locals used to sneak down to the lake for private bonfires and pot parties. (Sidenote: maybe the reason I'm not invited is because I call them "pot parties.")

Spots of moonlight dappled the forest floor, tiny little dots of light dancing along the pine needles. Nerves tickled my stomach. My breath came out in heavy puffs of clouds. The tip of my nose and cheeks began to tingle from the cold, and my fingers and knees grew stiff.

We neared Sherman's Cove, the location of Lookout Point.

I slipped off the trail and into the shadows, quietly moving through the brush.

The silhouette stopped and turned, seeming to look right at me.

I lunged behind a tree and froze, my heart leaping into my throat. I realized then that I wasn't 100 percent certain that the person I was following was, in fact, my mother.

I peeked around the tree as the dark, shadowy figure suddenly pivoted. This time, I looked at the shadow through a new lens.

No, it wasn't my mother. This person was much taller than my five-foot, two-inch mother.

Holy *shit*.

This person was tall and lanky and *definitely* sneaking. For some reason—instinct, perhaps—I thought of Leif, of him not answering his phone earlier. Not answering my many, many repeated calls.

The silhouette hurried through the woods, their head down, shoulders hunched, hands in their pockets, eventually disappearing out of sight.

Had they seen me?

I stood frozen behind the tree, suddenly becoming very, very frightened.

I thought of Marissa, and that her body had been found not ten minutes from where I was standing. Pictures of her body had been posted on social media, and I recalled what it looked like sliced to bits.

I thought of the rumors that plagued these very woods. The spirits that supposedly haunted them, the faceless, cloaked figures. I imagined them watching me from behind the trees. I saw them, shadows moving, a wall of inkblots taking shape right before me.

My imagination got the better of me that night.

I took off in a sprint, quickly finding the trail and running for dear life. My pulse roared in my ears, my breath wheezing in and out in quick, panicked pants.

Once back at my truck, I threw myself inside, locked the doors, and slid down to the floorboard to catch my breath.

I couldn't remember another time I'd been that spooked. It was as if I could *feel* the energy of the murder still lingering on the air, poisoning everything in its path.

Who had I just seen in the woods? Had they seen me?

And where the hell was my mother?

I started the truck and pulled out onto the road, my mind racing with a dozen half-formed thoughts, none of which made any sense. I kept looking in the rearview mirror, hoping to see the headlights of my mother's orange Mustang.

I braked at the stop sign in front of the two-lane road that led into town and to my house.

Where was she?

I stared in the rearview mirror, my stomach in knots.

Who had I just seen?

Was it possible that I'd just encountered the Pollock Butcher?

I accelerated.

Bam!

A vehicle slammed into the front fender of my truck. I'd freaking pulled out into oncoming traffic.

The impact thrust me from behind the steering wheel into the passenger seat. Tires squealed against pavement as the other truck spun out of control, barreling into the ditch on the opposite side of the road.

Shit!

Shaking the daze from my head, I snapped into action, lunged out of the truck, and sprinted across the road toward the brake lights glowing through the smoke.

The door swung open, and a man the size of a mountain jumped out. I skidded to a stop in the middle of the road.

Beckett Stolle.

Chapter Thirteen

Jo

"*Jesus Ch*—are you okay?" His whiskey-brown eyes shimmered in my headlights. Although they'd been calm at the bar hours earlier, they were now filled with panic.

I was too stunned to speak, from both the accident and the man barreling toward me.

"Are you okay?" Beckett asked again, slowing as he approached, scanning my body for any visible sign of injury.

"Yes," I said finally, a bit breathlessly. "Are you okay? Oh my God, I—I'm so sorry."

Beckett didn't respond. Instead, he meticulously looked me over, like a heifer being sold at auction, even lifting my arms like a rag doll. Once he was convinced I was unharmed, he frowned with disapproval at me. I felt like a schoolgirl in trouble, being caught by the principal after sneaking out of algebra.

He took my elbow and guided me off the road. "What are you doing out here?" he asked, assessing the damage to my truck.

My left headlight had been shattered and was now nothing more than a piece of silver metal hanging from wires. Around it, a nasty dent.

"What were you doing out here?" he asked again.

"I—ah, was on my way home from the bar."

"Not true." He crouched and examined the front tire. "*I* am on my way home from the bar. You left an hour ago."

"Don't call the cops."

He blinked, then stood. "Why?"

"Just—don't."

"Are you drunk?"

"No, jeez. Just don't."

"Okay . . . I won't call them, don't worry."

I looked away, my heart pounding.

If the cops showed up, they would look at my record; they would dig, and they would find out that I'd been arrested before. I couldn't risk that—I had way too much to lose. More than that, though, I didn't want Beckett to know about my past . . . or my present, for that matter.

I refocused on the accordion that was my fender.

"*Shit.*" I jabbed my fingers through my hair and whirled around, realizing I hadn't even checked the damage on his truck. *Selfish.*

Thankfully, the grill attached to the front of the hood had absorbed most of the blow. Unfortunately, however, it hadn't protected against the tree limbs he'd barreled into on his way into the ditch. Several nasty scratches ran down the side of a brand-spanking-new black Chevy.

I sucked in a breath, then turned back to him. "I am *so* sorry."

"You should be but not about my truck." Beckett glowered down at me, a completely different person from the flirtatious charmer at the bar hours earlier. "You should be sorry for yourself. What the *hell* were you doing? Were you on your phone? You pulled right out in front of me. You could have killed yourself or someone e—"

"I said I'm sorry," I snapped.

"Get your stuff."

"Get what stuff?"

"Whatever valuables you have in your truck."

"Why?"

"I'm taking you home."

"What? No, I'm fine. And my truck's fine."

"I'm taking you home, or I'll call the police and have them escort you home in the back of their car. You're obviously not fine because you just almost killed us both. I'm taking you home. Your truck will be safe here overnight."

I scoffed but bit my tongue.

Bottom line, Beckett was right. I could have killed someone, and this thought sent my pulse racing. And based on the look in his eyes, he wasn't lying. He would call the cops; I had no question.

Dammit.

My hands trembled as I clumsily gathered my things from the cab.

Dollar signs clicked off in my head as we approached his truck. The entire vehicle would need to be repainted.

"I'll pay for it."

Beckett grunted, opened the passenger-side door, and impatiently gestured me in.

A wave of embarrassment hit me as I climbed inside. I'd been so damn smooth at the bar, and now I was a hot mess, an idiot woman driver wearing an oversize puffer jacket that made me look like a red Michelin Man.

Beckett waited until I buckled my seat belt, then slammed the door, stalked around the hood, and climbed inside. The tension was thick as he started the engine and pulled onto the road.

"I'm going to ask you again, and this time, I'd appreciate it if you were honest. What were you doing out here?"

I bristled at his sharp, condescending tone.

"And why were you so distracted? Jesus, you literally pulled out into my headlights. I mean, there was no way you didn't see me."

"I said I'm sorry," I barked back.

"Answer the questions, Jo."

"*I'm sorry,*" I said, mocking him in an overly sweet and sarcastic tone. "It's Beckett *Stolle*, right?"

Unamused, he gave me a deadpan look.

"My point is, I barely know you, Mr. Stolle, which means I don't need to tell you anything. I said I was sorry, and I'll pay for the damage to your car. Now drop it."

"One, don't call me Mr. Stolle, and two, I wouldn't say that's entirely accurate, sweetheart. You just blew your way through the side of my truck. We're about to get to know each other very well. Why were you hiking in the same area a woman just got murdered?"

"I wasn't hiking."

He jerked his chin toward my boots, caked in fresh mud.

Annoyed, I sighed and stared out the windshield for a minute while attempting to create the perfect lie. There was no way in hell I was going to tell Beckett that I'd been following my crazy mother who'd sneaked out of my house after she thought I'd gone to sleep.

No. I was *not* going to go there.

"I thought I saw someone out in the woods," I said finally.

Beckett turned his face toward me. "What?"

"There was a man—I think—in the woods, alone. I saw him. And considering what just happened to Marissa Currie, I thought it was suspicious."

"So, you got out to investigate?" he snapped, displeased by this decision. "Why the hell would you get out of the car and go after a man you saw in the woods, alone, in the middle the night, right next to where a woman had been sliced open from head to toe?"

I released a frustrated groan. "I don't want to talk about it. Listen, I'm sorry about your truck. Send me the bill. I'll get it taken care of."

"Where do you live?" he mumbled.

"Next left up here, past the corner."

⌒⊙

We drove up my driveway, the headlights of his truck reflecting in the walls of windows and steel.

"This is your place?" he asked.

"Yes."

"I wondered who lived here. It's nice."

Just then, the front door flung open, and there she was—my mother, in all her tennis-outfit-and-diamond glory.

My heart stuttered in my chest as relief washed over me.

Wiping her hands on a dish towel, Melinda frowned into the headlights. It was as if she'd never left the house at all.

"Who's that?"

"My mom."

Beckett's brow arched.

"I know, she's hot. I know."

"No, she's—she's literally sparkling. Like . . . shining . . ."

"Oh, that. Yeah. She wears glitter lotion all over. Don't." I held up my hand. "Just don't. I can't."

A grin split his face. Apparently, my sudden fluster amused him.

"You live with her?"

"No—*God*, no. This is *my* house. She's visiting. She leaves tomorrow morning."

We rolled to a stop in front of the porch.

Beckett was studying me with a small curve on his lips. It absolutely infuriated me.

Melinda jogged down the steps.

"Nooo . . ." I muttered every vile word I'd ever heard in my life as I desperately searched for the door handle.

Before I could tell him to stay, Beckett was pushing out of his door with a shit-eating grin on his face.

"Hello, there," Beckett said in a thick Southern drawl sure to melt any mother's heart.

I practically lunged out of the truck as they exchanged names and handshakes.

"What's going on here?" Melinda asked, curious and yet intrigued. "Is everything okay?"

I stared at her, completely flummoxed. She was acting as if she'd never left the house.

"Mom, where did you go?" I asked.

Beckett looked at me.

Melinda frowned. "Nowhere. Jo, honey, are you okay? Is everything okay?"

"No. I mean yes. Everything's fine. Mom, did you—did you go anywhere tonight?"

Melinda glanced at Beckett, then back at me. "When?"

"Now. Like, thirty minutes ago."

"No. No, honey. I've been here."

I felt like I'd stepped into the twilight zone.

"Where's your truck?" she asked, now bordering on panic, considering my odd, disheveled mental state. "And why—"

"Your daughter's truck found its way into my Chevy this evening, Mrs. Bellerose. But she's fine, and I'll get it all taken care of."

"*What?*" Melinda squeaked. "You were in an accident? I didn't even know you left!"

"*Mom*—seriously, *please*. Everything is okay." Humiliated and beyond confused, I turned my focus to Beckett. I wanted this night to end. "Thanks. I'll, uh, I'll—"

"Oh no, no, no." Melinda winked at me. "Don't let me interrupt." She waved a hand in the air. "Carry on. Please, Mr. Stolle, *do* carry on."

My cheeks flamed with embarrassment.

Chuckling, the devil's spawn turned on her perfectly tanned heel and sashayed back into the house.

"She's something else," Beckett said, still with that irritatingly beautiful grin.

"Take her. Please. I'm sure she'd love it."

"I'm not really into blondes." He flicked my black hair.

I blinked at this flirtatious move. Then, just wanting it all to go away, began making my way to the porch. Beckett fell into step beside me, awkwardly walking me to the door.

"God, this feels like high school," I muttered.

"You're acting like you're in high school."

"What's that supposed to mean?" I asked as we stepped onto the porch.

"What is it about your mom that's got you all riled up?"

"How much time do you have?" I said sarcastically.

But when I looked up, Beckett wasn't smiling. Instead, he was staring down at me with a smoldering look that raised goose bumps over every inch of my skin.

Before I could catch my breath, Beckett Stolle stepped forward, took my face in his hands, and kissed me. A soft, sweet, sensual kiss that curled my toes and left me absolutely breathless.

"What was that for?" I whispered against his lips.

"In high school, I never walked a girl to the door without stealing a kiss." His hands dropped from my face, and he took a step back. "I'll see you at seven o'clock tomorrow morning."

My eyes fluttered open, my world suddenly so very upside down.

Beckett smirked, his eyes twinkling, his lips gorgeously puffy. "Seven okay, or would you prefer six?"

"I don't prefer anything at six in the morning."

He winked. "Seven, then. I'll pick you up and take you to your truck. How do you take your coffee?"

"My what?"

"Coffee."

"Uh, cream and sugar . . ."

Beckett dipped his chin. "Good night, Miss Bellerose. Lock the door once you get inside."

I forced my jaw to close and wobbled a little as I stepped inside. Once the door closed, I released my weight and fell back against it, sucking in a breath for what felt like the first time.

What—*the hell*—just happened?

I listened to the sound of his boots crunching over the gravel, his truck door slamming, his engine firing up.

I turned and peeked through the side window, catching the tail-lights of Beckett's truck as it faded into the darkness while the heat from his kiss tattooed itself on my soul.

Chapter Fourteen

Hey, your kid might be crazy. Might want to keep an eye on him . . .

Crazy. I still think about this word a lot. Are we born crazy, or does life, after years and years of abuse, deliver one final blow that sends us into psychosis?

Honestly? I think a little of both.

Genetics are a powerful thing, I believe, and unfortunately, I hit the mental illness jackpot with mine.

I was abused for so long that I didn't know that hitting your child daily wasn't a normal thing. Like taking a shower, eating breakfast, brushing your teeth, a back of the hand to the face was as routine in my life as self-care.

You hear stories of abuse, most start with, He came home drunk. Not mine. Mine started with, He woke up.

Hiding was impossible. Not only was the house small, but he knew all my spots. Yet, I still hid, body trembling, my stomach churning with fear as I waited for that veiny, calloused hand to grab me by the shirt collar and drag me out.

He never used an object to beat me. No, that would have been too cowardly. He used his fists—raw, unbridled hatred unleashed on the weak.

I never knew what I was being punished for. The first time he had an actual, legitimate excuse was when I painted a dead body in art class and the school intervened.

The beating started immediately when I walked in the door.

But this one was different.

This time, he stood in front of me, fists raised, a dark, evil look in his eyes, and forced me to fight back.

Forced me—a kid.

With tears streaming down my face and a puddle of vomit at my feet, I did as I was told. Like a weak, injured bird against a rabid dog, I fought back.

I cried the entire time.

I lost that fight, along with everything good in me. Whatever was good to begin with.

It took me many years to learn that I wasn't being punished for freaking the hell out of my teacher. I was being punished because I'd opened the door to an examination into my family's life. I'd brought attention to our little house out in the woods. I'd brought attention to him.

It was a mistake I had to live with my entire childhood. But believe it or not, that was not life's final blow that led to psychosis. That happened many years later.

I was told there are no mistakes. Only opportunities. This was what they told us during training.

The statement is total bullshit.

Things happen, errors happen all the time. Life-changing mistakes, split-second decisions that can single-handedly change the course of your life.

Just like the mistake of painting the dead body in art class, I lost the car keys. I fucking lost the keys.

A rookie mistake, one that could link me to Marissa Currie with a single DNA swab. My prints were in the system. I'd be linked immediately.

What were you doing with Miss Currie's keys?

There was no reasonable answer. Not now.

One stupid mistake, and everything had gone to shit.

This wasn't like me, and I didn't like the panic that blew through my body, making itself at home, a constant undercurrent of stress under my skin.

Never go back to the scene of the crime. It was the number one fucking lesson in homicides for dummies.

I did—and I wasn't the only one there.

At first, I thought, this is it. I'm busted. One of the Feds or local cops were making one last round around the scene, and bam, *there I was, presenting myself on a fucking platter. It didn't take me more than a second, however, before I realized the person following me through the woods was a woman and a ridiculously incompetent amateur, at that. This eased my worry, but just barely.*

I quickly doubled back, unbeknownst to the woman, and just like that, the hunter became the prey.

I followed this mystery woman back to her red Chevy, one that I realized I'd seen a time or two in town. I made a mental note of the license plate as she drove away.

Fucking idiot.

In under six hours, I had her name, address, occupation, blood type, and entire fucking family tree.

I wasn't sure if she'd seen my face or any detail to identify me, but it wasn't a risk I was willing to take, especially since things seemed to suddenly be going sideways.

So, plans changed.

The mistakes that were made must be remedied. The woman who saw me in the woods must either be taken care of or keep her mouth shut.

My plan was made in minutes.

Josephine Bellerose became my new focus.

Chapter Fifteen

Jo

Not even seven in the morning, and already, I was exhausted. Physically, mentally, and emotionally.

Physically because I'd been awakened at four by the thuds and pounding footsteps of my mother packing up for her drive back to Houston. Despite being just over five feet tall, Melinda walked with the heel strikes of an African savannah elephant.

Mentally because when I'd asked my mother—again—if she'd gone out the night before, she vehemently denied it. Was she lying? Or was I losing my damn mind? I spent what little sleeping hours I'd had dreaming about my mother, sliced bodies, inkblot cards, and Leif Ellis—who still hadn't returned my calls. And who I needed now more than ever.

The story went like this:

Leif Ellis was a Skull Hollow native. A former high school soccer stud who had become disabled after an unfortunate incident turning his ankle during the state championship. An unsavory metamorphosis came soon after—high school athlete turned pot-smoking hippie, turned raging hydrocodone addict (within two months of the accident), turned badass biker, turned small-town pill peddler.

I began keeping tabs on Leif when several of my clients had mentioned—confessed, more like—to buying excess pills from him. This was when my connection to the Medicine Man became somewhat muddled.

After my third client had mentioned him, I began my own investigation, sleuthing my way from contact to contact, location to location, using my medical credentials to pull confidential information on the man.

My intentions were pure in the beginning. I want to make that clear, so I'll say it again: my intentions had been pure.

My plan was to make contact, threaten to report him if he sold any more illegal pills to any of my clients, and then be on my merry way.

I only wish it had gone like that.

Leif and I met for the first time outside of Jolene's bar one hot summer night. I was three whiskeys deep and stumbling on my new Jimmy Choos when I saw him, texting on his phone in the shadows.

Like the flip of a switch, I went from Amy Winehouse to Nancy Drew, slipping into my undercover persona that I sometimes wonder if I created out of sheer boredom. Again, my intent here had been to call him out on his shit. Instead, I left the meeting with an unlisted phone number, a bottle of gabapentin, and a weird feeling in the pit of my stomach.

The next morning, I tucked the pills in a safe under my bed, convincing myself that it wasn't *all* bad that I, the town psychiatrist, had just illegally purchased pills off the street, because, well, it was one fewer bottle on the streets for really screwed-up people to buy. You know, people *not* like me.

The next week, I texted him, got a few more bottles, and hid those pills as well.

The next week, the same, and on and on we went, until the fateful evening that changed it all, forcing our acquaintanceship into an actual relationship.

I arrived at our agreed-upon drop location where Leif, the sixty-something-year-old former biker, was getting his ass *kicked* by a couple of drunk cowboys who were apparently displeased with the amount of money Leif had taken from them during a friendly game of poker hours earlier.

That night, I threatened to kill two people, lying, saying I had a gun in my truck.

That night, Leif slept on my couch.

For several days, I stayed by his bleeding, broken body as he detoxed and healed from the beating, ensuring he kept breathing.

After that, I drove Leif six hours to a rehab facility, where he emerged clean and sober two months later with a dopey smile and the promise to keep clean. I'd received a five-figure bill. After that, the man started playing the bongos and grew dreadlocks, but kept selling.

Leif and I had a tenuous relationship, one born in the shadows of secrets, thriving only because we both had dirt on each other. I, single handedly, could get Leif Ellis locked away for the rest of his life. Similarly, Mr. Ellis could return the favor and strip me of my career and ruin the life I'd worked so hard to create.

We had a deal, he and I. To take our secrets to our graves—and to always, always answer each other's phone calls. This was the first time the old hippie hadn't lived up to his side of the bargain, and my instinct was screaming at me that something was going on.

And finally, and perhaps most jarring, was the reason for my emotional exhaustion—that kiss. That *damn* kiss.

That toe-curling, stomach-tickling, breath-stealing kiss.

Beckett Stolle had knocked my world off its axis with a single kiss. Totally, unexpectedly, I might add—which made it all the sexier.

I looked in the mirror for the twentieth time, secured a rogue strand of hair that had escaped the confines of my topknot. I angled my head to one side, assessing this move, then pulled the strand loose once again, allowing it to frame my face.

It was the third time I'd messed with that single strand of hair.

I loathed myself. I couldn't remember the last time I'd cared so much about my appearance.

Damn Beckett Stolle. Damn that *kiss*.

I looked at the clock *again*—6:45 a.m.

My stomach flipped—*again*.

With a dramatic roll of my eyes (at myself), I pushed away from the mirror, turned off the bathroom light, and stepped into the pigsty that had become my bedroom.

Clothes were everywhere, scattered across the bed, dangling from the dresser, crumpled into piles on the floor. Dresses, skirts, jeans, slacks, business suits, and one pair of leather skinnies—because Beckett was definitely the kind of guy who would like that sort of thing. Despite the selection, each outfit had been discarded after I'd deemed it substandard for a man who could kiss like that.

Not a good start to the day.

I looked at the clock again—only one minute had passed—and then into the full-length mirror. In the end, I'd gone with skinny jeans, knee-high brown leather boots, and a chunky cashmere sweater with a skull and crossbones stitched in the center.

My favorite sweater. Chic and totally badass.

The rumble of an engine pulled my attention to the window. Of *course* his truck growled like a powerful and sexy jungle cat.

I darted into the bathroom for one last check on that unruly strand of hair that, apparently, was going to make or break my entire life. I tucked it behind my ear. After clicking off the light, I grabbed my cell phone from the bathroom counter and hurried into the bedroom.

Where was my purse? My pulse skyrocketed as I tossed clothes into the air, searching for the Chanel bag that matched the boots.

A knock sounded at the door, and I froze.

He came to the door?

Do I get another kiss?

After finally finding my purse buried under a stack of inkblot cards, I hurried to the door. The blast of frigid air was no match for the scorching heat that flew up my body.

He looked stunning.

Wearing a dark-navy suit and a crisp white dress shirt, the rough and rugged Beckett Stolle looked like he'd just stepped out of *GQ* magazine. His hair was combed, and his scruff shaved, exposing a razor-sharp jawline that made my mouth water.

The man was a vision, igniting every sexual sensor in my body with little pops of lightning.

Be cool, be cool . . . think femme fatale, hard to get.

"Good morning, beautiful."

Be. Cool.

"Right back at you."

He gestured to the suit and shrugged. "I have meetings today."

"With the president?"

"That's this afternoon." Beckett winked and motioned me outside. "Don't forget to lock up."

He waited until I did so, his scrutiny burning into the side of my face. My entire body vibrated with adrenaline, that heady, addictive feeling of lust. Despite my shaky knees, I pulled back my shoulders and did my best "aloof."

We walked down the steps.

"A few Feds are coming in this morning to look at our facility," he said, referring to why he was dressed to the nines.

"Well, if it's a female Fed, I'd say you have nothing to worry about."

"Because a tailored Tom Ford suit is the only thing a woman needs to fall to her knees?"

"No, a perfectly scented cologne is. What are you wearing?"

"It's called Enigme—French for *enigma.*"

"Interesting."

"Precisely."

I laughed.

"So," he said, "did you make an appointment to replace the headlight on your truck?"

"You mean from the accident that was"—I made a show of checking a watch that I wasn't wearing—"not even seven hours ago?"

"Plenty of time to make a phone call."

I thought of my truck and how it had been sitting on the side of the road all night. "No. I haven't made an appointment yet."

"You going to?"

"Yep." *Nope.*

I glanced up at the sky, dark and crowded with thick clouds.

"It's supposed to start sleeting on and off this afternoon," he said. "The storm is moving quicker than anticipated."

"It isn't supposed to hit for two more days, right?"

"Sooner now."

We approached his truck, the scratches appearing deeper and much angrier in the light of day.

"Don't worry about it," he said, catching my cringe.

"I'll get it fixed."

"I said don't worry about it."

Beckett opened the passenger door and gestured me inside. It felt like a date, and again, I wondered if I'd be granted another one of his earth-shattering kisses.

The cab smelled of rich leather and freshly brewed coffee.

Beckett slid behind the steering wheel, plucked one of the coffee cups from the cupholder, and handed it to me. "Cream and sugar and a little something extra."

"Whiskey?" I examined the camouflage mug.

"Is it a whiskey kind of morning?" He started the engine.

106

"You could say that. It's been a long time since I've been in a car accident."

"It'll rattle you; I know. Hopefully, your mom provided some sort of comfort last night."

I snorted.

Beckett peered at the house. "I was disappointed that she didn't greet me at the door like last night."

I grinned. "I'll bet you were."

He winked as he shoved the truck into reverse.

"She left this morning," I said. "Before dawn. I don't even think she went to bed last night."

"She doesn't seem to be the type to sleep much."

"She isn't, and therefore, I don't sleep well while she visits . . . which has become more and more frequent over the last six months."

"Why's that?"

"Midlife crises that she has no one else to take out on? I don't know," I grumbled.

"You're not a morning person, are you?" he asked as we drove down the driveway.

"Guilty. You are, I'm guessing."

"Yes, ma'am," he drawled, and I pulled a face. He grinned. "Try that coffee, Maxine. Might turn your morning right around."

"Maxine? As in—the grumpy old lady in those old cartoon strips?"

"They're taped all over the walls at the breakfast burrito place I hit every morning. My favorite is 'My idea of a Super Bowl is a toilet that cleans itself.'"

"Mine is 'If at first you don't succeed, you probably had a man helping you.'"

"Ouch."

I grinned, then sipped the coffee.

A multitude of flavors hit my tongue. A smooth balance of sweet and bitter, a warm, earthy spice barely noticeable but definitely there.

In it, the perfect mix of cream and sugar. And it was fresh, too, as if it had been brewed in his truck seconds earlier.

"What kind of coffee is this?"

"Good, isn't it?" he said as we pulled onto the dirt road.

"Yes, and different."

"It's called cask coffee. It's been aged in whiskey and rum barrels."

"And there's no whiskey in it?"

"No. Sorry to disappoint."

"Well, it's still delicious—and less dangerous, for that matter."

"The key to the freshness is that I get it in whole beans. I grind them every morning. People underestimate the difference in the quality of coffee when you do that."

"I didn't take you as the type of guy to grind his coffee beans every morning."

"More of an instant kind of guy?"

"Yeah . . . kind of. Between this and that suit of yours, I'm beginning to rethink my initial assessment of you."

"Which version of me intrigues you more? Instant or whole bean?"

"Definitely whole bean."

"Ah, she likes the suit, then."

"I do. I haven't seen a suit like that since my father took me to Sotheby's in New York when I was a little girl."

"Is that where you got that diamond tennis bracelet around your wrist?"

"You noticed?"

"I had to put on my sunglasses before I even turned into your driveway."

I laughed. "No, this was a gift from my mother, just because. She's into tennis everything all of a sudden."

"That's one hell of a just-because gift."

"You should have seen the last one. An obnoxious gold statue of a mermaid with an emerald cut ruby clasped in her hand. It currently sits in the back of my closet. Makes one hell of a thong holder."

"Tell me more."

"Just focus on the road."

He sucked in a breath. "Careful, Miss Bellerose, or I might have to go and kiss you again."

"Coffee first."

Smooth, Jo. Very smooth. I bit back a smile. *She still has it.*

We pulled onto the main highway.

"I want to know more about this figure you saw last night in the woods," he said.

"Me too. Trust me—I'd like to know more about it too."

After replaying the image in my head, I was certain that the person I'd seen in the woods wasn't my mother.

So, who was it?

Was it Leif?

Was it the Pollock Butcher?

Was Leif the Pollock Butcher?

Had I laid eyes on the Pollock Butcher?

"Did you see his face?" Beckett asked, reading my thoughts.

"No. I didn't see his—*or her*—face. I did realize, this morning, while thinking about it, that the person wasn't carrying a flashlight. They were just hiking through the woods in the dark. Odd, isn't it?"

"Not if you're extremely familiar with the area."

"Good point."

Deep in thought, Beckett said, "Grady Humphries, Marissa's boyfriend, was born and raised in Skull Hollow."

I nodded. "That's true. Do you think it was Grady?"

"The motive is there, but nothing else fits. I think the Feds think it's him."

"But he has an alibi, right? That's what Mia told me."

Beckett nodded. "That's what I heard too."

"Who is it? His alibi?"

"No clue."

Deep in thought, I sipped my coffee.

After a minute of silence, Beckett looked at me, lingering a moment before refocusing on the road. "I trust that you will no longer stop in the middle of the woods and get out to investigate when you see a stranger lurking in the shadows."

We rolled to a stop behind my truck. I was relieved to see it hadn't been vandalized or broken into.

"Thank you." I gripped the door handle, paused, and turned back toward him. "I really am sorry. Please send me the bill for your truck. You can either send it to my house or the office, but please send it."

"Please don't go chasing strangers in the dark, Dr. Bellerose."

I smiled. "Thank you for the ride—and the fancy whiskey-barrel coffee."

"Anytime," he said.

Anytime . . . I thought as I slid behind the steering wheel while he waited for me to pull out.

Chapter Sixteen

Jo

I could feel the energy of the room before I even stepped inside the waiting room of the Dragonfly Clinic.

"Jo . . ." Mia looked up from behind the reception desk, where she was hovering over Stella, who was typing on the computer, her neon-green nails clicking feverishly against the keyboard. I recognized the look on Mia's face—forced politeness masking urgency.

And then I saw why.

Jamie Ledger stood anxiously at the side of the desk, her short blonde hair a frizzed, tangled mess, sticking out at all angles as if she'd stuck her finger into an electrical socket. Her eyes were bloodshot and rimmed with dark circles, her gaze darting around the room in a wild, manic manner. In contrast to the faded hoodie she was wearing, a dozen silver bangles hugged her skinny wrists, clanking against each other as she nervously wrung her hands. Quite frankly, Jamie Ledger looked like one of my patients who had recently been released from a 5150 hold.

Next to her, and in stark contrast to her mother's nervous energy, Aria Ledger stood tall, seemingly unaffected by her surroundings. Her blonde hair ran in long strings over her shoulders, which were draped in a loose-fitting gray sweater. A pair of baggy Levi's hung low on her waist, and I got the impression she'd lost weight recently.

Aria looked at me as I walked in. Her mother rushed me.

"Dr. Bellerose, I'm hoping we can meet with you today, too, after Dr. Frost."

Mia shot me a fervid look that clearly said, *Keep your mouth shut. I'm dealing with this.*

Jamie continued. "I—I know it's short notice, but Mia offered her services." She placed a shaky hand on her daughter's arm.

Jamie's anxiety was so palpable, it actually made me nervous. Apparently, Aria wasn't the only person in the room who would benefit from talking about the traumatic event of walking up on a dead woman in the woods.

But was that all it was? I got the sense there was something else bothering Jamie Ledger, something that made her nervous, scared.

"The last few days have been a lot," she said quickly.

"I can imagine."

Jamie exhaled, and I caught the scent of stale alcohol on her breath. "It's all over—the gossip. We can't go anywhere—everyone's talking . . . saying the craziest things. My poor baby."

Aria's gaze flicked to me. She didn't like being called *poor baby*.

And it was then that I realized she looked much older than her seventeen years. Taller, stronger, both in stature and presence. I wondered if she exercised. Jogged, perhaps? Was that how she'd lost weight? Was that why she'd gone to the lake that day? To exercise?

"I'd be more than happy to meet with you both today," I said, avoiding the I've-got-this-under-control lightning bolts shooting from Mia's eyes. "I'll work it into my schedule, whenever is best for you."

"Mrs. Ledger," Stella said, "can I see your insurance card again, please? And the paperwork?"

I walked up the stairs to my office.

While powering up my computer, I did my best to eavesdrop on what was going on downstairs but to no avail. As the laptop beeped and belched to life, I walked over to the windowed wall that overlooked the lobby, where Aria had drifted away from the reception desk and was staring intently at the stack of inkblot cards I'd strategically placed on the waiting room table. I did this to serve as a conversation opener while clients were waiting for their appointments—and to gauge their willingness to participate.

The teenager became completely transfixed as she flipped through the stack.

A little tingle of excitement sparked in my stomach. Before I could stop myself, I walked back downstairs. Mia and Jamie were in deep conversation, failing to notice my reemergence as they discussed the different routes Aria's therapy could take.

I walked over to Aria. "You're interested in this," I said quietly, not a question.

She looked up, her eyes twinkling with interest.

Smiling, I nodded. "Me too."

I picked up the card Mia and I had argued about the morning before. The one in which Mia, in her grouchy morning sickness state, had seen two animals fighting, and I—in stark contrast—had seen two people meditating.

"What do you see here?" I whispered, not expecting a response, as I knew Aria was primarily nonverbal.

She didn't say anything at first, simply studied the picture with keen interest.

Then she spoke—one single word. "Blood."

It was as if time suddenly stopped. The room fell silent, both Jamie's and Mia's attention whipping in our direction at the unexpected sound of Aria's voice.

I flicked a wrist behind my back, a not-so-subtle gesture to request they remain quiet so that I could explore whatever was happening here.

"Tell me where you see the blood," I said, keeping my voice level despite the excitement that was now rushing through my body.

Aria traced her finger along the outline of the black inkblots, eventually settling on the bottom splatters of ink.

"There?" I asked.

She nodded.

"Do you see anything else?"

She shook her head.

The creak of a floorboard gave Jamie away as she started to approach. Again, I flipped an angry wrist—*Give me one minute. One freaking minute to explore this.*

I pulled another card from the stack, this one a large puddle of ink, a huge, imposing figure that appears to hover over the viewer. To me, it looked like an animal hide or a rug. It was a very important card in the test.

The intention of this card is to represent the test taker's view of authoritative figures—how they feel toward authority, or in some cases, the male gender in general.

It can be a very telling card. The test taker's response indicates how they feel about the ruling presence in their life, whoever (mom, dad, boyfriend, law enforcement, teacher) or whatever (perfectionism, drugs, alcohol) that might be. In my experience in using inkblots with clients, I have found this one to be the breakthrough card.

I slid the card in front of Aria. "What do you see here?"

"Death."

There was no hesitation. No question.

"Death?"

"Death," she said, pulling her hands away from the table and wrapping them around herself.

The card—or her perception of it, at least—made her instantly uncomfortable. It pulled an intense emotion from deep within Aria's buried conscience, and that emotion involved death.

Death of an authoritative figure, I wondered, and thought of her mother hovering behind us. Or was it something deeper? Death of a part of Aria, of a ruling urge or addiction?

Or was I thinking far too much into it? Could it be metaphorical death of a relationship? Aria was at the age when romance and dating took center stage.

Or was she simply picturing Marissa Currie's face in the inkblot? The slaughtered woman she was found sitting next to in the woods.

Whatever had died, according to her subconscious mind, had now become a roadblock in her willingness to participate any further. She was withdrawing, emotionally and physically, from the table.

I spoke quickly. "What else do you see?"

"That's enough," Jamie snapped, pulling Aria into her arms and shooting me a look of disapproval.

Mia and I exchanged glances. Unlike Jamie, Mia understood that what had just happened was an incredible breakthrough. Until now, Aria had only said two words in regard to finding Marissa Currie: *yes* and *no*. But now, two more words had been added: *blood* and *death*.

Aria aggressively withdrew from her mother and looked at me.

I stepped forward, addressing Jamie. "She's okay, Mrs. Ledger." I looked at Aria and smiled. "She's just fine."

"Are you, baby? Are you fine?" Jamie asked her daughter.

Acting on instinct, I said, "Would you be interested in doing some art therapy, Aria? Painting on an easel?"

Mia lightly touched Jamie's arm as Jamie inhaled to protest.

Focusing on Aria, I continued. "We could do it in my office or wherever you would like. But based on your interest in the inkblot test, I think art therapy might be something you'd enjoy, and it also might help you cope with what you've been through."

"Yes," Aria blurted, her voice jarringly loud. Confident.

"Great." I shifted my focus to Stella. "Will you please schedule Miss Ledger for art therapy as soon as possible?"

"Now."

All heads turned to Aria.

"Now?" I asked Aria, unsure if I'd heard her correctly.

"Now."

I smiled. "Well, all right, then. Let's head up to my office."

Chapter Seventeen

Jo

I led Aria up the stairs. Jamie and Mia followed closely behind.

I motioned Aria into my office, then turned, stonewalling Jamie and Mia.

"Please," I said quietly. "It's important that Aria has space to do this. Not just physically but mentally and emotionally as well."

Mia nodded, understanding. Too many bodies in the room. Too many emotions, too much tension in the air.

"We have a small seating area over here," Mia said, urging Jamie away. "Let's go there. Would you like some coffee? We have . . ."

I shut the office door as their voices moved down the hallway.

Aria was standing by the window, staring at the cold, bleak landscape outside.

Quickly, I straightened the painting area I'd haphazardly set up in the back of the office to use while getting my certification. Then I grabbed a stool, placed it in front of an easel, and dragged the small rolling table of paints and brushes next to it. I hadn't planned on the space getting used anytime soon but pulled together what I had as quickly as I could, creating a calm, welcoming, and most importantly, easy place for Aria to express the untold stories of her subconscious.

After cracking the window to allow for fresh air, I gestured to the stool. *God, I'd kill for a smoke.*

"You ready?" I asked.

Aria turned from the window and nodded. I watched her intently as she settled in, taking a long moment to study the canvas. I took in the lines of her face, the crease of concentration above her brow, the intensity that suddenly washed over her.

A few seconds passed by.

A full minute.

Five excruciating minutes ticked by as Aria sat frozen in place, staring blankly at the canvas.

"Would you like some music?" I asked quietly.

Aria thought for a moment, then nodded.

I turned on one of my favorite coffeehouse instrumental playlists. A soft beat filled the air, accompanied by an acoustic guitar.

Aria picked up a paintbrush and began.

I scribbled down the word *music* to remind myself to add this to Aria's chart. Music was her happy place, her calming force.

The painting came together quickly. The chaos in Aria's mind transferred fluidly from her brain, through her hands, onto the canvas. She painted in confident, sharp strokes, passion bursting from her fingertips.

It was fascinating to see, to watch. Spurts of emotion, followed by brief moments of calm while she assessed her work.

I made an effort to notice even the most minute details—the way her eyes flashed with energy with certain brushstrokes, the way they fluttered the second before the brush hit the canvas. The way her shoulders tightened and then released, depending on what section of the canvas she was painting in.

I study each image from three separate perspectives: One, by breaking down the picture by colors, lines, patterns, etc. and then identifying the feeling of each. Is it happiness, sadness, chaos, or calm? Or is it a combination of all four? Two, by recording the sensation that I, the therapist, feel while looking at the picture. Does the image feel cramped, open, claustrophobic, free spirited, or angry? Three, by considering what the image looks like as a whole. What does it remind me of? If anything? What is odd about it? What's in the center—the focus? This perspective mirrors the Rorschach test strategy that I had become so interested in.

After a session concludes, it is my job to connect the analysis of these three perspectives to the trauma that the artist—the client—is relaying through her fingertips onto the canvas. Art therapy is all about uncovering and gathering the clues in the image, then creating a path to recognize, expel, and banish the intrusive, negative thoughts and replace those emotional vacancies with hope.

I made a point not to watch the clock, not to make notes, but to watch her so that I wouldn't miss a thing. My focus was tunnel visioned, my brain mentally cataloging every motion so I could make a record of the experience immediately after, study the notes, and then make my own interpretations over a bottle of wine.

I'd read that many autistic children had heightened intelligence in one or more areas of the brain, despite what appeared to be total disorder in the application of skills. In Aria's case, I began to think her superpower was an extraordinary kind of communication. A heightened way of making her point, a heightened way to portray her thoughts. Not just through painting but through nonverbal cues as well.

Aria spoke with her eyes. With the brush in her hand. With the way she moved. A laser-like intensity that left no question that she was speaking to you—without actually speaking to you.

Aria was a beautiful, anomalous creature, and in those few minutes of watching her paint, I became entranced. I felt like I was watching something magical. A gift from God, a different kind of being, one with a diagnosis that is often misunderstood, but in reality, isn't a diagnosis at all—it's simply her, *she*, in her own beautiful way.

Jamie appeared in the doorway, peeking through the small window, hoping to glimpse the daughter she didn't understand.

I stayed rooted in place and forced a smile.

Jamie responded by tapping on the window like a child at an aquarium.

I quietly crossed the room and cracked open the door.

"Can I come in?" Jamie whispered, her breath laced with black coffee, her overactive nerves now short-circuiting. "Please."

"It would be best—"

"Please."

I looked over her shoulder, searching for Mia. She was nowhere in sight, likely with a client. I could hear Stella downstairs on the phone.

Dammit.

"Sure," I said, biting the inside of my cheek.

Jamie slipped past me, slinking into the shadows against the wall. I joined her, and together we watched her daughter paint.

Sleet began to ping on the windows, a loud and erratic *tick, tick, tick.* Another intrusion, another request to come inside. The universe, anxious to read its child's message.

Finally, Aria set down the brush.

I didn't need to look at Jamie to see that her jaw was on the floor.

I stepped forward—in almost a protective stance, I noticed—shielding Aria, her creation, her emotions right there on the canvas, from her mother who didn't understand.

Aria stared at the canvas.

Awestruck, I stared at it too. Because before me wasn't just a painting; it was a story. A tale of violence, of pain, right there in the bleeding brushstrokes. The splatters in the corners, the strokes of red in the center; each wave stacked onto the other until eventually fading into angry slashes and more splatters. Each pattern of waves eerily similar.

It was unquestionably a story. A communication.

Written in blood.

"Oh my God." Her mother gasped. "She's painting what she saw," Jamie whispered as if her daughter weren't coherent enough to hear or understand her. "On the dead woman she found in the woods. Marissa Currie. She's painting the blood she saw."

Jamie was right. Aria had recreated the exact image that had been painted on Marissa Currie's torso, painted in her own blood.

The fourth creation of the Pollock Butcher.

But was Aria painting what she'd seen?

Or was she painting what she'd done?

Chapter Eighteen

Beckett

The first round of Winter Storm Agnes had begun, intermittent showers of freezing rain and blustery winds, accompanied by a bone-chilling drop in temperature. It was the beginning of what was predicted to be one of the worst ice storms in recent history.

While most of Skull Hollow's citizens had retreated indoors to huddle around their fireplaces, I'd spent the day walking the woods around County Road 49, searching for any tracks from the mystery person Jo had claimed she saw lurking in the shadows the night before.

The more I thought of the situation, the angrier I became. Why would a woman, alone, get out of her car to investigate a stranger in the woods—in the middle of the night?

It made no sense.

And why was she so adamant about me not calling the cops?

Jo was lying, keeping secrets, and I didn't tolerate that well—especially from her.

Why? Because her lying to me indicated that she didn't trust me, and that bothered me more than I cared to admit. I wanted Jo to trust me, to confide in me, to *want* me to protect her.

I wanted Jo to like me.

Why? Because I liked her.

A lot.

I wanted to find the tracks of whoever she saw, not only because they might lead to whoever was slicing up local women, but also because finding them would give me a reason to call her. To tell her who it was that she saw and then casually ask her to dinner—for the second time.

Unfortunately, no tracks were found, and on my way back to the office, I received a call from the head of the FBI team assigned to Marissa's case, requesting the equipment and expertise of the LYNX Group to assist in searching the lake around Lookout Point.

The team was growing desperate. It had been just over two days since Marissa Currie's body was discovered. Hours of interviews, dozens of false leads, and a handful of weak evidence had yielded no substantial movement in the case. The Pollock Butcher appeared to be gone in the wind, leaving nothing but nightmares in his wake.

That is, until Alek, Dane, and I showed up.

Within two hours of using LYNX boats and high-end sonar equipment, my team had located a submerged vehicle a quarter mile south of Lookout Point, just beyond an old drop point for fishing boats. The area had been searched previously by local authorities, and I made a mental note to check who, exactly, had conducted the search. It was a major miss, one that could have cost the success of the investigation.

By dusk, two tow trucks and a team of crime scene techs had arrived on site.

Klieg lights had been erected along the shoreline, the loud fluorescent lights shining down on the white car being pulled from the lake. The small one-room structure known as Lookout Point now served as a command post that included two space heaters and a pot of coffee. In the distance, yellow and white lights twinkled from the boats slowly searching the pitch-black lake for additional missed evidence.

Namely, the knife used to slice Marissa's body to shreds.

I'd just pulled my own boat to the dock and was making my way to the crowd.

At least a dozen people stood anxiously around the tow truck, their hands shoved into pockets, shoulders hunched against the wind. The team of divers sat huddled under solar blankets, sipping on Styrofoam cups of coffee, waiting to be dismissed. A three-man crew from the local towing and recovery outfit worked the trucks, fighting the mud that was growing slicker by the minute. After multiple hours and numerous attempts to gain traction on the damp, muddy shoreline, the engine blew on one and patience cashed out.

It was a slow, laborious process.

After a quick chat with the Feds, I found Sheriff McNamara at the front of the crowd, watching the car being pulled from the water. "Is that it?" I asked as I walked up. We stood with our backs to the crowd.

"Yes, sir—a white four-door Corolla with a license plate number that matches Marissa Currie's car. This indicates that Marissa drove out here on her own accord and wasn't abducted by her killer. And that her killer got rid of her car after he killed her. Why?"

"Maybe he was in the car with her or had been in the past. Maybe he was worried about his DNA being discovered inside her car."

The sheriff nodded. "Have your men found anything else out in the lake?"

"No. I've instructed them to keep at it."

"Good."

"Any bodies in the car?"

"No. The diver did a thorough check before we began pulling it up. The windows were up, no one inside. Nothing suspicious on his initial look. Took underwater pictures."

"I'd like to see them."

"I'll see what I can do." The sheriff frowned in deep thought. "So . . . what? Miss Currie drives out to Skull Lake to meet someone at Lookout Point, namely her killer. Or maybe she was out for a hike."

"No, that wouldn't make sense. This part of the trail is off the grid. Only seasoned hikers know about it. No one comes out here without a purpose."

"Good point. Okay. So, let's say she was coming out here to meet her killer . . . for what? How did he lure her out here?"

"What do her cell phone records show?"

The sheriff glanced over his shoulder at the Feds with hostile, slitted eyes. "From what I've *gathered*"—he paused to emphasize his annoyance that he wasn't being filled in on case details—"Marissa's phone records show only normal activity. Calls for takeout, bill pay, et cetera. And the only people she communicated with—of interest, anyway—were one of her girlfriends who worked at the chicken plant and her boyfriend, Grady Humphries."

"Let me guess. The girlfriend has a solid alibi, just like Grady does."

"Righto."

"Any calls to Leif Ellis? The drug dealer she was rumored to have been seen talking to last week."

"Nope. There is *nothing* to *anyone* indicating a meetup here two nights ago."

"She could have used a different phone to communicate with whoever she was meeting. A burner phone yet to be discovered."

"True."

"Or her killer drove with her," I continued. "She picked him up, and they came together."

"If so, this points to whoever the hell she was rumored to be messing around on Grady with. The affair. The guy she was cheating on Grady with is the guy who killed her."

"And that guy is the Pollock Butcher?"

"Shit, I don't know." McNamara shook his head, clearly frustrated.

"What do you know about this Leif Ellis guy? A former biker, known drug dealer. Someone to watch out for, in my opinion."

"Agreed, but . . . I personally know that guy. Old hippie. We used to run into each other at the farmers' market all the time. I can't see him slicing up multiple women and painting on their bodies. Yeah, he's a bit odd but just doesn't seem the sort. I don't see him as the Pollock Butcher."

"Whoever it is isn't only smart but an avid outdoorsman. No one could dump that many bodies in the woods and not leave a single trace. He knows what he's doing."

"Agreed."

"Is the scenario the same with every one of the victims?" I asked. "Body found in the woods, sliced, painted, and their car disposed of?"

"No. In the other cases, the women's cars were found somewhere nearby. And their keys, phones, and purses were left at the scene."

"This is important."

"Why?"

"It means the Pollock Butcher is going off the script that has worked for him thus far. Which means he's thinking either emotionally or reactively, not methodically anymore. Something with this one—with Marissa Currie—has triggered something in him. Something is making him feel like he needs to change things up."

"Or he's spooked. Maybe something has him spooked."

I nodded.

The car shuddered with a jolt as the crane dipped unexpectedly. A collective gasp, punctuated by a few curse words, swept through the crowd.

"Christ Almighty." McNamara shook his head. "They've got a damn eighteen-year-old driving that motherfucker. I'm going to go see how I can help."

I surveyed the boats in the distance. "I'm going to check on Alek and Dane, see if they've found anything interesting out there."

"Yeah," the sheriff said over his shoulder, "like the murder weapon."

I nodded but bit my tongue.

They wouldn't find the knife that killed Marissa Currie.

The Pollock Butcher might be going off script, but he wasn't that careless.

Chapter Nineteen

Jo

The streetlights clicked on as I slipped into the only remaining parking spot at the Sunrise Café.

Freezing rain sparkled in the dim orange glow of the lights, but there was nothing magical to it. Instead, a palpable, nervous energy had settled in town. Everything was dark, gray, muted, haunting. A local homicide and impending ice storm were taking their toll on the citizens.

I had a headache. I was tired, hungry, and generally pissed off. The Dragonfly Clinic had been slammed with walk-ins and calls from clients trying to get in before the storm hit. I was busiest of all, as missing therapy wasn't nearly as catastrophic as running out of Prozac.

My afternoon was spent at the courthouse for a witness testimony where I'd been subpoenaed to the stand to validate and explain my medical diagnosis of a client who was currently being tried for second-degree battery. I despised testifying. It always felt like I was trying to convince everyone in the room of the validity of my profession.

In the little spare time I had between appointments and phone calls, I studied Aria's painting and recorded my analysis of what it could mean—all four thousand of my interpretations. When I needed a break from that mental jigsaw puzzle, I called Leif, over and over again.

Still, no answer. It was unacceptable and, quite frankly, pissed me the hell off. Leif was avoiding me, and I became more and more convinced that it had been him I saw in the woods that night.

The café was packed to the gills. Most people were waiting for takeout to eat with their families, one last good meal before the weather hit and the electricity went out, as was expected.

In contrast to the cold air outside, the café was humid and hot, the air thick with the aromas of grease, coffee, and burned toast. I imagined the furnace was on full blast, the locals unaccustomed to dealing with such dramatic temperature shifts. The waitresses looked haggard, eager to get home and out of the weather.

Round, ruddy faces turned toward me as I paused by the checkout counter and loosened the scarf around my neck, scanning the floor.

"Hi there."

Charlene, a veteran Sunrise Café employee, breezed up to me, deftly sliding a tray of dirty dishes on the counter beside the register. I almost didn't recognize the fifty-seven-year-old Skull Hollow native and wouldn't have if not for the color of her trademark raspberry-red lipstick.

Stella was right; Charlene had cut her hair and looked vastly different. Her former long, stringy gray strands were now a helmet of pin-straight, chin-length, platinum-blonde hair framing a round, happy face with stenciled-on eyebrows and rose-colored blush. Dangling from her ears were gold hoops you could stick a fist through. She wore a white apron over a traditional blue diner dress and blinding-white Nikes with pink laces.

I thought of my mother. Was the waitress also in the midst of a midlife crisis?

Charlene Webley was on her fourth marriage, sixth home, and third goldendoodle named Debbie. (Charlene believed in reincarnation.) The only thing constant in the woman's life was her job and her ability to regurgitate every single piece of gossip that had come through her diner in the last twenty years.

"Jo, right?" she asked.

"Yes, ma'am," I said. I wasn't a regular diner at the café.

"Thought so."

There was an awkward beat between us. I'd lived in Skull Hollow long enough for everyone to know my name, and it was a testament to my hermit lifestyle that the locals still felt the need to confirm it.

"Is Leif Ellis here?" I asked.

Charlene glanced back at the kitchen, then up at the clock. "I think he just got off, or at least should be getting off. Can I help you with something?"

"No, thank you. I was hoping to catch him before he left. Would you mind telling him I'm here?"

The waitress studied me closely in a way that instantly put me on edge.

Of all the time Leif and I had spent together and all the experiences we'd shared, I'd never—not once—gone to his place of work and asked for him. Not only because I knew it was risky on my behalf, but also because he'd specifically told me never to do it.

Desperate times called for desperate measures. He should have answered his damn phone.

"Just a minute." Charlene held up a finger before turning and disappearing into the kitchen.

I waited and waited.

And waited.

I could feel the crowd staring at me, this odd, black-haired doctor from the city. I looked at my feet, my head down with insecurity.

No.

I cleared my throat, lifted my chin, and pulled back my shoulders.

They don't know you. Screw them.

Finally, Charlene reemerged from the kitchen.

"You just missed him," she said, avoiding eye contact.

"Did I?"

"Yep. Sorry."

I lingered on her long enough to make sure she knew that I knew she was full of shit.

"Thanks."

I spun on my heel, pushed out the door, and hurried around to the back of the building—where Leif, sure enough, stood under the awning, bundled in an oversize leather jacket, scarf, and black beanie. He was smoking a cigarette.

And he wasn't alone.

I immediately recognized the frizzed blonde hair, the pale skin, the skinny stature.

What *the hell* was Leif doing talking to Jamie Ledger, Aria's mother? I didn't know they knew each other. Jamie and Leif had at least a fifteen-year age difference and nothing in common, best I could tell. Was she buying drugs? Surely not. Not out in the open like this, and not after her daughter, her family, had been thrust into the public eye. It would be too risky. Right?

I considered hiding behind a nearby dumpster to eavesdrop but then remembered that I'd already been seen by everyone in the café and assumed prying eyes were on me still.

My body stiffened with a surprising rush of anger.

What had Leif gotten himself into?

A twig snapped under my feet.

Shit.

Leif's face dropped when he saw me.

Jamie's bloodshot eyes rounded like a child caught doing something naughty. A small white bag was clutched in her hand. She immediately stepped away from Leif, a feeble attempt to distance herself from him.

The woman looked worse than she had when I saw her earlier that morning, as if she'd been crying. She was wearing the same baggy hoodie and yoga pants.

Where was Aria?

"H—hi, Dr. Bellerose . . ."

"Hi, Jamie," I said, glancing at Leif. "How's Aria?"

"Good. She's home with Cyrus." Jamie glanced at Leif. "I'll see you around."

Without waiting for a response, Aria's mother hurried to her gray truck. I noticed the front vanity plate that proudly depicted the firefighter's flag. A nod to her husband.

Leif took a long drag from his cigarette once Jamie was out of earshot. Glaring at me, he released it slowly. "I thought we agreed to never show up at each other's place of work."

I slammed my hands on my hip. "I didn't realize you and Mrs. Ledger were friends."

He glanced over his shoulder as Jamie's truck pulled onto a side street.

"We're not. She just came in for some takeout, and we ran into each other out here."

"That's what was in the bag she was holding? Takeout?"

"Yes," he said, catching my implication that he'd just sold her drugs.

"Where the hell have you been?" I snapped.

Leif took another annoyingly long drag, eyeing me over the tip of his cigarette. He blew the smoke to the side. I wanted to walk into it and inhale every bit of nicotine into my lungs.

"You okay, Bellerose?"

"I said, where the hell have you been?"

"And I said, I thought we agreed to never show up at each other's place of work."

"I wouldn't have to meet you like this if you'd answer your damn phone. Answer my question—where have you been?"

Leif tossed his cigarette onto the cracked concrete, then stomped it out. "Busy."

"Busy doing what?"

His eyes narrowed. "Since when did I owe you a recap of my daily activity?"

"Since I held your head while you detoxed all over my toilet for four days."

"Listen, young lady—"

"*Don't* call me that."

"This goes both ways. You've got dirt on me, and I've got plenty on you." His bushy brow cocked. "Are you already out of that stash you bought from me last week, *Doctor* Bellerose?"

Anger, frustration—*embarrassment*—blazed inside me.

"Listen, asshole, I didn't spend five figures to send you to rehab to turn around and wreck it all. Someone's got to hold you accountable."

"There's really no need anymore. I've decided to stop selling."

I snorted out a laugh. "What, are you serious?"

"Dead serious."

"So, just like that, you're an honest man?"

"Just like that."

"I don't believe you."

"I don't believe you're here because you care enough about me to hold me accountable for my sobriety. You're here because you're covering your own ass."

"Where have you been?" I snapped, avoiding his comment—the truth.

"Busy," he hissed back. "They've got me pulling doubles here."

I envisioned the dark silhouette running through the woods two nights earlier. Was it him?

I crossed my arms over my chest in a rather childish show of I'm-not-leaving-until-you-talk.

"Dammit, Bellerose." He shook his head. "You'd be a lot happier if you'd learn to just let shit go."

"Talk."

Leif released a heavy exhale, peering toward the woods, and for the first time, I saw stress pull at his face. Real, heavy emotion.

"Talk," I said. "Please."

He looked at me. "They questioned me about Marissa Currie."

"*What?*"

"Yeah."

"Who questioned you?"

"The Feds."

"What were you questioned about?"

"Someone saw me with her last week, outside of Jolene's bar."

"What were you doing with her?"

"Nothing. I'm not the dude she was sleeping around on Grady with, if that's what you're asking."

"Were you selling her drugs?"

He looked away.

"Leif—"

"Yes. Just a little pot. One of the girls here—I guess a friend of one of her friends—said Marissa was asking where she could get some weed, and she was pointed in my direction."

"What girl?"

"One of the part-time waitresses here. Amy. Don't worry; she was questioned too."

"Do they think you did it?"

"You mean *kill* her?"

"Yeah. Is that the vibe you got?"

"No—I . . . I don't know."

Leif glanced at the door. He wanted away from me, away from this conversation. He wanted me gone.

"Where did you do the exchange? Where did you give her the drugs?"

"Here. Slipped it in a napkin when she and her boyfriend came in."

"Grady Humphries."

"Right. She left cash on the table—looked like a tip—and the waitress gave it to me. Done deal. No biggie."

I frowned, contemplating this small but potentially huge detail for a minute. "Have you ever sold to Grady—her boyfriend?"

"No. I don't think he uses."

"Really?"

"Yeah, I would know. He drinks and is a total dick. That's all I know."

"You think he was a dick to her? To Marissa?"

"If you're asking me if I think he killed her, then no. I don't know." Leif shrugged. "I just don't see it."

"Did you kill her?"

"What the—" His face scrunched in disgust. "Get the hell out of here, Bellerose."

"What were you doing a few nights ago when I called you so many times?"

"I told you," he said in a slow, measured tone. "I was working."

"What about after work?"

"Home."

Lie.

We stared at each other with the suspicion and readiness of two soldiers meeting on opposite sides of the battlefield.

"Well," he said, "as you can see, I'm alive and everything's okay."

"Well, answer the phone next time I call you."

"Stay away from my work. Seriously, Jo."

"Then answer your phone."

We took a step away from each other. Neither of us liked this relationship, but it was what it was.

I watched Leif disappear back into the diner.

What were he and Jamie Ledger, Aria's mother, whispering about? And what the hell wasn't he telling me?

Chapter Twenty

Beckett

After what seemed like an eternity, Marissa Currie's white car was fully recovered from the lake and back on solid ground.

Despite freezing rain and rapidly declining weather conditions, the crowd had grown. I didn't recognize many of the faces, and this made me uneasy. Men huddled around the Corolla, sipping coffee and smoking cigarettes, like a block party of rednecks on a lazy Sunday afternoon. A crowd lurked behind them, puffs of steam rolling from flapping jaws as conspiracy theories of Marissa's death were eagerly shared.

An FBI crime scene tech dressed in full hazmat gear was busy conducting her initial examination of both the exterior and the interior of the car. Next, the car would be shipped to a local warehouse, where it would be dismantled and scanned for trace evidence that might not have washed away.

A short, petite brunette bundled in a red scarf and tweed coat stole my attention.

I wove my way through the crowd, tunnel visioned on the administrative assistant to the county coroner's office. A young, excitable woman, Stephanie Johnson enjoyed Zumba, rum-fueled drinks with umbrellas, and having her toes nibbled after being spanked—the latter revealed after one too many of the aforementioned umbrella drinks.

"Well, if it isn't Beckett Stolle." Her blue eyes slitted as I approached. Inwardly, I cringed.

So, she was still mad. This confirmed what I knew to be true of all women. Even if they tell you they aren't looking for a relationship, they absolutely, unequivocally, in fact, *are* looking for a relationship and *not* a one-night stand.

"Good to see you," I said politely, attempting to defuse the tension between us. Then I went with a joke. Because what was the assistant county coroner doing out here, anyway? "Is there another dead body somewhere around here?"

"Yours if you don't get to the point."

I cleared my throat and cut to the chase. "Did Dr. Mackenzie finish Marissa's autopsy today?"

"He did."

"And?"

"And what?"

"What did he find?"

Stephanie pursed her lips and regarded me closely, allowing a minute to pass as she feigned commitment to the confidentiality agreement she'd signed upon accepting a job at the coroner's office.

I knew better. Everyone in town knew better. It was widely known that the only thing Stephanie Johnson enjoyed more than getting spanked was spreading gossip.

However, having nibbled her toes personally, my understanding of the administrative assistant went a bit deeper than that. I knew that Stephanie teetered on the line of histrionic personality disorder, someone who derives their self-worth by getting attention from others. Likely driven from low self-esteem, Stephanie's drug was attention. (Dr. Bellerose would be very pleased with this assessment.)

"The Feds are keeping details close," Stephanie said finally, succumbing to her craving for my undivided attention. "No one seems to know what's going on here anymore."

I closed the few inches between us. Lowering my voice, I said, "Except for you, right?"

And just like that, Stephanie forgot all about that pesky little non-disclosure agreement.

"The stab wound in the back of Marissa's neck was the same as all the other Pollock Butcher victims. They were all immobilized in the same way. It's him. There's no question."

"Any idea what kind of tool was used?"

She frowned. "A knife, obviously."

"Right, but I mean, what did the official report suggest of the specifics? The size of the blade, the width, type of blade edge . . ."

"Oh." She thought for a minute. "I didn't really get into that part. But I know it was a small laceration—and I know this wasn't the official cause of death."

Possibly a pocketknife, I thought, something that the killer could carry around easily in his pocket without being noticed. This also suggested the killer was extremely confident, as he would have had to get very close to his victim to stab her in the back of the neck.

This validated the assumption that the Pollock Butcher had made enough of a connection to his victims that they felt safe and allowed him to get physically close. Had he met them before? Or had he simply lured each victim to himself in a manner that made them feel safe and comfortable?

Was he posing as a trail guide, perhaps? Someone from the Skull Hollow Parks and Recreation team? Or was he simply charming and skilled at small talk?

I thought of Ted Bundy. A good-looking, charismatic psychopath with a, quote, kind and loving personality, according to his neighbors. Bundy was able to lure women to himself easily and make them feel safe with very little interaction. This was unusual for serial killers. Bundy appeared to be a one-off, which was why his case was studied ad nauseam. Most serial killers had outward signs of psychopathy. Ted Bundy was more than socially competent; he was also charming.

So, what did this mean?

Was this who we were looking for? A Ted Bundy type? Someone who, by society's standards, was considered popular? Someone others liked? Gravitated toward, perhaps?

"What about Marissa's toxicology report?" I asked.

"Clean. No drugs or alcohol in her system at the time of death—wait, I take that back. She had some sort of allergy medicine in her system, but that was it."

This surprised me. Despite the fact that Marissa Currie was dating a known troublemaker like Grady Humphries and had been seen most recently with Leif Ellis, a known drug dealer, the woman was clean.

"What is the official cause of death?"

"Hemorrhagic shock after deep myocardial injury—he stabbed her right in the heart." Stephanie's eyes flared with sick excitement. She liked the macabre nature of it.

I made a mental note of this and tucked it away.

"This is also congruent with the Butcher," she said. "All his victims are stabbed in the heart before he slices them up. In this scenario, the victim loses consciousness from shock within the first fifteen seconds and then completely flatlines within three to five minutes. Final death would come within eight minutes. Which means they're technically still alive when he starts slicing their veins and painting them."

"Did Marissa have any defensive wounds?"

"Nope, not a one. But Mackenzie made a note that Marissa could have fought back at some point, but because of the way her body was so sliced up, any minor defensive wounds might have been impossible to see."

"Did anyone come by the office asking to see the autopsy report?"

"You mean aside from the Feds and Sheriff McNamara?"

"Right."

"No, not that I recall."

The sheriff's voice boomed over the crowd as he yelled to one of his sergeants. The crime scene tech was wrapping up her initial examination of Marissa's car. I wanted to catch her before she left.

"Thanks, Stephanie," I said. "Be careful getting home."

As I walked away, she called out, "Why didn't you ever call me back, Beckett?"

I turned, staring at her a minute. "You're a beautiful woman, Stephanie. And you deserve much better than the half-assed effort I would put into any relationship."

She blinked.

As I walked away, I realized Stephanie wasn't the only one surprised by my admittance.

So was I.

I thought of Jo and my intense attraction to her. Was that all it ever was with me? Attraction, the chase, then—*bam*—boredom?

It didn't feel like that with Jo. It felt like more.

Why?

Because she is more.

McNamara spotted me as I approached the crowd.

"Did your boys find anything?" he asked, advancing.

"No. They're about to pull in the boats for the night."

"No keys?"

I frowned. "Keys?"

The sheriff jerked his chin toward the car being examined. "No keys in the car."

"Really?"

"Yeah. The tech checked everywhere—the floorboard, under the seats. The windows were up, so there's no chance they fell out. Surprised the hell out of me too. For the car to be in neutral, the keys would've had to have been in it."

"Not if it were a remote key. The killer could have had it in his pocket as he pushed the car into the lake."

"Then what? He kept the keys? That's reckless—keeping a piece of evidence that would undeniably link him to Marissa's car."

"Could be a souvenir," I said. "Not uncommon. But . . . back to the spooked theory. What if the killer wasn't thinking correctly? Clearly? Didn't mean to keep the keys? Maybe he meant to put them back in the car before it submerged. Remember, the Pollock Butcher had never disposed of a victim's car before. And he's always left the purse, keys, and phone at the scene. He's gone off script with Marissa."

McNamara chewed on this a minute. "So, we're looking for those things and the murder weapon."

"Two knives."

"What?"

"The knife the Butcher used to stun the victims in the back of the neck, and the one used to penetrate the heart."

The sheriff turned toward me. "How the hell do you know these details?"

"Probably the same way you know half the shit you've told me since the Feds took over. I asked around."

He sighed. "Damn Stephanie. Damn small town."

"Not anymore," I said, nodding toward the crowd, the navy wind-breakers marked *FBI*.

McNamara scoffed. "They don't know these woods like me, like you." I nodded.

"Not many people know them like you and your team."

"Where are you going with this, Sheriff?"

"Just saying. A small set of keys and a knife—or two—takes a keen eye to find in this kind of terrain. Be a shame to be missed."

I dipped my head, understanding what he was telling me—*search again, under the radar. Look harder.*

This was perhaps what I liked most about Sheriff McNamara. The man was old school when it came to getting shit done. Use whatever you can, whoever you can, and use every tool in your toolbox to get it done.

The sheriff did what he did because he loved his community. While the Feds approached the investigation as an assigned case, McNamara approached it with his heart. He wanted the Pollock Butcher caught, not for the attention that would come with national headlines, but because it was *his* town that was being terrorized now.

I nodded. "You'll hear from me early tomorrow morning."

"Thanks. Be careful on these roads. Just got a call from Nancy that someone slid off about an hour ago. They're already starting to get slick, and the bad ice isn't even supposed to start until tomorrow afternoon. The roads will be covered in wrecks, distracted drivers not using common sense."

I thought of Jo, her silhouette behind the wheel as she pulled right out in front of me.

Distracted driver, yes. But why?

I nodded.

After checking in with Dane and Alek to ensure they were good, I made my way back to my truck with one thing on my mind.

Jo Bellerose.

I settled in behind the steering wheel and looked at the cardboard box on the passenger seat. *Distracted drivers . . .*

I pictured her face, the fear and panic as she jumped out of her truck and sprinted to mine. Then I pictured her eyes as I cupped her cheeks and kissed her.

I turned the engine, hesitated, then looked again at the box—at the headlight I'd purchased at the auto shop earlier that day. Not for my truck, but for hers. A spontaneous decision inspired by the woman I hadn't been able to stop thinking about. The one I knew wouldn't take the time to fix her truck.

Yep, Jo Bellerose needed someone to change that light for her.

And I sure could use another kiss.

Chapter Twenty-One

Jo

I turned into my driveway, irritated at Leif and wondering what the hell he was keeping from me, and on edge from the weather.

Ice was beginning to form on the roads and bridges. The trees would follow next. I found myself worrying about my patients, about their medications. If the pharmacy closed down for a few days, would they be okay? If not, how could I help them?

I thought of the stash of expired pills in my safe. Began making plans.

My truck's one working headlight swept across the dense woods that surrounded my home, and something tickled in my stomach. An unease, deep inside. I straightened in my seat, suddenly becoming very alert.

Slowly, the headlight illuminated the front of my house.

I gasped and slammed on the brakes, sending my purse and briefcase tumbling onto the floorboard. I sat frozen for a minute, completely dumbstruck at what I was staring at.

My home had been vandalized. Someone had vandalized *my home*.

A shot of white-hot anger flew up my spine. This was *my* house. The only thing I had.

Mother. Fuckers.

I hit the gas, my tires spinning before the truck slid to a stop in front of the porch. I threw open the driver's door and stormed out, my heart pounding and fists clenched. I had absolutely no doubt that I would have physically attacked anyone who approached me in that moment.

My pulse roaring in my ears, I crossed the small driveway, surveying the red paint that had been splashed across the front of my house. Splattered on the windows, the awning, the wood slats that lined the porch. The front door was almost completely covered.

As the scene unfolded around me, common sense began to slowly awaken.

Turn off your truck. Close your door. Get your keys. Call someone.

But I didn't listen. Instead, I marched up the porch steps.

That was when the smell hit me. A sharp, sweet metallic scent.

No . . .

I stopped at the top of the steps, staring at the red paint splattered across my front door. Except it wasn't paint . . .

It was blood.

Chapter Twenty-Two

Beckett

Jo stood frozen like a statue on her porch, her back to the driveway. She was staring at her front door, in some hypnotic state. Like a ghost, unmoving, the strands of her long hair so black, they glowed blue in my headlights.

And then I noticed the red. It was everywhere. Splashed like war paint across the front of her house. I didn't need to examine it to know it was blood. I'd seen enough blood-splattered walls in my time overseas.

I pressed the brake, sliding to a stop behind her truck. Still, she didn't move. Had she not heard my truck coming up the driveway? Beginning to worry that something was wrong with her, not just the house, I slammed the truck into park and pushed out of the door.

"Jo," I said loudly, climbing out of the truck. "*Jo*," I said louder when she showed no sign of acknowledgment.

My pulse rate skyrocketed. I broke into a jog, leaping up the steps, ignoring her truck that was still running.

"Jo."

Slowly, she turned.

I'll never forget the look on her face. Her skin was pale, almost luminescent against her pitch-black hair. Her lips were dry and bloodless, her eyes wide, wild with emotion.

Instinctively, I reached out for her hand. "Are you okay?"

Jo responded by holding out her trembling hands but was unable to speak. Her fingers were cold as I pulled her to me.

She blinked, the movement jerking her back to reality. "Yes—Yes. I . . . I drove up, and it was like this—what are you doing here?"

"I came by to fix your headlight."

The admission sounded stupid, but it was the least of my worries at that moment.

Jo frowned, glancing at my truck.

"But it looks like there's something much bigger we need to take care of first. Have you called the cops?"

"What?" she asked, still dazed.

I gestured to the blood splattered on the front door. "The cops. This. Have you called to report it?"

"Oh."

By the look on her face, I could tell that she hadn't even thought about it. A sharp pang of protectiveness shot through me. She wasn't thinking straight.

"Come over here." I gently led Jo to the corner of the porch, the only area the blood hadn't defaced. "Do you have a phone on you?"

"Shit. Yes. But it's in my truck, on the floorboard, I think. I—I . . . skidded to a stop. It fell. Will you get it? I need . . ."

"Stay here."

I jogged to her truck and turned off the ignition. Sure enough, a mess covered the floorboard, where the entire contents of her purse had spilled. I replaced the briefcase on the seat, then carefully examined her purse. I noticed the buttery-soft leather, the Prada label—and the two bottles of prescription pills that had tumbled out, along with her phone.

I glanced up. Our eyes met.

Quickly, I stuffed everything back into the bag and jogged back up the steps. As I handed Jo the purse, I studied her in a new light.

There was only one kind of prescription pill women carried around in their purses—the ones to take in emergency situations brought on by extreme stress. I didn't know why, but I didn't see Jo as the type to take pills. I should have looked at the labels, but something inside me already knew that I wouldn't like what I saw.

Her hand trembled as she pulled out her cell phone.

"Would you like me to do it?" I asked, feeling like I needed to fully insert myself in this situation now.

"Please." She thrust the phone at me, almost dropping it.

I called 911 and relayed the situation. Once I confirmed someone was on their way, I hung up.

"I don't know who would do this . . . I can't imagine." Jo clutched her purse in her hands, staring at the blood on the walls.

"Any crazy ex-boyfriends?" I asked.

"Yes. Many. But not around here."

The comment might have been funny under normal circumstances, but neither of us laughed.

"I thought it was paint when I pulled up. But then I realized it was blood when I walked up the steps." She looked at me, her fear palpable. "I don't think I would've gotten out of my truck. I didn't realize—my God. Blood? *Whose* blood?"

"Maybe not whose, but what kind of blood," I said. "It could be an animal's."

"Wh—" Her voice pitched. "You mean like fucking *Carrie*? The movie? You think someone killed a bunch of pigs to do this?"

"Better than a bunch of humans, right?"

She blinked. "Good point."

"Take a breath, Jo. We'll figure this out. The cops will be here soon. They'll take samples and run a test to let you know exactly what the blood is—if it's human or animal. And they'll go from there."

"If it is human, will the blood tell us whose it is, specifically?"

"Possibly, yes, if the DNA is already in the system."

She refocused on the house, obviously baffled. "Who—why?"

"Think for a minute. Have you had an argument lately with anyone? Wronged anyone? Have you had any conversations lately that were out of the ordinary? With any of your clients? Have you seen anything—"

She spun toward me. Together, we looked at her broken headlight, then back to each other.

Her hand lifted to her mouth. "Oh my God," she muttered between her fingers.

My stomach twisted. "The man you saw in the woods . . ."

"Yes."

Fuck.

"Do you think this is related?" she squeaked out.

The cool, calm, smooth Jo Bellerose I'd met in the bar was no more. And I got the feeling that whoever that woman was, was an act. I recalled the way she'd been with her mother, the odd interaction and obvious tension, how nervous she'd been when I walked her to the door, and how dangerously disheveled she'd been when she ran her truck into mine.

Jo wasn't as stable as she wanted everyone to think she was. This concerned me, and I found myself hesitating with my response.

Did I think the fact that Jo's house was splattered with blood the day after she saw a man creeping through the woods, in the same area Marissa Currie had been brutally murdered, was connected? Yes, I did. In fact, there was no question in my mind. Whoever she saw also saw her, or maybe her truck later that night, and wanted her to keep her mouth shut.

My jaw clenched; I looked away.

"I saw something I wasn't supposed to, didn't I, Beckett? The man in the woods. I saw the Pollock Butcher. Oh my . . ."

Jo reached for the railing to steady herself. The woman was two seconds from a panic attack.

"Hang on, Jo. Sit down. Just breathe." I wrapped my arms around her waist and slowly lowered her onto the porch. "Put your head between your knees. Breathe."

When she calmed, I gently leaned her back against the wall and shifted in front of her.

"Jo, will you please tell me whatever secret you're holding on to?"

"I'm not—"

"I don't believe that you just happened to be driving by Lookout Point and saw someone."

She exhaled. "I was following my mom, okay?"

"Your *mom*?"

"Yes—at least, I think so. She denies it, but I saw it. I saw her leave the house."

"Why did you follow her?"

"Because it was weird. It was late, and I could tell she was sneaking out. She didn't turn on her headlights until she was out of the driveway. Trust me, I know that move."

"Me too. Do you have any idea why?"

"No—not at all."

"But she was here when I brought you home after the accident."

"I know, I know," Jo snapped, growing frustrated.

"Did you see where she went?"

"No, I lost her after she turned onto the road that leads to the lake."

"Could it have been her you saw in the woods?"

"No." Jo scrubbed her face. "Whoever I saw was much taller than my mom."

I frowned. Something wasn't adding up, and still, Jo wasn't telling me everything.

"Jo, did you recognize who you saw in the woods?"

"I—yes, possibly." She shook her head, angrily pushed off the porch floor, and began pacing. "But no—no. There's no way. If who I saw that night was who did this," she gestured to the blood covering her house. "He didn't—couldn't have done it . . . I *just* saw him. He's been at work all day. I'll confirm it, but there's no way . . ."

I stood. "Who?"

"No, I—"

I stepped forward and grabbed her hand. "Jo, *who?*"

"Leif Ellis."

"The Medicine Man—the drug dealer?"

"Yeah."

The same fucking man who was seen with Marissa Currie days before her murder? Coincidence?

I thought of the pills I'd just seen in her purse. "Jo—"

"Don't take that tone with me." She jerked her hand out of mine, her voice loaded with anger, embarrassment, fear. "It's none of your business."

"This is now absolutely my business. How do you know the Medicine Man, Jo?"

She groaned, jabbed her fingers through her hair, and began pacing again. "It's personal and really no big deal."

Female translation: it's a *big* fucking deal.

"And besides," she said, "Leif didn't do this. I know he didn't. I literally just saw him at the Sunrise Café. He's been working this afternoon. And even if he wasn't, I know he's not like this. It wasn't him." Defiant, she spun toward me. "I know it wasn't."

"Okay." I held up my hands in surrender. "Okay."

Jo suddenly stilled as she recalled something. "When I saw him . . . he was talking to Jamie Ledger."

Christ, the crazy mother of Aria, the girl who found Marissa's mutilated dead body. Everything connected. Incoherent, broken strands that, when separate, didn't seem to fit, but each leading to the same place—the Pollock Butcher.

Jamie Ledger, Aria Ledger, Leif Ellis, Marissa Currie. What was the connection between them all?

"Are you sure the person you saw in the woods was a male?"

"My immediate assumption was that it was a male, but . . . I don't know. You think it could have been Jamie?"

"Anything is an option right now."

Jo looked back at the blood. "I can't see that woman slinging blood all over my house."

Honestly, I couldn't either, but we couldn't rule her out.

"The cops will take pictures and samples of the blood. Hopefully, we'll get something to help unravel this thing."

"What will the pictures help determine?"

"They'll run a BPA—blood pattern analysis—on the patterns of the blood."

"What's that?"

"It analyzes the way the blood was splattered onto the surface. This can reveal some very important things about a crime scene—a homicide, specifically. Like, where the blood came from, what caused the wounds, from what direction the victim was wounded, and what movements were made after the assault. And even further, does this pattern analysis align with witness testimony? It's a huge part of forensics in a crime scene."

"How do you know all this?"

"I interned for a bit with the Criminal Investigations Division of the Marine Corps. Analyzing crime scenes has always interested me—a natural fit for search and rescue. Kind of like your inkblot analysis, come to think of it."

Jo gestured to the bloodstained door. "What does your analysis of this blood tell you?"

"Well . . ." I stepped next to her, and together we studied the pattern. "So, bloodstains are classified into three basic types—passive, transfer, and impact stains. Passive stains are drops coming off a body or a weapon. Transfer is like when blood is smeared on the wall, leaving wipes or patterns. Impact stains are from blood projecting through the air."

She wrinkled her nose. "The gross stuff."

"Yeah, the gross stuff. So, it's the *shape* of the blood spatters that they analyze."

"What do you see here?"

I stepped back and looked around. Then slowly retraced my steps, finding drips of blood on the cold, crunchy ground.

"You can see here"—I motioned to the drips—"that whoever did this was probably carrying a bucket, and moving quickly, based on the drips. And they fade here, where someone would park, which means they drove here."

"Do you see tracks?"

"No, we trampled them with our own trucks."

"Dammit."

"And no visible boot prints."

Jo chewed on her lower lip, deep in thought. "So, they drove right up to the house? That's ballsy."

"Yes, it absolutely is."

Thinking of what the sheriff and I had deduced about the Pollock Butcher, a confident Ted Bundy type, I continued. "And they were carrying the bucket with their left hand, which means they're probably right handed since they flung the blood with their right hand." I followed the blood trail. "You can see the splashes from the bucket right here." I pointed to the bloodstained floorboards, then focused on the walls. "My best guess is that they had a paintbrush, dipped the brush into the blood, then flung it onto the house."

"That's a lot of blood," she said, staring at the door.

"Yes, it is. But that's not what concerns me."

She frowned. "What concerns you?"

"The way they transferred it." I looked up at the ceiling, at the railings, at the floor. "They were swinging the blood erratically, getting it everywhere, probably getting it all over themselves and not caring."

"So, this means they're reckless," she said.

"No. It means they're angry." I turned to her. "This is a message, Jo. A threat, plain and simple."

"What message?"

"To keep your mouth shut."

"Well, that's easy, because I don't even know who I saw."

"But they don't know that."

"Beckett . . . I need to call my mom."

Chapter Twenty-Three

Jo

"Mom."

"Jo, baby, is everything okay? It's late."

I heard the rustle of sheets in the background. I'd awoken her, and I felt bad about that. No matter how mad or frustrated I was with my mother, it pained me to cause her worry.

In that vein, it was an easy decision to *not* tell Melinda about the vandalism. She would freak out, jump in her Mustang, and be back in my house, in my hair, in under three hours. I didn't need that mess. I also didn't need her I-told-you-so's, as she would undoubtedly blame the vandalism on one of my "crazy" clients.

"Everything's fine." I stepped off the porch and walked to the edge of the woods, out of earshot. Luckily, Beckett picked up on the cue and left me alone, though he didn't go far. He was careful to keep me in his sight at all times. "Mom, I want you to tell me where you went the other night, when I got in the accident."

"I told you. I didn't go anywhere."

"That's not true," I snapped in an immature, whiny tone that made me want to punch myself in the mouth. "I *saw* you from my bedroom window. I watched you pull out of the driveway."

"Jo, I didn't go anywhere. It wasn't me."

"Liar," I hissed.

"Josephine Bellerose, how dare you."

I inhaled, biting my tongue. "So, you did *not* leave the house two nights ago?"

"No."

Liar. Just like my father, she lied to her family.

Anger pulsed.

"Fine, Mom. Keep your damn secrets."

I clicked off the phone and stared into the tree line.

How could she lie to me? Her own daughter.

But . . . was I really sure it was her? An orange Mustang? Did I actually *see* the color of the car? Because . . . why would she lie?

I began to shake, my entire body trembling with emotion.

What was happening? It felt like my life was suddenly spinning out of control.

Just then, a pair of headlights reflected off the trees in front of me. I turned as Sheriff McNamara's truck bounced up the driveway.

I looked at Beckett, who gave me a dip of his chin intended to reassure me but that instead sent my stomach twisting.

I watched as he stepped off the porch, his large, masculine body outlined in McNamara's headlights as he strode to the car. Beckett was in his element, responding to an emergency, coddling the victim, handling the procedural side of things, taking care of everything that needed to be done in a cool, calm manner.

A real-life hero, right there in my driveway.

My hero.

Sheriff McNamara got out of his truck, his gaze meeting mine.

I would *not* tell him about my mother. I wouldn't tell him that I'd watched her sneak out of my house and then followed her, thereby spinning me into this whole damn mess. I wouldn't defend myself when she would tell him I was "mistaken."

Why? Because I didn't want her here, to get involved, to make it a huge spectacle.

Lie.

The truth was . . . I didn't want people to think I was losing my mind.

Chapter Twenty-Four

Jo

I was interviewed twice, same questions each time. Samples of the blood were taken.

My house had been searched, every doorknob and window checked, my things turned upside down. The woods had been searched, by both the sheriff and Sergeant Rosa. All this while I stood on the corner of my porch, as instructed, sick with nerves.

The weather wasn't helping calm the energy. The night was as black as coal, spitting freezing rain between gusts of bone-chilling wind.

I told the same story I'd initially told Beckett. The only thing "odd" that had happened to me in the last few days was that, on my way home, I had seen someone in the woods and gotten out to investigate.

Despite not finding any valuable evidence, one thing was for certain. Everyone believed this grotesque vandalism was tied to the man in the woods. And because of the painted blood, it was also tied to Marissa Currie, which meant it was also tied to the Pollock Butcher—which meant the concern, sense of urgency, and attention to detail were kicked up a notch.

The FBI was notified, and they arrived less than five minutes later.

It was chaos, a swarm of strangers stampeding their way into my privacy. And while what had happened was bad enough, I was now also worried about my past being unearthed for the gossip-hungry citizens of Skull Hollow to consume and spread like wildfire. I didn't need that. My clinic didn't need that.

But surprisingly enough, it was Beckett who I cared about the most. I didn't want him finding out that I'd been arrested. And he would because the man wouldn't leave my side. As everyone slowly began to drift away, Beckett remained.

Beckett.

He'd stood by my side—not in front of or behind me—the entire time, never interrupting while I spoke but quick to step in when he could tell I had nothing more to say. He was a wall, tall and strong, between me and everyone else. Screening, protecting, guarding.

It surprised me that I didn't mind this. In fact, I liked it. Appreciated it. Needed it, I realized.

Before Beckett, I'd handled things on my own, and in the rare moments that I had a man in my life at the time something went sideways, that man had backed off, assuming that I, the badass independent woman, could handle it myself.

Except for Beckett.

There was a shift in us that night, subtle but definitely there.

∽

It was almost ten o'clock by the time everything wrapped up. Only one vehicle remained.

Sheriff McNamara emerged from the side of the house while Beckett and I were cleaning blood from the window. Recentering the hat on his head, the sheriff stepped onto the porch. He looked tired, his usual brightness heavily shaded, his face etched with worry lines and wrinkles I'd never noticed before. He was stressed, this incident adding a new level of panic to an already dire case. I wondered if he'd slept since Marissa Currie's body had been found.

"Well"—he scanned the driveway—"looks like everyone's packed up. Sorry you've had to deal with all this tonight."

"Thanks," I said, because, really, what else do you say to that?

"Have you got somewhere else to stay tonight? A safe house?"

A *safe house*?

"Yes, she does."

My attention snapped to Beckett.

McNamara's gaze pinged between us. Apparently, he was picking up on the romantic energy between Beckett and me for the first time. As if the fact that my house had been painted with blood wasn't going to be enough gossip for the morning papers.

"All right, then . . ." McNamara cleared his throat and handed me his card. "Call me if you think of anything that might help with the investigation or if you get scared or anything at all—call me. I'll be up."

I slipped the card into my pocket. "Thank you."

"No problem." He looked at Beckett. "Get to wherever you're going quick. Roads are getting slicker by the minute."

With a tip of his hat, Sheriff McNamara turned and descended the steps.

"Why didn't you tell them about Leif Ellis?" Beckett asked the second the sheriff was in his truck and out of earshot.

"I told you. It's not him. He was at work all day. I'm not going to make such a huge implication like that unless I'm absolutely certain."

"I understand, but Jo, everything needs to be examined at this point. If there is even the—"

"Leif didn't do this, and there is no way that man is the Pollock Butcher." I felt my frustration slowly creep into anger. I was too tired to be questioned again. Too tired to analyze. I was hungry, emotional . . . and scared.

"Every detail, Jo, is important. Everything links. If it feels weird, you need to tell the cops. Period. Trust me here, I know how even the most minuscule thing can make or break a mission, or an investigation, for that matter."

I looked away, beginning to feel sick.

"Just think about it. Think about telling them. And think about telling me, someday soon, why you're so sensitive about Leif."

I looked up at him.

Beckett didn't push, simply stared back. He lifted his hand and tucked a strand of hair behind my ear, leaving a trail of heat from his fingertips that reminded me of our kiss.

Butterflies mixed with the nerves in my stomach.

"I'm going to check the perimeter of the house," he said. "And if it's okay with you, I'd also like to check the inside again now that everyone's gone—while you get your stuff packed."

I groaned.

Beckett's brow arched in a way that told me there was going to be no argument about this. For the first time, I realized that I wasn't the only one who was tired. *Selfish*.

"You're not staying here tonight, Jo."

He was right. I'd be stupid to stay in my just-vandalized home alone while a murderer was on the loose in Skull Hollow.

"Fine. I can call . . ."

Who? Who would I call?

Mia was the only friend I had who I was close enough to and would let me crash on her couch. But Mia was struggling through her first pregnancy and very likely had her head in the toilet at the moment. I didn't want to—wouldn't—intrude on her and add to the stress she was already going through.

"I've got a place close to LYNX headquarters," Beckett said. "You can stay there until we get all this figured out."

Stay—*the night*—with Beckett?

No.

I didn't feel ready to stay with a man I had a legitimate schoolgirl crush on. Emotionally or physically. I hadn't shaved. I had a zit on my nose. I hadn't flossed, and I hadn't washed my hair in two days. I hadn't analyzed every single angle of every single outcome of what a romantic encounter would involve.

Sex? God, no. I wasn't ready for that.

Was I?

No.

"No. It's fine. I can call a hotel, or . . . I can even sleep in my truck somewhere. It's fine, I—"

"Don't worry. I won't stay with you. You'll be alone but very close to the LYNX office where I'll be, along with a bunch of dudes with guns."

"Beck—"

He held up his hand, officially done with the dramatics. "Jo, I've got some shit I need to do tonight, and I'm hungry. I don't have time to stand here and argue back and forth when you and I both know that the end result is, without question, that you will be staying at my place."

I bit the inside of my cheek, then nodded.

He regarded me for a second, surprised at my submissiveness.

So was I.

"Go pack," he said. "I'm going to do a perimeter check, then inspect inside your house. After that, we'll head out." He took my hand and stroked his thumb along the back of it. "One thing at a time, Jo. And that thing, right now, is to pack an overnight bag."

One thing at a time.

Just *one thing at a time.*

But why did it suddenly feel like the entire world was tumbling onto my shoulders?

Chapter Twenty-Five

Beckett

I took my time checking the perimeter, looking for any tracks the officers might have missed. Alone, in the solitude of nature, where I could hear my breath, my steps, the wind through the trees. Where I could close my eyes and listen, feel the air around me, allow my instinct to hunt out even the most minuscule inconsistency in the nature around me. Because there, in that small, seemingly trivial space, was where the clues hid.

This was why I was good at my job. I knew how to slip into that space. How to live there—sometimes for far too long.

I halted when I stepped into the house, taking in the gleaming silver, the sharp lines and angles, the black-and-white monochrome of the modern interior design.

It was stunning and very different. Unexpected.

Just like Jo.

A staircase was suspended by wires. A loft looked down to a living room that, during the day, I imagined was flooded with natural light from the floor-to-ceiling windows. The kitchen was open, a juxtaposition of simplicity and the most complex-looking appliances I'd ever seen. Her coffeepot had six blinking lights and four levers that looked like arms.

I should have been surprised by the masculine feel of the house, but I wasn't. And oddly enough, I found myself aroused by the boldness of the design. Jo was anything but normal and average, and I imagined a life with her would be full of surprises.

I could hear her shuffling around somewhere down the hall. Her bedroom, probably, packing. So, I began my internal audit.

I checked the windows and locks, the doors, the floors, anything with a handle. I looked for any sign to indicate that whoever had doused her home with blood had been inside, but there was nothing.

I made my way—carefully—up the suspended staircase, relieved when the floating structure remained stationary under my weight. Space Mountain? I could ride that thing ten times in a row, blindfolded, backward, upside down. But a gently swaying rope bridge? I puked every time. In fact, it was an ongoing joke among my military buddies.

The loft upstairs served as a home office. All black leather, sharp lines, and the same masculine, monochromatic theme.

I checked the windows, felt the latches. Looked for prints, tracks.

When I knelt down to check a scuff on the baseboard, my attention was pulled to a safe tucked far under her desk, away from prying eyes. The safe's door was slightly cracked open.

My brow cocked.

After peeking up from behind the desk to ensure I was still alone, I refocused on the safe. There was no question that whatever was in the safe was meant for Jo's eyes only.

A hundred different scenarios barreled through my head.

Old pictures of past boyfriends? A collection of taboo sex toys—was she into that stuff? If so, was I? Yes, I would be—with her. Or maybe a stack of cash? A stack of condoms? Female hygiene . . . stuff?

The angel and devil warred on my shoulder. The battle didn't last long.

I quickly—and quietly—rolled away the office chair and crawled under the desk. After one more peek at the doorway, I leaned back on my haunches and opened the metal door.

I wasn't prepared for what I saw. This, coming from a man who served seven tours overseas and conducted more raids on terrorists' homes than I can count. Thing about those raids was that I was prepared for what I saw. I knew what to expect. Bearing witness to the most vile, heinous things wasn't really a surprise.

This was a surprise. The stacks and stacks—*and stacks*—of prescription pill bottles in the safe were nothing less than shocking. The pills were "hidden" behind a stack of old cigars. I wrinkled my nose, cursing them as I set them aside.

My pulse started to thrum as I picked up each bottle one by one, reading the labels.

Xanax.

Two bottles of Ativan.

Four bottles of amitriptyline.

Gabapentin—multiple strengths.

Four more bottles of Xanax.

Klonopin.

And for the grand finale, six—*six*—bottles of Valium.

Each bottle was prescribed to a different patient, different addresses, different directions. I didn't recognize any of the names.

Fake?

I thought about the pills I'd seen in her purse and then about the accident, about how adamant she'd been that I not call the cops. Because she had illegal pills on her? Because she was high? No. I'd been around plenty of intoxicated people. Hell, I'd been trained to recognize it. Jo wasn't high that night; she was scared.

Something clattered downstairs, and my head slammed into the bottom of the desk. I shoved everything back into the safe, repositioned the rolling chair, and shot to my feet. I pulled in a breath, smoothing my pants, my mind racing.

A very interesting development, indeed.

It appeared the badass, independent Jo Bellerose wasn't nearly as put together as she would like everyone to believe. The woman who seemed stronger than most had a weakness bigger than most—one that was deadly.

I made my way back downstairs, contemplating this new twist in the mystery that was Jo Bellerose.

Behind every addiction was a reason, and I wondered what hers was.

In an instant, it seemed, this woman who had intrigued me since before I even met her, the woman who had given me butterflies before I even knew her name, had become an all-consuming obsession. A rock that I had to crack open.

Exactly who was Jo Bellerose?

Chapter Twenty-Six

Jo

I surveyed the items I'd absentmindedly shoved into the overnight bag that I would take to my *safe house*. In this dire emergency situation, I, Josephine Bellerose, had packed:

Three silk pajama sets—one red, one black, one with hot tamales printed all over it.

Seven pairs of fuzzy socks.

Fourteen pairs of thongs.

Two pairs of jeans, three cashmere sweaters, two bras.

Two toiletry bags, one stocked with bathroom essentials and the other with every piece of makeup I owned.

An entire bag of jewelry.

A hair dryer, a curling iron, a jumbo can of dry shampoo.

Gas-X.

Phone charger.

A pair of six-inch stiletto Louboutin heels.

Self-tanning lotion.

A pack of vanilla cigarillos.

A tin of Altoids.

A twelve-pack of condoms, ribbed.

And for the grand finale, a gold-and-diamond belly chain I'd purchased in Vegas on my twenty-first birthday.

As I stared down at the contents inside the Louis Vuitton duffel, two things became painfully obvious. One, my brain had officially stopped working; and two, I had a major—make that *massive*—crush on Beckett Stolle.

Dammit.

I was about to dump everything onto the floor and start over when I heard the growl of an engine fire up outside—my not-so-subtle cue to hurry. *Beckett's hungry,* I reminded myself, recalling his earlier comment.

I quickly zipped closed the duffel, flung it over my shoulder, and after turning off the lights, hurried through the house, checking each room, though I didn't need to. Beckett had already turned off the lights and secured every window and door in my home.

After locking the front door behind me, I observed the bloody smears once more.

My stomach rolled. I couldn't believe this was happening.

"Ready?"

Startled, I turned. Beckett stood at the bottom of the steps, his hands in his pockets, unfazed by the sleet pummeling his head and shoulders.

I shoved my keys into my bag. "Sorry."

Beckett took the duffel from my shoulder and laid his palm on the small of my back. Goose bumps rippled through my body.

"Careful," he said. "It's getting slick." He opened the passenger door for me and helped me inside.

I watched him round the hood, the sleet like a million diamonds falling around him in the headlights. My heart stumbled.

I looked at my bloodstained house, then back at Beckett, and suddenly felt I had no control over my life.

Reaching down, I patted the side pocket of my duffel until I felt the bottle of pills I'd stuffed in at the last minute.

Beckett settled behind the steering wheel, and together, we set out into the cold, dark night.

The beginning of an adventure I would never forget.

Chapter Twenty-Seven

Jo

The roads were empty. The cab was filled with the roar of sleet pummeling the top of the truck, the asphalt ahead of us shimmering with black ice.

As we drove, my mind raced with jumbled, incoherent thoughts.

Why hadn't I demanded to take my own truck? To follow him, so that I would have my own vehicle. So that I could leave whenever I wanted to—or needed to. What would the mailman think when he drove up to the house tomorrow morning and saw all the blood?

Did I lock *all* the doors?

What about work tomorrow? How would I get there? Was I going? Or would I need to be available for any questions the cops might have?

Would the entire town hear that someone doused my home in blood? What would my clients think?

Who the hell was I to serve in an authoritative position meant to fix someone's life when my own was such a mess?

"First thing tomorrow morning," Beckett said, pulling me from my erratic and not-helpful thoughts. "I'll get some of the guys and we'll start cleaning your house."

I released the breath I didn't realize I'd been holding.

Clean the house. Wash away the blood. Yes, this would be step one. Good.

"I'll take you to work—" he continued.

"No, it's my house. If you're going to be there, so will I. I'll help clean it up."

"Come, don't come. Help, don't help. It's up to you."

I frowned. Did he really think I would let a bunch of people into my sanctuary without me there?

"Listen," he said. "We all need help navigating this crazy life every now and again. And I've got a feeling this is one of those times for you. Accept the help, Dr. Bellerose. Tonight, we'll get you settled. Try to get some rest. Your body is in overdrive. If you don't sleep, tomorrow is going to be ten times worse because of it. Right now, you need to focus on calming your body and mind."

"And how do you suggest I do that?"

"I'll be there."

"Because that solves everything?"

"Because I'll help relax you."

I blinked, unsure if the glaring sexual innuendo was intended. I imagined that Beckett Stolle knew exactly how to make a woman relax. Hell, I'd bet the man knew how to make a woman completely comatose for days.

I meditated on this exact thought until we pulled into a long, narrow driveway that wound through a thicket of pines. The needles shimmered in the headlights, making the trees appear as if they were glowing. It was beautiful . . . magical, even.

The driveway took a turn, and as the headlights illuminated my temporary safe house, I couldn't help but be surprised. Floored, actually.

When Beckett had said he "had a place" close to LYNX headquarters, I'd imagined a home that resembled the large, imposing, sleek structure that served as the search and rescue headquarters. Perhaps with bars on the windows and bulletproof siding.

What I got was a tiny, dilapidated stone cottage the size of my closet.

His lips twisted in amusement at my reaction. "You expected something different?"

"Yes. Yes, I can say, with all confidence, I expected something totally different."

"What did you expect, exactly?" He parked in front of the door—no garage—and turned off the engine.

"Well, something . . . a tad larger?"

"Something nicer, you mean."

"No, I didn't say that."

He grinned. "Not all of us were brought up with silver spoons in our mouths, Bellerose."

I snorted. "You mean shoved in our mouths."

"There are those mommy issues again."

"Not funny." I looked away and grabbed my duffel, noting how completely off kilter I was. I didn't like being unceremoniously yanked from my comfort zone and thrown into a situation for which I was totally unprepared.

As I grabbed the door handle, Beckett gently pulled the duffel from my other hand.

Stubborn, I yanked it back. "I can carry my own bag."

The door popped open, and I fell out of the cab, stumbling as my feet hit the ground. Humiliated, I slammed the door.

Beckett was by my side in an instant. This time, I let him take the bag, avoiding eye contact at all costs. He looped the bag over his shoulder, and we made our way to the cottage.

"This was an old war bunker, built sometime in the late 1800s. The walls are strong." He stepped up to the door, a deep mahogany brown. "But the character is even stronger."

He unlocked and pushed open the door. The scent of leather filled my nose, followed by a rush of warm air that enveloped me like a hug.

Beckett motioned me ahead, and with butterflies in my stomach, I stepped into the one-room—yes, one large room—cabin. The scent of warm ashes in the fireplace and coffee beans mingled with the leather.

Cozy was the single word that entered my head.

Despite the weathered exterior, the interior appeared to have been completely renovated.

A massive Persian rug covered most of the cottage, deep shades of red, blue, and brown highlighting aged hardwood floors that had been buffed and polished to a gleam. Two massive leather couches sat in front of a large stone fireplace that served as the focal point of the room. Covered with flannel throws, the couches were colossal and fluffy, the kind that would swallow you up in the most wonderful way when you sank into them.

On the other side of the room was a small kitchenette with only the necessities, a bed that looked to be no more than a double, and beside that, an extremely narrow door that I assumed led to the world's smallest bathroom.

Only two windows—one framed a small shed and a large woodpile in the backyard and the other in the kitchen.

Beckett made no excuses for his place as he hung my duffel on a hook next to the door. And he didn't need to, I realized, because despite the size—or maybe because of it—it was truly a beautiful home. Safe, warm, masculine, and *incredibly* romantic.

"Hungry?" Beckett pulled a bottle of water from the small refrigerator in the corner.

"I'll take a water."

Along with a bottle of water, he pulled out a box of pizza. "Cold or hot?"

"I prefer my water cold, thank you."

"The pizza, Jo."

"I'm not hungry."

"Then you haven't had Paolo's Primo Pizza."

"Paolo's what?"

"Primo Pizza. You know, that new pizza shop that opened up a few weeks ago."

"The one in the Kum and Go gas station?"

"That's the one."

I watched in horror as he opened the box and slid two pieces into a microwave.

I'd only been inside the Kum and Go once before, and that was for an emergency run for cough drops before a deposition. Inside, I'd counted seven roaches, three moldy boxes of mini apple pies—on sale for ninety-nine cents—and one almost fully exposed butt crack.

Beckett looked over his shoulder and grinned. "You're familiar with pizza, yes?"

"Yes, but not particularly with Kum and Go."

"Me either. Don't worry." He winked.

I grinned.

The microwave dinged, and when he opened the door, the mouth-watering aroma of melted cheese and marinara sauce hit my nose. My stomach growled.

After grabbing the roll of paper towels—the entire roll—Beckett strolled into the "couch area" of the room and set the "table" (i.e., the coffee table).

He gestured to the couch, and I sat. "Dig in."

"Into the gas station pizza."

"Don't knock it till you try it."

I watched as Beckett devoured half a slice in one bite, sending a stream of melted cheese down his chin. I wanted to lick it off.

He made a flamboyant display of enjoying chewing.

I smirked and nibbled off a piece of my slice. The pizza was outstanding.

"See?" He grinned, a smear of marinara at the corner of those perfect, plump lips.

I nodded. "It's pretty damn good."

"Right? You should try the Hawaiian."

"I don't like fruit on my pizza."

"You also thought you didn't like gas station pizza."

"True. Quite the day of firsts I'm having, aren't I?"

His hand slid onto my thigh. "We'll get it figured out. Tonight, just turn off."

Turn off.

"Eat." He took another bite. "So, here's the rundown. There's no central air or heat in this castle and no television."

"No air?" I squeaked. "There's no air-conditioning in the place?"

Beckett looked at the window, frosted around the edges. "Just go stand outside for a minute."

"No, I mean, during the summertime. I'm pretty sure having air-conditioning in Texas during the summer is necessary for survival."

He snorted but didn't respond. A ridiculous statement, apparently. I remembered the gossip I'd heard about his time in the military. Weeks spent in the desert. He'd probably learned how to deal with the heat. Princess Bellerose had not.

Beckett shoved the last bite of pizza into his mouth and pushed off the couch.

"Make yourself at home," he said, beginning to stack logs on the fire—something I realized he'd intentionally waited to do until he ensured I ate something.

I took my plate to the "bed area" of the room and set it on the nightstand. After retrieving my duffel from the hook and setting it on the bed, I ran my fingers over the soft cotton duvet. The sheets were a bamboo blend, soft as silk. The pillows, big and fluffy. The large flannel throw, warm and fuzzy. Clean, comfy, safe.

I felt the heat of his gaze on my back. I turned, my pulse picking up steam. Our eyes met like a clash of electricity, the memory of our kiss now front and center in the small room.

"You don't have to leave," I said quietly.

He stared at me a long moment with a flicker of heat. "Okay."

My heart skittered. *Okay.*

"I'll sleep on the couch," he said.

A blow of disappointment settled hard in my gut. I wanted him to *want* to sleep next to me. I wanted to cuddle up to him, wrap my arms around that superhero chest, smell that clean scent of his. I wanted to have sex with him—which wasn't mutual, apparently.

Did he regret the kiss? Was he not attracted to me?

Was I not good enough? The weird girl who just had her house painted in blood.

I looked down and turned my back, refocusing on the bed. And in that moment, I wanted nothing more than to curl into a ball and cry.

Chapter Twenty-Eight

Beckett

It was a test, and she'd failed miserably.

I only offered to sleep on the couch because my mother raised me to be a gentleman. Because I didn't want to take advantage of a woman in a vulnerable and emotional state. I would never do that—unless the need was mutual.

Not only hadn't Jo Bellerose asked me to join her in the bed, but she had also turned her back to me and not uttered a single word the rest of the evening, leaving no question about her lack of interest in me.

After all, it was me who'd initiated the first kiss. I was the one who'd coerced her to stay with me. I was making all the moves.

I didn't sleep that night.

Shortly after the awkward sleep-on-the-couch moment, Jo slipped into bed, not bothering to change her clothes or wash her face or do the hour-long evening ritual most women performed with unfailing commitment. Following her cue, I took my place on the couch and pretended to sleep until, finally, Jo fell asleep sometime after midnight.

I tiptoed across the room, knelt at the bedside, and with the stealth of an Arabian lizard, sifted through Jo's fancy designer duffel bag, praying I wouldn't find what I was looking for.

Unfortunately, I did.

Tucked into a nearly invisible side pocket was a bottle of prescription pills with the name scratched off. Ativan, four-milligram tablets, filled to the fucking top of the bottle. Literally a three-month supply—at least—in one bottle.

My stomach dropped.

With the bottle clutched in my hand, I stood by Jo's bed for longer than I cared to admit, staring down at the angelic face that had completely captivated me. I wanted to touch her hair, long and black, fanning over the pillow—*my* pillow—like waves of silk. I wanted to kiss her lips, pink and plump.

I wanted them to be mine.

I watched the glow of the fire dance across her cheeks, the heavy rise and fall of her chest. Silently, I thanked the universe for giving her this moment of peace. The only other time I'd seen her at peace was the second after our kiss.

I couldn't stop thinking about that kiss, the way my body had responded like an IED had gone off inside me; the way my skin had tingled with heat; the way, for only a moment, I had forgotten everything else in the world.

That is—until I found her stash of pills.

I realized I'd never actually seen her take a pill, and that all the bottles I'd found were completely full. Something wasn't adding up, and for the remainder of the night, I pondered this until, eventually, Jo woke just after sunrise.

She shot up in bed like a jack-in-the-box, momentarily confused by her surroundings. A sleepy yet panicked gaze scanned the room. Her hair was plastered to the side of her face, her eyes puffy, her cheeks rosy with lines of indents from the pillow.

Under different circumstances, I would have laughed at this incredibly cute image. But far too quickly, the haze of sleep faded and the memories of the night before came barreling back to her. Once realization set in, her mood turned vile, grumpy, argumentative, and surprisingly short tempered. I found myself walking on eggshells, approaching her like one might a temperamental toddler.

I informed Jo that a team from LYNX was already on the way to her house to clean the exterior. To my surprise, she said she was going to go into the office instead of being there while they cleaned, as she'd demanded the night before. I asked her why, and she said she had a meeting with Aria for art therapy.

All the better, I thought, because now I didn't need to come up with some bullshit reason to stay with her all day to ensure her safety. She would be safe at the clinic, around her friends, and only a block from the police station. Meanwhile, I could begin my hunt for whoever had vandalized her home.

Over breakfast, Jo filled me in on her last meeting with Aria, about the waves of red Aria had painted on the canvas and about the odd behavior of her mother, Jamie.

Odd behavior . . . kind of like stashing pills everywhere.

I watched Jo like a hawk that morning, wanting to catch her in the act of taking pills. But unfortunately, she slipped into the bathroom with her entire duffel bag of tricks.

I became obsessed, lingering outside the door, secretly listening for the rattle of a pill bottle.

No. Something wasn't adding up.

∞

Twenty minutes later, we arrived at her place so she could get her truck.

There was a lull in the sleet, and the roads had been properly salted. But this false sense of security wouldn't last long. The worst of the storm was predicted to hit at nightfall.

The LYNX trainees had already started power washing the exterior and had also replaced the headlight on her truck, as I'd demanded.

I had expected another show of emotion from Jo, another moment of her freezing in place, staring at her house, disbelieving of what had happened. Instead, Jo surprised me. She greeted the boys with a warm smile before breezing through the front door.

Was she high?

I lingered outside, pretending to examine the boys' work, until Jo returned minutes later in a fitted white pantsuit that hugged her curves just enough to make you wonder what she was wearing underneath—if anything at all.

She thanked me, though it felt automatic and insincere. Her mind was somewhere else.

On work, I thought.

On Aria.

Not high. No, Beckett, not high.

I followed Jo to her office, unbeknownst to her.

Once I ensured she'd arrived safely, I drove to the LYNX headquarters, my mind solely occupied by the wonder that was Jo Bellerose.

Regardless of the pills right in front of my face, I couldn't shake the impression that Jo didn't seem like someone who was addicted to pills. So, what the fuck was up with her stash? And why was she so damn protective of Leif Ellis? Why was she so sure he wasn't the Pollock Butcher?

This constant flow of questions had me huddled behind my computer in my office, researching everything that was absolutely none of my business—and to say that I was surprised at what I saw was an understatement.

Josephine Nichole Bellerose was arrested on October 14, 2004. As a juvenile at the time of her arrest, the report should have been sealed, but I was able to get into it.

When I found the arrest report, I assumed it involved drugs—something related to pills, right? Wrong.

At age sixteen, Jo was arrested and charged with harassment.

Harassment.

Her case was forwarded to the juvenile court, where she received a sentence of six months' probation and three months' community service.

After having Loren, our office manager, hunt down the reporting officer, I called her up, catching recently retired Officer Rhonda Camps on vacation in the Keys, knee deep in her third margarita. Within three minutes, I learned that Rhonda was a recently divorced, flapping jaw of gossip. Naturally, I seized the opportunity with gusto and in an hour-long conversation had gleaned far more information about Jo Bellerose's past than I was comfortable with.

Jo's mother and father, Melinda and Gary Bellerose, had had a tumultuous marriage filled with rumors of infidelity—on both sides. Jo's neighbor, a world-class baker according to Rhonda, had told Rhonda in confidence that there was constant fighting and yelling at the house over the course of many years. I could only assume Jo was subjected to this volatile behavior between the two people responsible for modeling what an appropriate relationship was *supposed* to look like.

The day after Jo's sixteenth birthday, Gary packed a bag and walked out on Melinda and Jo for another woman. Melinda was inconsolable, according to Rhonda, despite being left with a boatload of money.

Jo, at the height of teenage angst and invincibility, reacted the opposite, directing her anger toward the woman who, in her mind, had destroyed her family.

Jo began stalking her father's mistress, watching her father, the man who Jo looked up to, arrive and leave the woman's house with a big ful-filled smile on his face. The woman took notice of Jo's amateur sleuthing and began telling people she thought Jo was watching her. Said she was scared and feared for her safety.

On October 14, Jo was confronted by her father, scolded, and told never to return to his mistress's home.

Jo's response? Confront her father's mistress and make sure she knew she'd ruined Jo's entire life. This didn't go well. The woman called the cops, and the rest was history, along with Jo's reputation.

According to Rhonda, that was when Jo had become "emo," wearing dark clothing, black eyeliner, the whole nine yards.

Was that also when she began taking pills?

This question led me down a rabbit hole of addiction websites. With Jo's image in my head, I found myself taking notes and creating a checklist of sorts.

People with addiction have an intense focus on using a certain substance, such as alcohol or drugs, to the point that it takes over their life. As a result, addicts experience different modes of thinking and altered brain functions that affect their daily lives and relationships.

I thought of Jo's hoard of pills—*intense focus*. And how this stash could end the career she seemed to love so much—*takes over their life*.

I thought of Jo's intense need for solitude, the emotional armor she wore everywhere she went, and her weird obsession with the inkblot test—*different modes of thinking*.

I studied the common habits of addicted people:

Lying and being secretive. *Check. (The pills, her relationship with Leif.)*

Isolation. *Double check.*

Neglecting responsibilities. *Check. (Being late, forgetting appointments, not fixing her truck headlight.)*

Being irresponsible. *Check. (Leaving her keys on the bar top, getting out of her car in the middle of the woods, not thinking to call 911, then choosing not to tell the cops all the details, etc., etc., etc.)*

Change in physical appearance. *Check. (Emo during her teenage years.)*

❦

The day passed slowly, my investigation broken up by multiple meetings, phone calls, and a few fires that needed extinguishing. I was staring at a picture of Jo that I'd found in the Dragonfly Clinic's Instagram account when my door was flung open.

Alek strode in, dressed like a dirty politician in a slick designer suit and diamond-and-gold cuff links that probably cost more than my truck.

"Another meeting?" I asked.

He frowned. "No."

"Funeral?"

"Not today."

"Girl?"

"No—but that's exactly what I came to talk to you about."

I straightened, clicking out of the Instagram feed that filled my monitor.

"Why did you pull away three of my trainees to go wash a house?" he asked.

"Because they're my trainees too."

Alek narrowed his eyes.

"Fine. A friend of mine needed help."

"The *friend* who stayed at your house last night?"

"Are you spying on me?"

"No, just a guess—which you just confirmed."

My jaw twitched.

"Talk," he said. "Because I had those guys scheduled for a session this afternoon."

I sighed and leaned back in my chair, threading my fingers behind my head. "You heard about the commotion down County Road 49 last night?"

"I know something happened. A robbery or home invasion or something?"

"No. Someone's home got painted with blood."

"Human blood or animal?"

"We're waiting on the test results."

"Let me guess—the owner of the home is the girl who stayed with you."

"Right. Her home was *painted* in blood—just like on the bodies of the victims of the Pollock Butcher."

"Ah, she's the next target."

A sharp pain speared through my gut. "It's a possibility, yes. She saw someone in the woods next to Lookout Point, the day after I found Aria near Marissa Currie's body. This person knows she saw them."

"And wants to take care of loose ends now."

"Exactly."

"Where is she now?"

"At her office. I'm watching her."

"Good. Speaking of the Pollock Butcher, you know Marissa Currie's boyfriend, Grady Humphries, has been left alone through this whole mess because he had a solid alibi, right?"

"Yeah."

"I just found out who that alibi is."

"Who?"

"Jamie fucking Ledger."

"What?"

"Yep. Apparently, Marissa wasn't the only one being unfaithful in their relationship—if that's even true at all. Grady has been banging Jamie on the side. She was with him the night Marissa was murdered. The Feds are keeping a tight lock on the information for now."

I frowned, taking a second to allow the information to process. "So, Grady was dating both Marissa and Jamie, and Marissa wound up dead."

Alek nodded. "Jealous woman—a story as old as time."

"Definite motive there. Maybe Jamie wanted Grady all to herself. Didn't like the thought of him being with another woman."

"That's fucked up, considering she's married."

"No shit. Does Cyrus, her husband, know?"

"If not, he'll find out soon enough. They always do."

"Has she been formally questioned?"

"No idea, but regardless, she has an alibi, too—Grady. They're both covered."

"Unless they're both lying."

"A Pollock Butcher team, then? Maybe they've been doing it together for a while. Slicing up innocent women. Jamie lures them, and Grady goes in for the kill."

I recalled Jo telling me that she had a meeting with Aria that morning. Jamie's daughter.

I didn't like how many connections were involving Jo, and suddenly, more than anything, I wanted to know where Jamie was while Jo's house was being doused with blood.

After dismissing Alek, I picked up the phone and dialed Jo's cell phone. No answer.

I tried again, and again. Voice mail.

Tapping the phone on my chin, I thought it through. Jo needed to know about this new development. She needed to drop Aria as a client. The connections were becoming too overlapped.

I dialed the clinic directly.

"Dragonfly Clinic, how may I help you?"

"This is Beckett Stolle. I'd like to speak with Dr. Bellerose, please."

"I'm sorry, Dr. Bellerose is with a client right now."

"It's important."

"As is her time with her clients. Is there a message I can pass her?"

I looked at the clock—3:47 p.m.

"Is she with her last client of the day?"

"I believe so, yes."

"Fantastic. I'll wait on her then."

"Uh—on the phone?"

I grabbed my keys and pushed out of my chair. "No. In the parking lot."

Chapter Twenty-Nine

Jo Bellerose reminds me of Clarisse McClellan, a character from the book Fahrenheit 451. A naive, curious woman who doesn't know when to stop. Blissfully ignorant, the kind of woman who seeks justice and understanding, having no idea what real life is like. What real pain is. She pushes and pushes and pushes because she doesn't know what it's like to experience the consequences of her actions.

I've read the book several times. There is something about the main character, Guy Montag, that spoke to me. He is the type of man who takes pride in his work, does his job to the best of his ability, until a growing discontentment takes over, and he begins to challenge the meaning of life and everything around him. In doing this, he digs himself deeper into a dark hole of internal torment and despair. He suffers many losses and unfortunate events until finally he snaps, setting his nemesis on fire and watching him burn alive. It is arguable whether Montag would be considered crazy or just someone who was beat up one too many times.

Jo Bellerose knows nothing of this. She knows nothing of the real definition of pain, of human suffering, of keeping her fucking mouth shut. She knows nothing of consequences.

She is like most in this godforsaken town.

Secrets, secrets, secrets.

Skull Hollow is full of them. A cauldron of lies slowly churning around each other, intertwining, getting mixed up together. Lies become muddled, confused, and eventually morph into entirely new lies, linking new sets of people, so that eventually we are connected somehow in what was supposed to be a simple white lie. A rolling boil of deception, soon to bubble over and destroy everything in its path.

I was at the center of it all, the puppet master deftly managing the threads.

I slowly made my way through the furniture store, weaving through the crooked, ill-thought-out pathways customers were forced to take while considering the "refurbished" pieces, priced three times their worth.

I trailed my finger along the back of a faded pleather couch, pretending to test the fabric, to determine if the sickly piece would fit next to the recliner in my living room.

Mrs. Breen, a sixty-something at the local title office, greeted me warmly, slipping into casual small talk. I learned that her son had just moved back into town, bringing with him a girlfriend, a brand-new baby, and the request to revive his old bedroom until he got his finances in order. Breen was searching for a new crib to accommodate the enabling of her loser son. I asked about her daughter, Emily, who I'd shared a drunken, sloppy kiss with outside of Jolene's bar years earlier. She was now married, pregnant, and happy.

Good for her.

After a quick hug and a promise to visit Breen's booth at the church bake sale that weekend, I made my way to the back of the showroom where, just past the checkout counter, I could see into the back room.

Our eyes met.

My pulse picked up as we stared at each other, everything around us fading to black. The lights, the sounds, the movement, all gone.

I saw the dozens of seashells that covered the workbench in front of him.

His face flushed as he frantically glanced around the room, searching for an interruption—any interruption.

Something was off.

I could feel it in my gut.

Chapter Thirty

Beckett

The sky was ominous, blanketed by thick, menacing gray clouds. Despite it being only late afternoon, my headlights clicked on. An icy wind howled against the side of my truck. Speckles of sleet popped against the windshield before slowly vanishing.

Skull Hollow was practically shut down in anticipation of the incoming ice storm. The hourly weather reports had become increasingly grim, another quarter of an inch added to each update.

There was something in the air, beyond the storm, a sense of impending doom that made the skin on the back of my neck prickle. The same feeling I would get moments before a mission began.

Something was coming. I could feel it in the depths of my soul.

My thoughts spun as I drove across town.

The early rumor that Marissa had been cheating on Grady was either not true or had gotten muddled in translation. Because now it appeared that *Grady* was cheating on Marissa and with none other than Jamie Ledger. And she was his alibi for the night Marissa was murdered.

So, did this clear him of being a suspect in her murder? Or did it implicate Jamie's potential involvement? Did Jamie kill Marissa Currie out of jealousy?

Also, what were the odds that Jamie's daughter, Aria, was the one who found Marissa's body? There had to be a link there . . . right?

And then there was Leif Ellis, the Medicine Man. The seemingly random dude who had been seen with both Jamie and Marissa during the last week, who also had a strong—and mysterious—connection with Jo. How the hell did he tie into all this?

Grady, Jamie, Aria, Leif, Jo.

How did they all connect?

The burning question—for me, at least—was who Jo had seen in the woods that night. Because whoever that was, he or she was now after Jo. And at the end of the day, this was all that mattered.

I pressed the gas, driving too fast for the slick roads, the need to get to Jo suddenly overwhelming. I made a note of this feeling, of how abnormal it was for me to feel so protective of a woman I barely knew.

I was emotional about Jo. Not only attracted to her—both physically and mentally—but also drawn to the mysterious and enigmatic aura that surrounded her. I worried about her. Thought of her constantly. I wanted to help her—I *cared* to help her overcome whatever demons she was battling.

I was fucking head over heels for Jo Bellerose, and this made me all sorts of uneasy.

༄

I was surprised at the number of cars in the Dragonfly Clinic parking lot, considering the weather.

It was a testament to the importance of mental health intervention. Rain or shine, no matter what was happening in the world, the need for mental health care was always there. Disorders of the brain don't pause for the weather. They are a constant battle that needs constant attention.

In that moment, I had an epiphany of sorts. I understood Jo's dedication and commitment to her work. Her passion for it. The woman had built her entire life around helping others. She made her clients her number one priority—even though her own life was currently in shambles.

A strong woman. Determined. Steadfast.

So, why couldn't she help herself, I thought, thinking again of the pills.

So, I will help her.

I parked in the only remaining spot at the edge of the lot and found myself scanning the surroundings, looking for anything out of the ordinary, anything that triggered my instinct.

As I crossed the lot, I studied the gunmetal-gray SUV parked next to the front door. I recognized the firefighter-flag vanity plate. Jamie Ledger was here.

My pace increased.

I opened the door and scanned the reception area.

Jamie sat on the edge of the couch, her elbows on her knees, her head bowed in her hands. Her blonde hair was oily and stringy, hanging dispiritedly around her face. She was wearing a baggy mismatched sweat suit with stains on the cuffs. In summary, she looked like an inmate at the county jail—no, she looked like a junkie.

One thing stood out to me: the tiny cross earrings she was wearing. I recalled the cross key chain her husband carried. Why did it surprise me so much that they were a religious family?

"How may I help you?"

I shifted my attention to the receptionist I'd spoken to minutes earlier, Stella Bloom.

Unlike Jamie, Miss Bloom was wearing a neon-green business suit and looked like she'd just stepped off a fashion show runway. Her long red hair fell in waves around her shoulders, reminding me of Ariel from *The Little Mermaid.* (Not that I'd seen it.) She looked like a happy hummingbird, the ideal person to meet at the front door of a mental health clinic. I imagined Miss Bloom soothed clients immediately, temporarily taking their minds off their troubles.

"Is Jo available yet?" I asked.

"I'm sorry. I didn't catch your name," she deadpanned.

So, not a hummingbird. More like a guard dog.

"We just spoke on the phone. I'm Beckett Stolle."

"Ah. Yes."

Stella scrutinized me from head to toe, sizing me up. Had Jo told her she'd stayed the night with me? Probably. And why did I like the thought of Jo talking about me to her friends?

In my peripheral vision, I noticed Jamie's attention was fixed on me.

"Let me check." Stella focused on her computer, typing at rapid speed, and I got the feeling she was placating me. Probably typing a bunch of incoherent words in her Notes app while she "checked" with Jo.

"I'm sorry. She's still with her client."

Aria.

Without another word, I pivoted and took the stairs two at a time. At the top, I could see Jo standing inside her office, in the corner of the building, framed in glass.

To say I was alarmed by Jo's appearance was an understatement. She looked vastly different from the woman I'd followed to work earlier that morning.

Her hair was haphazardly piled on the top of her head, held loosely in place by a dirty bandanna. She'd removed her white suit jacket, revealing a wrinkled, half-tucked blouse with an ink stain in the middle. Her skin was pale, her eyes wild as she paced back and forth like a feral tiger at the zoo. Her shoes were off.

She was off. Jo looked about as mentally stable as Jamie Ledger downstairs.

Her focus was laser locked on the canvas that Aria Ledger was painting on. She didn't notice me.

"Mr. Stolle." Stella grabbed my arm, breathless from jogging up the stairs in sky-high heels.

I jerked out of her hold, my attention on Jo. She wasn't okay—and getting to her, helping her, was my only priority.

"Mr. Stolle, I won't hesitate to call the cops if you don't get your ass back downstairs this instant."

This got my attention.

"Now." The guard dog grabbed my arm and, this time, began pulling me down the stairs.

I took one more glance at Jo, who still hadn't noticed me.

"Is Jo okay?" I asked Stella as she dragged me downstairs.

"Yes. She's fine."

"She doesn't look fine."

"She's tired; I know that. I tried to get her to leave earlier, but she didn't want to cancel her appointment with Aria."

Jamie was no longer in the waiting room when we reached the bottom of the stairs.

Stella frowned, then looked at me.

I nodded to the window where, just outside, Jamie stood hunched under the awning, a cloud of cigarette smoke swirling around her head.

"I'm going to step outside for a second," I said. "Please let me know the moment Jo is out of her session."

Stella peered at Jamie, then back at me. She dipped her chin, a look of concern washing over her face.

I pushed out the front door and into a blast of icy air. Jamie startled at the sound and turned toward me.

"Mrs. Ledger, good to see you."

"Mr. Stolle." She studied the cracked concrete. "I—I don't know if I ever officially thanked you for finding Aria."

"It's my job." I dipped under the awning, close, but careful to keep my distance. "How's Aria?"

Jamie's hand trembled as she took a long drag from the cigarette, then blew out the smoke. "I think she's doing better. She asked to come here to paint again today. I think the painting is helping her."

"That's good. How are you doing?"

"Fine." She looked away.

"Yeah?"

"I—it's been a rough few days. I . . ."

Jamie wanted to tell me something, just like her daughter had. I could feel it in my gut. Instead, she threw down her cigarette and frantically began digging in her purse for another. A dotted line of bruising ran down the side of her neck. Small, speckled contusions, like fingertips pressing too hard into the skin.

My instinct piqued.

I edged closer as she lit the second cigarette. "I can see it's been a rough few days."

Jamie inhaled, then turned her face fully toward me, her eyes watering from the cold or from tears, I couldn't tell. This was when I noticed the bruising on her left temple.

Jamie Ledger had been in some sort of physical altercation.

Grady?

Was Jo next?

A switch flipped in me, the temper I'd spent years learning how to rein in heating to a rolling boil in my veins. I would kill anyone who tried to hurt my woman like that.

Just then, the front door burst open.

"What the hell are you doing—" Jo froze the moment she saw Jamie. "Oh, sorry. Aria is in the bathroom. We just finished up."

"Thank you." Jamie took one last drag of her cigarette before tossing it to the pavement, then slipped past me and disappeared back into the office.

"What are you doing?" Jo barked. "Stella said she almost called the cops on you." She frowned, scanning my expression. "Wait—what's wrong?"

"Get in." I took her by the arm.

"I—"

"Jo, get in my truck. I am not in the fucking mood."

"Okay, okay, but I need to get my purse. I'll be right back. Okay?"

"Hurry."

Aria and Jamie passed Jo as she ran inside. Aria's eyes again locked on mine. She stopped, a deep breath escaping her lungs. She took a step forward, her hand fluttering upward, and for a minute, I thought she was going to grab my arm.

Jamie looked at me, then back to Aria, confused by this behavior.

I wanted to say something, anything, to try to communicate with Aria, but Jamie grabbed her daughter's arm and guided her away. I watched as they slipped into Jamie's truck, pulled out of the lot, and disappeared around a corner.

My heart was pounding, my instincts exploding, my head spinning with the thought that I was missing something. A clue right under my fucking nose.

This wasn't like me. I was confused, angry, my thoughts unclear other than one.

I wouldn't let someone hurt Jo.

I felt desperate and hated it.

Jo pushed out the door, her eyes wide with an epiphany of sorts. "Did you just see that?"

"See what?"

"The relief in Aria's face when she saw you. Her entire body responded to you, like you were a life raft. She literally grabbed for you." When I didn't say anything, Jo continued. "She's comfortable with you, Beckett, feels a connection, probably because you saved her."

"She feels safe with me."

"Yes, exactly. That's the reason for her intense focus on you."

I felt a rush of protectiveness for this girl I barely knew. And then there was Jo and the fact that I needed to protect her too. "Come on."

We fell into step together across the gravel. I opened her door of the truck, helped Jo in, then jumped into the driver's seat.

"Okay, Beckett, talk," she said. "What's going on?"

"There've been developments in the Marissa Currie case." I glanced to be sure it was clear, then pulled onto the road.

"Tell me."

"I found out who Grady Humphries's alibi is."

"Who?"

I looked at her. "The mother of the client you were just working with."

"*Jamie?*" Jo's voice squeaked.

"Yep. Jamie and Grady have had a side thing for a while. He was cheating on Marissa with Jamie."

"Are you serious?"

"As a fucking heart attack."

"So . . . did *she* kill Marissa? Out of jealousy?"

I shrugged. "To be determined."

Jo shook her head, trying to make sense of it all. "You mean to tell me that the mother of the girl who found Marissa's dead body is Marissa's boyfriend's alibi."

"That's right, and the woman who seems to be everywhere you go. Think about it. Jamie is everywhere you are. At your work, at the diner, talking to Leif. And by the way, did you notice the bruises?"

"On who? *Aria?*"

"No. On Jamie."

"Oh my God, no."

"They're there. Down the side of her neck and on her left temple."

"Who gave them to her, do you know? Could it have been Marissa? Fighting back before she was killed?"

"That's what we need to find out."

Chapter Thirty-One

Jo

Skull Hollow was a ghost town. The storefronts were dark; signs that read CLOSED DUE TO THE WEATHER hung from the windows. It had a creepy, apocalyptic feel to it.

We passed the Sunrise Café.

"Wait." Grabbing the dashboard, I scooted to the edge of my seat and peered down the narrow alley that ran between the diner and the furniture shop. "Stop."

"Stop?"

"Wait—no, don't stop." I whirled around in my seat, watching the alleyway as we passed. "Loop back around."

Beckett clicked on his turn signal. "What's going on?"

"I swear—that car . . ."

"What car?"

"The orange Mustang in the alley . . . I swear that's my mother's car."

"I thought she left."

"I thought she did too."

Beckett circled back and pulled into the post office parking lot.

"Wait, no, circle around again."

After three more loops around the square, we returned to the post office and parked. Beckett turned off the headlights.

A sickly streetlight illuminated the alley, just enough to make out shapes but not details.

"Do you have a pair of binoculars?" I asked.

"I do search and rescue for a living. Yes, I have binoculars. Would you like wide angle, night vision, zoom, or maybe a telescope?"

I rolled my eyes. "Just normal binoculars."

Beckett pulled a pair of shiny black binoculars out of a pocket in the back of his seat.

I looked through them and almost vomited.

"Other way." He grinned.

"Oh." I flipped them around. "God, these should come with a motion sickness warning."

"So should you. What the hell are we doing circling the square four times?"

"I want to see if that's my mom."

Beckett gripped the binoculars pressed to my face and repositioned my fingertips. "Feel this little wheel? In the middle here? Turn that, right, left."

"Oh . . . I see now. Thanks."

I zoomed in on the car. "That's it. Holy sh—that's it. That's her car. I recognize the license plate. *POO.*"

"Gross—what?"

"I know. The first three letters of her license plate are *P-O-O.* I made a joke about it—she didn't laugh."

"No, I wouldn't think a woman who wears tennis skirts on the regular would think potty jokes were funny."

I pulled down the binoculars and looked at him. "You just said potty."

"Yeah?"

I grinned. "That's a funny word coming from a guy like you."

"I feel like there's something sexist somewhere in that comment."

"Probably so. Okay, carry on with your cute little words, Stolle."

"Don't you mean *stool*?"

"Oh my God." I snorted, then refocused on the car across the street.

"So . . . what? She never left town?"

"Apparently not. She packed her bags, we kissed goodbye—hell, I even called her last night, remember? After we found the blood all over my house? I asked her where she went that night in the woods."

"Which she denied, correct?"

"Correct."

"Okay, so yeah, that's weird. If it is your mom, what would she be doing here? Parked in an alley? Everything's shut down."

"And knowing a massive storm is coming. Where the hell is she staying?"

Just then the side door of the furniture store opened. Leif Ellis stepped out, followed closely by Melinda Bellerose—*my mother*. Holding her hand, the former biker turned drug dealer walked my mom to her car.

She looked different, I noticed. Not as put together, uptight. Around her neck hung a necklace made not of diamonds but of seashells. Simple cracked seashells.

Since when was my mother into shells?

I watched Leif and *my mother* embrace, watched her nestle into his chest as he held her, stroked her hair.

And then, I watched them kiss.

Chapter Thirty-Two

Beckett

I watched the color literally drain from Jo's face as she peered through the binoculars. My view of the man and woman getting into the car was blurred, but based on Jo's unhinged jaw, the woman was her mother—and apparently her mother was kissing someone.

"Jo . . ."

No response.

"Jo, babe. What's going on?"

Keeping the binoculars in place, Jo turned her head, her eyes as wide as golf balls in the lenses. "That's Leif."

"What?" I grabbed the binoculars.

Sure enough, the Medicine Man was sliding into the passenger seat of Melinda's Mustang. Together, they pulled out of the alley and disappeared down the highway.

Jo gaped at me. "What the *hell*?"

"I'm assuming you didn't know about this?"

"No!" she squeaked. "Of course I didn't freaking know about this." Her fingertips gripped the dashboard as she watched the car fade into the distance. "What the—I mean, what the hell does she think she's doing? Follow them! Fucking follow them, Beckett!" Her jaw twitched with anger. "Dear God, when I see her, I'm going to—"

"Just hold on a second. Breathe, Jo."

Her gaze snapped to mine. If she were a cartoon character, smoke would have been rolling out of her ears.

"Breathe, Jo. Calm down. Sit back and put on your seat belt."

I waited until she did so, then pulled out of the post office and onto the highway.

"They took off that way." Jo pointed down the road.

"We're not following them, Nancy Drew."

"Why?"

"Because you're in no shape to see your mother right now, and she obviously doesn't want you to know she's here. I'm taking you to your truck, and we'll go home and assess everything over some cold gas station pizza."

"My mother is in a relationship with the local drug dealer, Beckett." Jo clenched her teeth, seething. "The guy that I paid five fucking figures to send to rehab."

I looked at Jo, and she realized she'd said too much.

"Jo, you've got to tell me what's going on. Tell me everything. Why are you so damn weird about this guy?"

No response.

"Tonight, Jo. We're going to have a long talk."

I turned into the Dragonfly Clinic parking lot, now vacant of cars.

"I'll wait," I said.

"It's fine."

"I'll wait."

"Don't worry. I'm not going home; I'm going to your place. I'm not stupid. Until the Pollock Butcher is caught, I'll stay there."

"Thank you."

Her response? Grabbing her purse and slamming the door.

Chapter Thirty-Three

Jo

"What the hell are you doing with Leif Ellis?"

My tires spun as I peeled out of the parking lot, one hand on the steering wheel, the other with a viselike grip on my cell phone.

"Jo, I—"

"Mom, don't even try to lie to me. I *just* saw you, Mom. Just now! You're here, in Skull Hollow, not in Houston. Where have you been staying? How long have you been here? Have you even left? My *God*, Mom—"

"Jo, please, let me—"

"Christ, Mom, do you know he's a drug dealer?"

"I know he's not perfect, yes."

"Not *perfect*? Mom—you're dating a drug dealer. You're dating a drug dealer, and you're worried about the people *I* hang out with? You're worried about *my* clients? What a fucking hypocrite!"

"Don't you dare use that language with me, young lady."

"Is this where you went the other night? When you sneaked out?"

There was a pause, and my stomach sank. I couldn't believe what was happening.

"Yes," she said finally.

"You sneaked out to see Leif?"

"Yes."

"So, you lied to me."

"It's not that simple, Jo."

"Yeah, I'll bet that's what Dad said to you, right, when you found out he was cheating? And how did that feel, Mom? Being lied to by someone you thought you trusted?"

"Please don't do this—"

"Why the hell did you meet him in the middle of the woods? What were you thinking?"

"The middle of the woods? No. No, I met Leif at the lake. He has a houseboat he keeps on Skull Lake." She exhaled, clearly frustrated now. "Jo, I am a grown woman. I—"

"Then act like it, Mom!" I yelled. "Get your shit together. Get your life together."

"I'm trying, Jo! Can't you see I'm trying?"

Melinda burst into tears on the other end of the phone.

I didn't care. I felt no empathy for her. If anything, the random show of emotion ignited my rage even more. Years of pent-up anger and emotions bubbled up to one catastrophic, explosive release.

I went *off*.

"Mom, do you even realize how much pressure you put on me growing up? My grades, sports, friends, boyfriends? I was never good enough for you. Never. Nothing I did was good enough for you."

"It's because I didn't want you to end up like me, Jo. A depressed waitress living from paycheck to paycheck."

"Until Dad came along, right? And you sure as hell had no problem spending Dad's paychecks once he took you in, did you?"

"That's uncalled for, Josephine—and by the way, look where that got me. Cheated on and left."

"*We* were left, Mom. *We* were left. But the difference between us back then? You were the mom. I was the kid. You were supposed to be the strong one for me, not fall apart when I wasn't mentally and emotionally mature enough to handle it all. Having a child is a responsibility, Mom, but you acted like it was a mistake, a regret. Like I was nothing more than an annoying gnat that wouldn't go away. You didn't want me; that's what it felt like. You didn't want me because I wasn't good enough."

A lump caught in my throat; tears filled my eyes. I realized I'd never told my mom she made me feel that way.

I wasn't good enough . . .

I'm not good enough.

I'd never said the words out loud, not only to her but also not to myself. Although I had built an entire career around helping others uncover hidden, buried triggers in their subconscious, I'd never dug into my own.

"That's not true," she choked out, sobbing. "I'm so—so sorry, Jo."

"Me, too, Mom. Thanks for fucking me up."

I disconnected the call, threw my phone into the back seat, and burst into tears.

Chapter Thirty-Four

Jo

I blinked, trying to regain focus.

My eyes were dry and stinging, my head pounded, and my body ached as I balanced on all fours, studying the line of inkblot cards I'd meticulously laid out in front of me. The images were beginning to blur together, my brain unable to fight the fatigue, both mentally and physically. Still, I stared at each one, trying to find the connection that I knew was right in front of me—and all around me.

Using duct tape, I'd hung all six of Aria's paintings that she'd completed during our art therapy sessions on the cottage walls. Below the canvases, I'd taped up photos of the Pollock Butcher's victims that I'd pulled from social media and their bloodied torsos under blurred faces that I'd printed from news articles. News articles and inkblot cards completed the crazy wall.

Scattered on the coffee table were photographs of everyone directly or indirectly involved in Marissa's life—and possibly death: Grady Humphries, Leif Ellis, Aria Ledger, Jamie Ledger. Next to them, I'd arranged more news articles I'd dug up on the Pollock Butcher, as well as a photo of my house, painted in blood.

All connections led to Aria. Each of her paintings resembled the image painted on Marissa Currie and the other women, as well as the splatters on my front door. The patterns, on Aria's paintings and on each of the victims, were extremely similar but different. Different waves, different angles at which each wave stopped.

Aria held the key. I just needed to know why, how? What was she trying to tell me in her paintings? Did each painting tell a story? Or was it one collective story?

The common theme, overwhelmingly, was painted blood in the pattern of waves.

Waves?

Waves of blood.

Waves . . . what did that mean?

Water . . .

Seashells . . .

My mother's necklace . . .

Leif? Had he given her that necklace?

Was Leif the Pollock Butcher—not Jamie and/or Grady?

More importantly, was my mother part of it all?

No. I couldn't imagine it.

I sat back on my haunches and rubbed my temples. My head throbbed. I had that sick, queasy feeling from not eating enough. I was light headed, confused, and pissed the fuck off.

Leif had to know Melinda was my mother. Did he tell her I bought pills from him?

Jesus Christ—did my mom know that I bought pills illegally? Would she go to the police?

As fucked up as it sounded, I could see her doing just that. Melinda would be so disappointed in me that she would want me to learn a lesson the hard way. Mom had always hated my job, hated the passion I put into it and the fulfillment I got out of it. She would call the police because she would want me to know she was right. That I couldn't do anything well. That I messed up even something that I cherished so much.

But she was my mother, for Christ's sake. Mothers were supposed to love their daughters, no matter what. They were supposed to coddle them in times of need. They were supposed to grab their shoulders and shake them when they strayed.

And then another thought hit me, one that cut much deeper than my mother reporting me to the police. If my mother did know I was buying pills from Leif, why wasn't she by my side? Trying to save me?

Like Beckett was.

Fucking Beckett. Damn him and all his ridiculous hotness, damn the way he gave me butterflies and made me melt with nothing more than a glance in my direction.

Beckett was the perfect man. This proven for the umpteenth time when he reluctantly gave me the space I so badly needed after arriving at the cottage. *I need a second,* I had told him. *I need to be alone.*

I didn't want the man I was falling for to see me so disheveled. To see me cry.

I was embarrassed, not only by my lack of control but of my crazy mother too. Did he think I would turn out like that? End up like her?

Without asking questions, Beckett had kissed my forehead, grabbed his suitcase, and after ensuring I had a list of every number where he could be reached, he went to the office to catch up on work.

I took solace in knowing that Beckett was only a mile away, that he hadn't gone far. I imagined him watching me through a fancy pair of binoculars from his office window, making sure I was safe.

He made me feel safe. He made me feel *loved.*

And why did I feel so undeserving of this?

This disgusting, vile feeling of self-pity and defeat reminded me of my teenage years. Feeling lost, like I didn't know who I was or where I was going. Feeling ashamed of my father for cheating on my mother, ashamed of my actions toward the other woman. Feeling like I was such a disappointment to my parents, that I didn't stack up to the woman they expected me to be. Feeling like I was never worthy of a boy's attention. Especially not someone as perfect as Beckett.

"Goddammit all to hell," I muttered, pushing off the floor and wiping the tears away. *"Goddammit!"*

I began pacing in front of the fireplace. The fire, I realized, had dwindled to nothing more than smoldering ashes sometime during my self-loathing. The cabin was freezing.

Beckett would be disappointed in me, I thought.

I tossed the two remaining logs onto the ash. Nothing happened.

Sucking back my tears, I grabbed my coat, pulled on my boots, and stepped outside. Darkness had fallen.

A security light on the roof spotlighted the woodpile at the edge of the property. Sleet sparkled in the dim yellow beam, and a thin layer of ice covered the ground. The conditions were getting bad, and fast.

I hunched my back against the biting wind and carefully stepped off the porch. My boot crunched into the layer of ice.

A sudden unease trickled up my spine. I got the feeling I was being watched.

I looked over my shoulder at LYNX headquarters, illuminated at the top of the hill.

He's right there, I told myself. *He's probably watching you right now.*

With that thought, I jerked back my shoulders and made my way to the woodpile at the edge of the property. Not surprisingly, Beckett had covered the pile with a large blue tarp to protect it from the elements, and it took me a solid five minutes to figure out how to untie the knots and pull it off the stash.

My fingertips were frozen, my ears and the tip of my nose tingling painfully by the time I piled the third log into my arms. While balancing the logs in one arm, I attempted to reattach the tarp with my other hand.

I failed miserably, stumbling and slipping on the ice, which sent me tumbling to the ground and the logs flying into the air. My ankle caught in the string of the tarp as I went down. I twisted awkwardly to fall on my side (instead of my face), but unfortunately, my ankle didn't twist with me.

Pain shot like lightning up my leg, and I screamed.

Blocks of wood tumbled down on top of me, one dragging down the side of my face, leaving a trail of splinters and scrapes. Moaning, I rolled around on the ice like a beached whale, trying to catch my breath and regain my composure.

Eventually, I was able to sit up.

I attempted to remove my boot, but the pain was too fresh. There was no question that, if not severely sprained, it was broken.

Shit.

I scooted on my butt toward the woodpile. Using the stacked logs as leverage, I attempted to stand and walk. I screamed out in pain and fell back onto the ground.

"Shit. Shit, *shit.*"

I stared at the cabin five yards away, contemplating. There was no stick to use as a crutch and nothing to grab onto along the way.

Grinding my teeth, I pulled myself up once again, sucked in a breath, and attempted a hop—and screamed louder than when I'd tried to walk.

I crumpled to the ground, rolled onto my back, and began sobbing. And for the first time in a long time, I didn't care what happened to me next.

I felt like I was living the past all over again, hurt by my mother, consumed by pills, feeling lost, alone, and scared. And worst of all, feeling like I didn't want to wake up in the morning.

Chapter Thirty-Five

Beckett

"It's getting bad outside."

Alek's reflection appeared in the window I was staring out of with my hand stuffed in my pocket, focused on a single dim light through the trees.

My cottage. My woman.

He stepped into the office. "McNamara just called. There are two accidents down by Black Hills Bayou. One car slid into the swamp."

I turned. "Everyone okay?"

"I think so. But one is a mom and her newborn baby on their way home from a checkup."

"Does McNamara need our help?"

Alek joined me next to the window. "I sent a few of the trainees over to the Bayou. They're on the four-wheelers. Dane's about to head over too."

I nodded. "Let me know if there's anything I can do."

Alek stood in silence next to me, scanning the grounds. "She okay?"

"Who?"

He jerked his chin in the direction of my cottage.

"She won't be okay until we find the Butcher."

"The Feds won't let it go," he said. "It's hit national news, and McNamara is also breathing down their necks. I've never seen him so fired up about a case."

"Have they made any arrests?"

"No."

"Did they talk to Jamie Ledger?"

"I'm sure they did the moment Grady confessed his relationship with her. Jealousy is a strong motive."

"I saw her and Aria at the Dragonfly Clinic this afternoon. She looked strung out."

"Doesn't surprise me. I'll see what else I can dig up tonight, but I do have news. The blood work on your girl's house came back."

I looked at him.

"It was animal blood, not human."

"What kind of animal?"

"Pig."

I thought of Jo's comment about the movie *Carrie*—almost like she knew. "More than one pig was slaughtered to cover the house the way it was. Who owns pigs around here?"

Alek shook his head. "No one I know, but I'm assuming the Feds are hunting down that angle."

I stared at the cottage. It was a good lead, one that I wanted to dig into on my own.

I thought for a moment. "What do pigs symbolize?"

"In Eastern culture, pigs are a symbol of good luck and success."

I shook my head. "No. In some religions, pigs are seen as unholy creatures, right? Unfit and even offensive. Jamie is religious, isn't she? Yes, she is. She was wearing a pair of cross earrings today." I turned from the window and clicked on my computer, then opened a new search window.

Alek hovered over my shoulder, reading the page I pulled up. "Pigs are a symbol of destruction and punishment in the Bible."

Punishment.

Was Jo being punished for talking about what she saw in the woods? Or who she saw?

"How long is she staying with you?" Alek asked.

"Until she's safe."

He took a step back, looked down on me. "You keeping your head on?"

I looked away.

"Don't lose focus. She's a beautiful woman."

More than beautiful.

I turned back to the window.

Alek took the cue. "I'm going to respond to some emails, then call it a night."

I nodded, only half listening, instead locked on the twinkling light.

"Why don't you do the same?" he said before disappearing down the hall.

Don't lose focus . . .

Exhaling, I turned, looking at the long list of unanswered emails on my computer screen.

She's a beautiful woman. Don't lose focus.

Tearing myself away from the window, I slid behind the computer and forced myself to concentrate.

Chapter Thirty-Six

Jo

It took me thirty minutes to drag myself across the yard and back into the cottage. By the time I slammed the door shut, I was sure I had frostbite on nearly every inch of my body.

After ensuring the door was locked, I slowly removed my boot, the pain nauseating. I grabbed my overnight bag and pulled myself onto the bed to elevate my ankle. My clothes were damp and muddy from dragging myself across the yard. The room was cold and dark, save for a small table lamp across the room that did nothing to illuminate beyond its three-foot pool of light. I didn't care.

Tears ran down the sides of my cheeks as I stared up at the ceiling.

I lay on my back, hands on my stomach, a bottle of prescription pills clenched between my fingertips. A clock ticked from somewhere in the room as I ran my thumb along the grooved edges of the pill-bottle lid.

My thoughts were slow and muddled, pieces of memories of my past slowly drifting in my mind like a petal being carried down a lazy stream.

I remembered the first time I had taken a pill at age fifteen. The way it made me light headed and nauseated. And the second time, forcing it down, hoping to have a better reaction, thinking maybe the light-headedness had just been a fluke.

Let's try again.

I realized now that I was already addicted at that point. Mentally, not physically. Not to the pill itself, of course, but to the chance, the opportunity in front of me to numb my life. I was desperately seeking an escape from my overbearing mother, my cheating father, my school-mates who, no matter how hard I tried, never fully let me into any of their circles. Unfortunately, I was too young to drive at that age, so the option for a physical escape wasn't present. It had to be mental.

This little pill, this little white tablet that I could hide in my pocket, in my backpack, in my bra, under my mattress—anywhere, could offer the escape I was so badly craving.

My entire high school experience had been consumed by this addiction. Four years of my life that I barely remembered. To this day, I didn't know how I graduated. I was high morning, noon, and night, completely shut off from the world. In college, I walked to class alone, ate lunch alone, barely spoke. Hid behind black eyeliner and black hair.

Until one day, I took one pill too many and thought I was going to die. I was in my bed, unable to move or speak, but I could hear. The room stopped spinning, and I knew I was about to take my last breath. This was it, the end for me. The next second, I was vomiting over the side of my bed.

Thankfully, I was one of the lucky ones who was jarred by this experience.

Absolutely terrified, more like.

It was the wake-up call that I'd needed and quite literally defined my life. I changed my major to psychology and minored in biology. I was accepted into medical school, where I set my sights on psychiatry and never looked back. My world revolved around prescription pills and the human psyche.

That was when I met Mia. She became the first real friend I ever had. My life had changed.

But had it really? Do we ever really change?

Because after all that—overcoming addiction, graduating from medical school, and being a light for others who were lost in the darkness—I contemplated taking a pill. That night, lying in Beckett's bed with thoughts of blood and murder running through my head, I considered taking a pill.

Just one. Just a little escape.

The wind howled against the cabin. The ice ticked against the windows.

My thumbnail dragged across the grooves along the pill bottle's lid. My pulse started to increase, a warm rush of adrenaline flushing my skin.

Just one.

Tick, tock . . .

I closed my eyes, focusing on my breathing.

Tick, tock, tick . . .

Just one, maybe.

Clink.

My eyes flew open.

Tick, clink . . .

A different sound mingled with the clock, one of metal against metal. My heart stuttered.

Someone was outside, trying to get in.

Was it Beckett? Why wasn't he announcing himself?

A shadow moved next to the window. Fear shot like ice through my veins.

I mentally battled with what to do next. Stay in bed, hidden, perhaps? Or should I get up and confront whoever it was?

I didn't have time to make that decision because the window shattered into a million pieces.

I propelled my torso forward as if attached to a spring, scrambled backward, and fell onto the floor. I tried to scream, but I couldn't. My throat was quite literally clogged with fear.

A dark silhouette busted out the remaining shards and leaped through the window.

Dragging myself across the floor, I frantically looked for some sort of weapon, but there was nothing.

He was too fast. The glint of a blade flashed as the man dressed in black clothes and a black balaclava leaped over the bed.

My back slammed against the wall, and a scream ripped through me.

The knife was raised, and the silhouette lunged toward me.

I threw my body to the side, bracing for death, my entire being tensing in anticipation of feeling the punch of the blade.

It never came.

The man was jerked backward and thrown into the couches across the room. Tables and chairs went flying. I blinked wildly, trying to understand what was happening.

Beckett's face filled my vision.

"Are you okay?" he asked, shielding my body with his, searching my neck and chest for wounds.

The silhouette stumbled forward, tripping its way to the front door.

"He's getting away!" I screamed.

"Are you okay?" Beckett bellowed in my face, jolting me back to the present moment.

"Yes. Yes. Beckett, he's getting away!"

Completely unaffected by this, Beckett scooped me into his arms and lifted me like a baby.

I squirmed against his hold. "*Beckett!* He's getting *away*! It was the Butcher, the man I saw in the woods. It was him. I know it. He's getting away!"

I was lowered onto the bed, and the floor lamp was flipped on.

Beckett's gaze raced over my body, searching still for any signs of injury. He zeroed in on my swollen ankle.

"What happened?"

"I fell outside while trying to get wood."

He looked at the fireplace, then back at me. "And to your face?"

"When I fell, a log fell on my face."

"Okay—what happened? Take me through it from the beginning."

"I—I was just lying here, and I saw somebody outside. I think they tried the doorknob first. I thought it was you, and I was confused because why wouldn't you knock. And next thing I knew, the window shattered, and someone burst inside."

As I spoke, Beckett ran his hands over my body, needing to confirm—for the third time—that I was okay. He lightly put his hand on my ankle, as if blocking it from any potential source of pain, then pulled his phone from his pocket.

"Are you calling the cops?"

"No."

"Why?"

"I'm calling Alek to come look at your ankle. He was a medic in the navy, and then Dane to see what tracks he can find."

"Do you think he can track him?"

The call connected, and Beckett barked out a list of commands to whoever was on the other end, from highest priority to lowest. After disconnecting, he refocused on me. Priority number one was for Alek to take a look at me.

"Dane can track anyone—if the ice allows," Beckett said, answering my question.

"You think the ice could have covered his tracks?"

"Yes, I do. It's coming down fast. But we'll also pull all the property's security cameras."

"Do you think the Butcher would be stupid enough to cross over onto LYNX property?"

"No, but we'll leave no stone unturned."

Frustrated at how calm he was being, I pulled my ankle out from under his hand. "Can't *you* go track him? Now?"

"I'm not leaving you."

His phone began beeping with a flurry of texts.

"We need to call the cops," I said.

"It's being taken care of—but there's no way anyone is coming out here tonight. The roads are covered. We're going to be stuck here for a while. Alek will be here on the four-wheeler in under two minutes." Beckett stood from the bed, turned, and froze. "What the fu—"

He was studying the corner of the room that was covered in inkblot cards, paintings of blood, pictures of the Butcher's victims.

Shit.

I sat up. "Uh . . . it's work stuff."

He picked up a picture of Aria I'd printed from the news. "What . . ." He turned, a line of confusion—concern—forming between his brows. "What are you doing, Jo?"

My cheeks heated in embarrassment. "I'm just trying to find the link . . ."

"Between Aria's paintings and the Butcher?"

"Yeah. Look, I know it sounds crazy, but something's there. Every one of her paintings appears to replicate the bloody patterns, or pieces of the patterns, on each of the victims—not exactly, but very close."

"Images of the victim's torsos have been leaked on multiple public platforms, and she obviously saw Marissa Currie's mutilated body up close. What makes you think she's not just painting what she saw?"

I shook my head. "No. She's trying to tell us something . . . I'm sure of it. One of her paintings doesn't match any of the victims. It's the very last one she painted. It stands out. It doesn't match any of them."

"Are you sure?"

I shot him a look.

"Sorry."

I scrubbed my hands over my face. "Why is it different? What the hell is she trying to tell us? . . . I've got to figure this out."

He frowned. "Jo, you need to leave this stuff to the police, the FBI."

I scoffed. "They haven't seen Aria's art therapy. I'm the only one who thinks there's a link."

"Why? Why haven't you talked to the Feds? Showed this to them?"

I opened my mouth but found myself speechless.

Why hadn't I? Because it was nothing more than a theory. No— because *I* didn't want to get involved more than I already was. Because I didn't want them digging into *me*. Because *I* had way too much to lose.

Beckett shook his head, replaced Aria's picture on the table, and pulled an ice pack from the freezer. He set it on my ankle.

I squirmed.

"It needs ice," he said softly. "And I need you to back off this Butcher thing. No more seeing Aria, no more digging into the past. You're obviously a target, and you need to be smart, Jo."

I looked at the ice streaming in through the busted window. "If the cops can't get here because of the roads, then whoever just attacked me can't leave either. Right? That's why you're not leaving me."

Beckett's jaw clenched, and he looked away.

I was right. He wouldn't leave my side, just like he hadn't during the circus that followed me after finding the blood painted over my house.

"I'm going to begin covering the window," he said, deftly avoiding a conversation that might lead to whatever was happening between us. "With the fire going, we'll be warm enough."

Silence settled between us as Beckett gathered his tools from the cabinets. After retrieving a tarp, a staple gun, nails, and a hammer, he knelt down at the window.

Ice pelted his head as he laid the tools out one by one, when suddenly he stopped.

I frowned. "Beckett?" Then I sat up. "Beckett?"

He didn't respond but glared at the bottle of pills I'd dropped on the floor.

Chapter Thirty-Seven

Beckett

Alek pulled up outside.

Before I could respond to Jo, I scooped up the pill bottle and hid it in the cabinet. I was glad Alek arrived at the exact second that he did, because I didn't know what I would have said to Jo in that moment. Something I would have regretted, I was sure.

I turned and found Jo staring at me wide eyed, nervous. My blood was raging.

These *fucking* pills. The secrets.

Why?

Alek knocked on the door.

I did my best to pretend to be calm and controlled as Alek tended to Jo's ankle while I secured the window with a tarp and staples. I kept stepping on a damn crime scene photo and an inkblot card, unbelieving of the fucking madhouse my cottage had been transformed into. The chilling paintings, creepy-ass cards. Every piece meticulously organized and laid out like an examination room at an insane asylum. And the damn bottle of pills on top of it all.

I could protect Jo from a madman, but I couldn't protect her from herself. Those goddamn pills were so much more dangerous than any serial killer. What the fuck was she doing?

I was mad. Scared. I felt betrayed.

Why? Jo didn't owe me anything.

Yes, she did, dammit.

She and I—*we*—were something. Something was happening between us, and I was going to guard whatever it was until my fucking death.

"It's not broken." Alek met me at the window as I popped in the last staple.

I glanced back at Jo, who quickly looked away.

"She's got a bad sprain. I've got it wrapped. You'll need to keep it elevated and put ice on it every few hours. I've got some crutches I'll bring down, but she needs to just keep off it and keep it up for the next twenty-four hours or so."

"Bring them first thing tomorrow morning. She'll try to walk."

Alek grinned. "I figured." Then he sobered. "Dane is in the woods now, looking for tracks—I'll keep you updated. I'm going to go review the security cams."

"Let me know."

"Will do. Keep your phone on you. I have a feeling it's going to be a long night."

"I do too."

Once Alek had gathered his medic bag and disappeared into the night, Jo and I stared at each other.

"We need to talk," I said through gritted teeth.

She said nothing.

I pulled the pills from the cabinet and set them on the bed, next to her. "We need to talk about *this*."

"It's my business, Beckett, not yours."

I gestured around the cottage—*that was mine*—and then to the window where I'd just chased off the man who'd tried to kill her.

"I believe we're way past that kind of deflecting, Jo. We are, quite literally, in this together now."

There was a defiance in her that neither aggravated me nor turned me on. Instead, it made me sad. This was a woman fighting her own demons. A battle deep inside that she kept locked away from everyone else.

And, *dammit*, I wanted to help her.

Please, Jo, let me help.

Chapter Thirty-Eight

Jo

Beckett sat on the side of the bed, careful not to jostle the pillows that Alek had stacked under my ankle.

My heart was racing. I couldn't bring myself to speak, to tell the story I was so ashamed of. A full minute passed as Beckett patiently waited for me to speak.

"I had this buddy once," he said, finally breaking the silence, "a real good friend of mine. We went into the marines together. I saved his life once, and he returned the favor one day in Afghanistan. There was an IED hidden on the side of the road where my team and I'd stopped to refuel the trucks. I needed to take a piss, and I stepped away from the group—less than a foot away from the IED. Less than one fucking foot. One step to the left, and I would've been blown to dust. To this day, I don't know how he saw the damn thing and I didn't. But he saved my life. I would literally be dead if not for him."

"What happened to him? You said you had this buddy *once*."

"He killed himself."

I blinked. "I'm sorry."

"He had PTSD that went undiagnosed. I was the one who found him, in the barracks, dead in his bunk . . . with a pill bottle that looked a lot like this one"—Beckett tapped the bottle that lay next to my arm—"clenched in his hand."

A chill snaked up my back.

"I'm not addicted," I said.

"The bottles of pills in your office suggest otherwise."

My jaw dropped. "You went through my stuff?"

"Yes."

"Y-you *jerk.*"

Beckett held up a hand, cutting me off. "While I was checking your house after it was vandalized, while you were packing, I saw the safe under your desk. The door was unlatched. I opened it and saw the bottles."

A rush of heat flushed over my skin. Not anger, but embarrassment.

"I can't believe you did that, Beckett. You had no right to go through my stuff."

"Well, I did, and it's done, and now here's another bottle with someone else's name on it, here in my cabin."

My racing heart turned into a banging drum.

His hand covered mine. "Look at me, Jo. Talk to me, please. I'm a decent listener, believe it or not. Just talk to me."

A moment passed as I fought a battle in my head, part of me wanting to lie, to say anything to avoid opening the box I'd nailed shut for years. The other part wanting to spill my guts and for Beckett to scoop me up and tell me everything was going to be okay.

"Talk to me, Jo, please."

On a pathetic exhale, I let go and unloaded, telling him all my secrets. In a mess of tears and jumbled sentences, I told Beckett about my mom, my dad cheating on her, my arrest, the first time I took a pill, the second. I told him everything.

Every. Single. Thing.

As I spoke, it felt as if the weight were slowly being lifted from my shoulders, pound by pound.

Beckett listened intently without saying a word, without expression.

"Anyway," I said after catching my breath, "that's the story. And I'm completely sober, by the way. I don't take the pills anymore."

"I believe you. So, why do you carry them around with you all the time?"

I shrugged.

"Jo . . ."

"It's a stupid security blanket. Just knowing that I have them if I need them is a weird comfort. I don't take them. I promise."

"You might not take them, Jo, but you're still severely addicted to the pills. Just not physically."

I looked down and began fidgeting with the blanket. Beckett was right. I was still addicted.

For decades, I'd considered myself recovered when, in fact, I was far from it, still secretly craving the opportunity for that oh-so-coveted mistake.

We sat in silence a minute, his hand slowly, comfortingly stroking the bottom of my leg.

"Where do you get the pills?" he asked. "And why so many? Why such a huge stockpile if you don't take them?"

"You've obviously never lived with someone with an addiction, have you?"

"No."

"Hoarding is common addictive behavior—you never want to run out. *Ever.* That little stash of whatever it is you're addicted to—booze, pills, porn—is tucked away, kept safe, until it is needed. Again, it's a security blanket."

"How long have you been hoarding them?"

"Five years."

"Why? What happened five years ago?"

I looked away. God, I was so ashamed. "It's so fucking stupid, Beckett."

"No, it's not. Addiction is serious, as are the reasons that brought you to it. Tell me. You got clean during college, but five years ago something happened to renew your interest in them."

I took a deep breath. "After I graduated with my MD in psychiatry, I began an internship at a clinic in Houston. I loved it. It was exactly what I needed and wanted to be. Except it was stressful. People don't understand . . . the stakes are very high when dealing with prescription drugs. There's a lot of internal conflict as well. There's a lot of worry and blame if things don't go as they're supposed to."

"What do you mean?"

"Meaning, if a patient doesn't respond typically to what you prescribe them. If their body doesn't do well with the drug, this can actually make things worse and even lead to suicide. I found myself really stressing out when I realized that most patients needed to go through several rounds of pills before they find the one that fits them. It's like trial and error with drugs, like Russian roulette."

I paused, looking up at him.

"It's a big deal. Most people have to 'try' at least two or three different classes of antidepressants before they find one that works for them. Can you imagine? You're already in a fragile mental state, and there I am, throwing drugs at you that literally alter your brain, knowing the first probably isn't only not going to work but will also make you a little crazier, or sicker, in the process."

"I can imagine that's a lot to shoulder."

I nodded. "It really is. I had a patient once who tried to kill herself because she had a negative reaction to the medication that I prescribed her. Technically, it wasn't my fault; it's all part of the journey to find the drug that works for you, but I felt like it was my fault. I started getting really stressed—like any normal person in a high-stress job."

Beckett nodded, encouraging me to go on.

"One day, one of my patients left a full bottle of pills in my office after her appointment—she'd come in, saying she hated the way they made her feel, and left them on my desk. I prescribed her another one and sent her on her way. I should've had her dispose of the pills correctly, but I didn't. She left . . . and I remember staring at that damn pill bottle, and I remember feeling that kind of wicked, exciting high of a craving. I had such a moment, sitting there at my desk, like I knew what was about to happen. I realized the craving had never gone away."

I shook my head, disgusted with myself.

"I took the pills and put them in my purse. That bottle sat in the bottom of my purse for seventeen days." I looked up. "Seventeen days, Beckett. I guarded that pill bottle like a mother would her child."

I looked down again.

"On the eighteenth day, I finally decided to take one. And you want to know the craziest part about that? There was nothing abnormal about that particular day. Nothing that pushed me to do it. It was just a normal, boring Wednesday. A client canceled on me, and I remember feeling a bit bored. And I remember shrugging, reaching into my purse, and simply popping one like it was no big deal." I felt the sting of tears, of shame, boil up. "The next morning, I felt so guilty. I took the pills and hid them in my safe, and I've never taken another one since."

"But you didn't throw them away."

"No, I didn't."

"And then?" he asked.

I looked at him, raising my eyebrows. "That's it. That's my story, Beckett. That is my absolutely pathetic, incredibly weak-human story."

"Except it's not only yours, is it? This is where Leif Ellis comes in, am I right? There's something you won't tell me about him, and I have a feeling this is the start."

I nodded. "Yes. I heard from several of my clients he was peddling pills. Leif and I apparently shared several clients. One day I called him, telling myself it was in the interest of my clients. I'd planned to tell him that I knew about his side business and as the town psychiatrist, I wanted him to stop. I knew way too many cases where a doctor had been called to testify about an overdose where one of their clients mixed drugs the doctor had prescribed with street drugs. It's a mess."

"So, your intentions were pure?"

I took a deep breath. "Honestly, I thought so then, but now I'm not so sure. Next thing I knew, I was buying from him. I don't know why. He said he just got a shipment of gabapentin in—this was my favorite drug. I asked where the shipment came from, and he said if I wanted to know anything else that I needed to meet him. I did and then left with forty-seven pills in my pocket. It was easy. I stocked them in my safe and felt this weird sense of independence, that now I could do anything, because I had the pills to catch me if I fell."

I sighed.

"This turned into a bit of a friendship, you could say. It sounds crazy, but Leif and I understood each other on a very real and somewhat dark level. And before I knew it, we both had dirt on each other that could ruin our lives. I sent him to rehab once to clean up his act and then paid for it. A little quid pro quo, if you will. He's been clean since, I think, but still sells. Says people are going to buy pills regardless, and at least this way, he knows the product they're buying isn't cut with fentanyl or something."

"And you bought these pills from him?"

"Yeah. I would tell myself that buying from him kept them off the Skull Hollow streets—stupid, huh?" I barked out a humorless laugh. "While he was telling himself pretty much the same thing—that he was selling to protect the community from bad drugs. Funny how someone can justify anything they want to, right?" I swallowed the knot in my throat and looked down. "Some nights, I just go sit in front of my safe and look at them. Isn't that crazy?"

"No."

"Yes, it is. How weak of me, isn't it?"

"No, you aren't weak, and neither was my buddy who swallowed a bottle of pills."

"That's completely different," I snapped.

"How?"

"Your buddy went to war and fought for our country and was a noble man. He had PTSD. He had medical reasons to be medicated. All the patients who come into my clinic have legitimate reasons for needing medication. They have an actual mental illness or have been raped or were molested in the past or stories you wouldn't believe, Beckett. Me?" I scowled in disgust. "Me? I'm just a stupid little rich girl who couldn't handle her parents and one day decided to take a pill."

God, I *hated* myself in that moment. I was so embarrassed.

I expected Beckett to stand up and walk away. Instead, he covered my hand with his.

"I'm proud of you," he said.

I looked up and blinked.

"I'm proud of you because you got clean."

A tear spilled onto my cheek. "Do you believe me? I promise I haven't taken one in so long. There are days I want to, but I don't."

"I do believe you. And I understand now why you hoard the pills."

"It's so ridiculous, I know."

"It's not ridiculous, Jo; it's completely understandable. But it's also playing with fire. And you, Jo Bellerose, are stronger than that." He wiped the tear from my cheek. "Thank you for telling me."

I squeezed his other hand. "Thank you for listening."

"Jo . . ."

My stomach sank. Here it came. The inevitable "this is all too much," and "let's keep this platonic."

Beckett shifted, his gaze flickering to the floor.

My heart began to race.

"Jo." He dragged his fingers through his hair. He was nervous all of the sudden, emotional.

"What is it, Beckett?"

"For a long time—no—for my entire life, I've held back. My only priority in life was my job, and everything else fell by the wayside. I never gave anything or anyone a chance, never was the man I needed to be to those who mattered most. I convinced myself that love not only wasn't necessary but was a form of weakness as well."

His eyes locked on mine, sending a rush of butterflies through my stomach.

"I want this, Jo. I want you to keep opening up to me. I want to keep opening up to you. I want you to trust me, to know that I will be there for you. I want you to depend on me—"

"Beckett, you don't have to—"

"No." He grabbed my hand, squeezed it desperately. "I know I don't have to. I *want* to, Jo. You, and all your baggage, are perfect to me. Show me *all* of it, Jo. Let me be your rock."

Tears swam in my eyes.

"I don't want to lose you"—he gestured between us—"this. Let me be there for you. Okay? That's all I'm asking right now. Let me in. Please."

And with that, Beckett leaned down, kissed my forehead, and then pulled me into his arms and told me everything was going to be okay.

Chapter Thirty-Nine

Jo

I woke up in Beckett's arms, in the same way we'd fallen asleep.

The cabin was flooded with a beautiful, bright, crystal-clear light. I turned my head and looked out the kitchen window.

Everything was white. The ground, the trees, the bushes, the sky. I'd never seen anything like it. Inches of twinkling ice. A winter wonderland right outside the window.

A fire was crackling in the fireplace.

I touched my fingertips to my forehead, where Beckett had kissed me hours earlier.

You, and all your baggage, are perfect to me . . .

A rush of emotions swirled inside me.

My gaze landed on the window that had been shattered, the blue tarp now covering it. I wiggled my toes, wincing at the pain. The memories came barreling back. My bloodied house, the attack, my confession, his comfort.

Let me in . . .

Let him in . . . Let this wonderful, perfect, handsome man into my life.

My heart.

Instead of feeling joy, I felt fear and insecurity. Because, really, who could put up with all this?

I glanced at the wall of blood paintings and inkblot cards. My pulse started to pick up with anxiety. This wasn't romantic. We were quite literally lying in a circle of death.

"Good morning," Beckett said, his voice husky and so incredibly sexy.

I swallowed hard, trying to rein in the sudden rush of emotion.

"How do you feel?" he asked.

How do I feel? Like a fucking mess.

I sat up, pulled off the flannel blanket that Beckett had covered me with, and inched my legs over the side of the bed. Pain ricocheted through my leg as my foot hit the floor.

"Shit."

Beckett was by my side in an instant.

I didn't know if it was the pain, the headache, or the fact that someone had tried to kill me, but a rush of anger as hot as fire shot through me.

"Here," he said softly, grabbing hold of my hands.

I was so mad. Misplaced anger, right there on the edge of his bed.

I looked away, hiding my swollen, makeup-streaked face and what was surely gnarly morning breath.

Beckett wrapped a hand around my waist and helped me stand. Knowing I needed to use the restroom, he guided me there and lowered me onto the closed toilet lid. Leaving for a moment, he came back and set my overnight bag next to the shower.

"Do you need—"

"*No.* Please. I can handle this."

He hesitated.

"Please," I snapped, feeling the sting of tears rise.

Reluctantly, Beckett turned away. The moment the door clicked closed, I surged off the toilet, hobbled to the door, and locked it.

I scrunched my face in pain and gripped the sink. I could have vomited but swallowed it back.

Inhale, exhale.

Inhale, exhale.

I found myself in the mirror and startled at the reflection staring back at me.

"Oh my God . . ."

My hair was a tangled mess, long black strings draping over my shoulders like a spiderweb. My face was pale, my eyes red rimmed and swollen from crying.

"Fix yourself, Jo," I muttered, scowling at myself. "Get it together. Jesus."

Cursing, I carefully squatted and pulled open my Louis Vuitton duffel and sifted through the contents. The pill bottle was missing, and I wondered what Beckett had done with it.

I washed my face, brushed my teeth, combed my hair, added an extra swipe of deodorant and even a dab of perfume behind my ears. After a sweep of mascara, a dab of blush, and a pop of lip gloss, I was beginning to look less like a dead body.

Getting dressed was a challenge, but twenty minutes later, I felt— mildly, at least—ready to face the day and the man who had seen me at my absolute worst.

I opened the door to find Beckett wearing a thin white T-shirt, even thinner gray sweatpants, and holding a cup of coffee in his hand.

He smiled as he handed it to me. "Whiskey-barrel-cask coffee. You liked it, if I recall correctly."

I blushed and took the coffee. "I did. Thank you."

This time, I graciously allowed him to help me hobble across the room to the kitchen, where bacon was sizzling in a pan.

Beckett had cleared the inkblot cards and news articles from the counters and placed them in an organized stack on the floor, next to another pile of papers. Aria's paintings remained tacked onto the walls.

Beckett lowered me into a chair, then pulled over another to elevate my ankle.

"God, I hate this," I muttered.

"Can't change it, but you can change your attitude about it."

"Thanks, Dad."

He grinned, then grabbed a pair of crutches that were leaning in the corner. "Here you go. Your new ride for a few weeks."

"Where did you get these?"

"Alek brought them down this morning, along with a few other things." He gestured to the bags cluttering the small kitchen counter. "Hungry?"

"Yes."

"Eggs, bacon, and toast coming up."

My stomach growled. I was starving. I sipped the coffee as Beckett worked his way around the smallest stove I'd ever seen.

"Did Alek have any updates?" I asked.

Beckett cracked two eggs into a sizzling pan. The cottage smelled divine. "Scrambled or sunny-side up?"

"You said we have toast, right?"

"Yep."

"Then sunny-side up, please."

He glanced over his shoulder. "Don't tell me you dip the toast in the yolk."

I nodded, preparing for the disgusted expression that always followed me telling someone that I did this.

"So do I," he said.

"No way."

"Yep. Have since I was a little boy. Takes talent to get the yolk just right."

"I have a feeling you're going to crush this challenge."

He winked. "Without question. So, yes, Alek had a few updates. Dane was unable to track the intruder; the ice was falling too fast. Our

Trail of Deception

best guesses are: One, he parked on a side road in a four-wheel drive and hiked his way here and back, then slid his way home. This is questionable, however, as the roads were almost impassable last night and surely someone would have seen him or he would have wrecked."

"What's best-guess number two?"

"That he lives close enough to hike here and back."

"That should be easy enough to check."

"Already done. Alek pulled the list of every resident within a five-mile radius. We're going to dive into it this morning. Also, Skull Hollow is totally shut down, and there's more ice in the forecast this afternoon. The weather is supposed to warm tomorrow, but we're stuck here until then."

Beckett slid a plate in front of me. Two eggs, sunny-side up—perfectly runny—two pieces of bacon, and two pieces of toast slathered in butter.

"You can do it."

"Oh, I have no doubt."

Grinning, he took his seat across from me, his plate filled with twice as much as mine. We ate in a comfortable, easy silence, listening to the ice tick against the glass and the flames popping in the fireplace. When I finished, I felt like a new woman as I pushed aside my plate, leaned back, and dramatically rubbed my stomach.

Beckett smiled. "Feel better?"

"Yes, thank you. For everything, Beckett." I took a deep breath. "I don't know how to repay you for all you've done for me."

"I can think of a few things." He winked.

I smiled, feeling a tingle of excitement at his dirty banter.

He stood and kissed my forehead, leaving a sensation of warmth on my skin as he cleared the table. "What now?"

"Well . . ." I looked around the cabin. "If we're stuck here until tomorrow, I'd love to shower."

"Together?" He turned, wiggling his eyebrows as he set the plates in the sink.

"Yep. You, me, and this swollen purple cantaloupe at the bottom of my leg."

"Ah, yes, you're right. Definitely not enough room for the three of us."

I laughed.

After wiping his hands on a towel, Beckett lifted me from my seat and cradled me against his chest.

I couldn't fight the stupid smile that crossed my face as he carried me into the bathroom. Then I couldn't fight the laugh as he had to carefully angle us into the teeny bathroom like a bad game of Jenga.

I was gently lowered into the shower, that thankfully, despite its size, was sparkling clean and appeared to be newly renovated. The door was frosted enough to avoid him getting a detailed view of my bits.

"Hand me your clothes and I'll put them on the bed."

"I'm not handing you my panties."

"Hard to get clean with them on, but fine. I'll turn around. You undress and toss them on the floor like a college kid. I'm right here if you need me."

"I'm not going to fall."

"That's right, because I'm right here."

"Fine. Stay turned around."

"I'll do my best."

It took a solid three minutes to wiggle out of my clothing in a way that didn't hurt my ankle. Each article was tossed at Beckett's feet—except the panties. I dropped those next to the shower door.

Pressing my back against the tile wall, I turned on the water, allowing it to warm before stepping underneath the stream.

"You good?" he asked.

"Yes, so good. Thank you."

"Good."

Instead of leaving me alone to shower, Beckett took a seat on the closed toilet lid, crossed his ankle over his knee, and settled in for a chat—right there in the bathroom while I showered naked three feet away.

"So, I was doing some thinking this morning," he said contemplatively.

"Yeah?"

"I think you have mommy-and-daddy issues."

"What?" I stuck my head out of the shower door.

"Yep." He nodded, grinning at the water dripping off my nose. "Pretty sure of it. And if you thought that was surprising, you might want to hold on to your ass for this next one, Jo."

I narrowed my eyes. "Lay it on me, big shot."

"I think you've got self-esteem issues."

My jaw unhinged.

"I know, it's rough."

"*You're* rough. That's a *huge* accusation—and I don't appreciate you being so smug."

"Smug or honest?"

I slammed shut the shower door. It bounced on its hinges, slid open again, and I cursed as I closed it again.

Honestly, the assessment didn't surprise me. I think I knew it, deep down inside, but much like the blow-up argument with my mother where I'd finally acknowledged how she made me feel not good enough, I'd suppressed this realization as well.

"Hear me out," he said. "It sounds like you were raised by two very polarizing personalities. I mean, hell, I even needed a deep breath after talking just five minutes with your mother. She's a lot."

"Yeah, I know."

"And your dad ripped apart your family."

"Where are you going with this?"

"Because of these two things, you became addicted to pills—to escape, as you said. But I think you're wrong."

"Am I? My twelve years of education suggest otherwise, Stolle."

"The number one reason people get addicted—trust me, I know about this—isn't the need to escape. It's the need for the feeling of a reward."

"What are you talking about?"

"A reward is something given to someone in recognition of their services, efforts, or achievements, right? It makes us happy, floods our brains with all sorts of happiness-inducing biological chemicals."

I didn't respond, now fully interested to see where this was going. I squirted a blob of shampoo in my palm and began lathering my hair.

"As a child," he said, "you received no rewards from your parents. And I don't mean physically. I mean the *feeling* of reward, of satisfaction. Your mother always told you to be more, do better, et cetera. She made you feel the opposite of satisfied. Your father walked away from you, which made you feel that you weren't worthy of any kind of reward. Understand?"

Again, I remained silent, but I nodded.

"The pills gave you pleasure, the feeling of a reward, so to speak, and would therefore flood your brain with dopamine—that really happy feeling you get when someone pats you on the back. This led to your physical addiction. Stop thinking you need to escape to be happy. That's not what it is. You need to learn to love yourself, to take pride in your accomplishments. Give yourself the old pat on the back."

"You're saying, then, that I sought rewards—or approval, satisfaction, or validation—by external sources such as pills, because I'd never felt it from my family or been taught how to find it within myself. Therefore, leading to self-esteem issues."

"Bingo, Doctor."

I slid open the door. "Wow. That's actually not bad."

"Thanks. See? I'm not just a jarhead."

I stepped back under the showerhead, rinsing the soap from my hair. As I contemplated this incredibly insightful analysis of myself, I thought of that Bible verse, something about, Why do you see the speck in someone else's eye but fail to notice the log in your own? I couldn't help but think of the irony of how many people I have diagnosed, yet never myself. This new self-awareness would surely make me a better doctor, help me to serve my clients better. And for the first time in a long time, I felt hope, like seeing the light at the end of a tunnel that I didn't even know was there.

"So, now that we know the source of the problem," he said, "we need to tackle it. I was thinking of a few things that would help. And they all revolve around structure."

"Don't use that word around me," I muttered around the water.

He ignored my ill-timed joke. "You're disorganized. Do you agree?"

"Yes."

"And this disorganization—like losing your keys, being late because of it, then being stressed because of being late—causes a slew of issues that trickle into every facet of your day, causing unnecessary stress and, therefore, making you feel like you're not—"

"Good enough."

"I was going to say *at your best*, but sure."

"And how do you suggest I tackle this?"

"Start by making clear schedules of your day. Get a weekly planner, a daily planner, write down your plans for the day, your errands, everything. I was thinking I could do this with you. I think it would be good for me too. I'd like to write down the goals of the day. Give you something to work for, you know?"

When I didn't respond, he continued.

"I think this is the first step in making routines, something I think you need in your life. Something you can count on so that your focus can go from point A to point B to point C. So that it's all not just a jumbled alphabet, and you're always playing catch up."

"No spontaneity," I said, scrubbing myself down with a loofah.

"Not for a while, no. We need to avoid multitasking. I think you should have reminders in your office and in areas where you do activities, reminding you to do one thing at a time. Do it to the best of your ability, finish it, and move on to the next task. And at the end of the day, I think we should sit down and look at this daily calendar and focus on the effort that was made and *reward* ourselves. You need to start looking at everything you do differently—focus on the accomplishment of it. Hell, Jo, just getting out of bed is an accomplishment for most people."

"Positive affirmations," I said, thinking out loud.

"Yes. Exactly. Tack those up around the house instead of bloody images."

I stepped under the showerhead and rinsed the soap from my body, my mind chewing over the last few minutes. I thought of the planner calendar Mia had bought me years ago, still wrapped in cellophane, shoved in a desk drawer somewhere. I thought of the key ring tracking device that I never really used. The inspirational daily meditation app that I installed months ago but have yet to click into. Effort. I needed to make the effort—more effort, where it mattered.

"Can I say something else?" Beckett asked, somewhat tentatively.

"At this point, yeah, anything."

"I think you should look at *all* your addictions . . . like, maybe scrolling social media too much or—"

"Don't patronize me. You're talking about my cigars."

"I am."

I jerked open the shower door and stuck my head out. "Do *not* mess with my cigars, Beckett."

"I'm just saying, it loops into that whole need for the dopamine rush. The buzz from a cigar is an instant reward—and by the way, I think you're embarrassed by it. Subconsciously, anyway."

My eyes narrowed.

He nodded. "Yep, I do. The way you held it away from me the first night we spoke, outside of Jolene's bar. The way you don't smoke around me, ever, and try to hide it from me, like the pills. You're sabotaging your own self-esteem by smoking."

"You're an ass, you know that?"

"Ah, but a correct ass, no?"

I slammed shut the door and shrank under the water. *Dammit*, he was right.

"Listen, Jo, life's tough, but the thing is, you can control your reaction to everything that happens around you. Let go of your mommy-and-daddy issues. Let go of the guilt of your past. Let go of the fucking pills, the cigars. And once all that is gone, you've got space to do what needs to happen . . . to meet yourself, who you truly are, for the first time. And I'll bet you're going to love her."

Tears welled in my eyes.

Beckett stood and leaned against the wall next to the shower. "Thing is . . . you are, without question, the most beautiful woman I've ever seen in my life. More than that, you're smart, capable, and strong as fuck, Jo Bellerose. You just have to realize that yourself. And I'm going to be right here with you the entire way."

When I didn't respond, he slowly opened the shower door.

I turned to him, buck naked, my eyes filling with tears.

"This is me, Beckett." I opened my palms, my lip quivering. "This is me. This is what you get. The mess, the train wreck, the cellulite on my stomach and on my ass. This is me."

"Baby," he whispered, his face dropping, "don't cry. Come here."

He reached for me, but I pushed his hands away.

"But what if you leave me too?" I asked.

"Baby, please," he said as he pulled me to himself. "You've already got me wrapped around your perfect little finger and have since the moment you poured a bottle of beer on my boots. I'm not going anywhere."

Beckett stepped into the shower and pulled my naked body to himself, the water drenching his hair, his clothes, but he didn't care.

Tears streamed down my face as he wrapped my arms around himself. I allowed myself to fall into him, ignoring the voice in my head telling me not to. Not to be weak, vulnerable. Not to let him see me this way.

I didn't care anymore.

He hugged me back, held me, laying sweet kisses on the top of my head while I cried.

For the first time, my brain turned off, my thoughts vanishing to nothing but the tears I shed. I took in his scent, the feel of his hard chest against my cheek, the comfort of his hold, the warm water washing over us like late-afternoon summer rain. I imagined it washing away everything. The pain, the past, the self-loathing that I hated so much about myself. The anger toward my mother and my father.

It all just washed away so easily in that moment, with him.

I looked up. Beckett wiped my tears, cupping my face in his hands.

Water streaked down his face, down mine, as he stared down at me with such intensity, such heat, that butterflies erupted in my stomach.

Without a single word, Beckett kissed me, and the final piece of armor—of insecurity—washed away.

I stripped off his shirt as he slipped out of his pants, our lips only losing contact for the brief second when his shirt was pulled over his head.

"Jo," he whispered, almost desperately, between kisses as our naked bodies pressed against each other. "You are everything."

Strong hands gripped my waist, lifting me off my feet. I threw my arms around his neck, wrapped my legs around him like a vise as he pressed me up against the shower wall.

"Don't leave me," I whispered as he trailed kisses down my neck, his hands cupping my breasts.

"Don't leave me," he whispered back. "I love you, Jo. I fucking love you."

"Kiss me. God, kiss me again, Beckett."

And he did just that, my body pinned between him and the shower wall, my legs open, wrapped around him. Heat pulsed below, and I began to throb with desire. I'd never wanted anything more badly in my life.

I reached down between us, easily finding his erection. He moaned as I wrapped my fingers tightly around it.

"Fuck me," I whispered breathlessly, squeezing him in the palm of my hand. "Fuck me, Beckett."

I guided his tip to my opening, replaced my arm around his neck, and held on as he speared into me.

I gasped, my breath escaping me. The world around me became a dizzying haze as our bodies combined into one.

This was life. This was everything.

We rode each other into oblivion, the water sluicing down our bodies. There was no bad in the world in that moment, no thinking, no worrying, no loathing, nothing but the purest form of joy, of pleasure.

Everything was good.

Everything was right as Beckett took me to climax, as he took me as *his*.

Chapter Forty

Beckett

My cell phone rattled on the nightstand. I looked at the clock—just after midnight.

Quietly, I shifted out of Jo's arms and picked up the phone. "Hello?"

"It's Alek."

I sat up. "What's wrong?"

"They just found another body."

"What?"

I immediately looked over at Jo to ensure her body was next to me and that she was indeed safe. She was asleep, her hair fanned over the pillow, her naked chest rising and falling heavily. Still okay. Peaceful.

Quietly, I got out of bed and walked to the kitchen window, naked. The security light pooled onto the ground, revealing a solid sheet of ice. Instinctively, I checked for tracks or any sign that someone had been lurking. There were none.

"Tell me everything," I said.

"You know cars have been stranded all over the road, right?"

"Yeah."

"Well, Jessie—the guy who owns the tow truck company that hauled Marissa's car from the lake—has been making his rounds with his buddy, helping pull people out. About twenty minutes ago, they got to that sharp bend right before you turn onto County Road 426."

"The road that leads here."

"Right. There was a car in the ditch. He parked, got out, and before they even got around to the driver's side door, they saw the body."

"Whose body?"

"Don't know—they don't know. A woman, middle aged. They just found it—her. I literally just heard it over the scanner."

My gut twisted. "You wouldn't be calling me if the middle-aged woman had died of something like a heart attack while trying to push her car out of the ditch."

"She was gutted, sliced to shreds, and painted in her own blood."

Shit.

"And they don't have any idea who she is?"

"No. I don't even know if the cops are there yet or if they can even make it. I'm about to head down there on the ATV now to see how I can help."

"You said the sharp corner, right? About two miles north?"

"Right."

"It's him." My jaw clenched. "The motherfucker never left after he attacked Jo. He's around here. Either at one of the houses in the area or hunkered down in a cave. He's here."

"I agree."

"What does the blood pattern on the woman's body look like?"

"No clue. All I know is that they said, quote, she's painted just like the Pollock Butcher does his girls. That's verbatim what the guy called in. I'll let you know as soon as I get there."

"No, I want to see it for myself. This is the last known location of the Pollock Butcher. The area needs to be searched by one of us, not some part-time county asswipe. Alek, we've got to find this son of a bitch."

"Agreed on all counts."

"I'll see you down there." I clicked off the phone.

"What's wrong?"

I turned. Jo was sitting up in the bed, wide awake, worry pulling at her beautiful, sleepy face. The comforter had fallen around her waist, exposing her breasts and bare skin that glowed like an angel against the flickering light from the fireplace.

God, she was perfect—and I would fucking *kill* anyone who touched a single hair on that beautiful head.

"What happened?" she asked again, shifting her weight to the edge of the bed.

"Stop," I said, hurrying across the room. "Let me help."

"Just tell me what's going on, Beckett."

"They found another body, a woman, cut up and painted."

Jo gasped, covering her mouth with her hand. "Who?"

"They don't know. The guy who found her didn't recognize her."

"Oh my God, Beckett."

"She's less than two miles from here. Stay there. I need to get you dressed," I said as I began gathering her clothes.

"We're going to the scene?"

"Yes. I need to check the area for tracks before the cops get there and trample over everything. Arms up." I slid a cashmere sweater over her head. "Alek is already on his way."

Jo nodded feverishly, kicking out her legs as I knelt down to slip on a pair of sweatpants. "Yes. Yes, whatever we can do to help."

I paused, looking up at her, feeling a rush of warmth in my chest. I've always prided myself on my rationality, my ability to think before I speak, but in that moment, I was completely overcome by emotion. "I love you so much, Jo. I don't care if you don't say it back. I love you. I love you, I love you, and I am going to tell you every day for the rest of your life."

"That's quite a commitment." She smiled softly.

"I'm ready."

"Let's get this done, first." She lightly cupped my cheeks, kissed me on the lips. "Let's end this crazy nightmare we've found ourselves in . . . let's get this son of a bitch, Beck."

I made short work of dressing Jo in four layers of clothing, including gloves, a scarf, and a beanie. Then I grabbed blankets and packed a quick bag to take with us to assist in any emergencies that—God forbid—might come up.

I carried Jo outside to the shed. After I unlocked the padlocks, I lowered her into the ATV, and together, we headed into the dark night.

The sleet had stopped. Only a few clouds lingered in the sky, crowding a full moon, and fortunately, its light. The woods were quiet, the creatures in hiding, hunkered down, seeking shelter from the storm.

The headlights formed a bubble of light around us, but beyond its reach was nothing but darkness. Ice was everywhere, coating the branches, the bushes, the ground. The trees wilted under the weight, as if bowing their heads in sadness while we slowly drove through the forest.

"I've never seen, or heard, the woods this quiet in my life," Jo said.

"I know."

"It's so creepy, isn't it? You'd think it would be beautiful. Enchanting, even. But it's not." Jo shivered, wrapping her arms around herself.

I pulled a blanket from the back and wrapped it around her shoulders. For once, I didn't know what to say to console her. Truth was, it was creepy as shit. There was something in the air that night, a presence you could feel as real as the biting cold.

We didn't speak the rest of the way.

I could feel Jo's nerves as she sat next to me. We were both on high alert, ready for whatever might happen along these two miles.

Chapter Forty-One

Jo

My head was spinning with two polar-opposite thought patterns.

Please don't let the dead body be my mom, and, *Oh my God, Beckett loves me.*

The moment Beckett said a woman had been found, it was my first thought. My mother had gotten herself into something she couldn't talk—or pay—her way out of. Or the Butcher killed her in his final warning to me.

In an instant, it seemed, every ill feeling I'd ever had about my mom faded away. It wasn't worth it. The stupid arguments, the grudges held on to for years.

It all felt so trivial all of a sudden.

And then—Beckett loves me?

I wanted to say it back. It was on the tip of my tongue, but for some reason, I couldn't say the words.

There will be time for that later, I reminded myself.

. . . Right?

Chapter Forty-Two

Beckett

Alek was already at the scene when we arrived. Both the tow truck and Alek's ATV had been positioned so that their headlights illuminated the rusted Oldsmobile stuck in the ditch.

As instructed by Alek, I assumed, Jessie and his buddy stood next to the truck, their faces pale, their eyes wide with adrenaline. Both men were wearing gloves, hats, and insulated coveralls depicting their company logo. Both men looked like they were about to shit themselves.

I remember the first time I saw a dead body, one that had been brutally murdered. It would stay with them for a very, very long time.

"I want to come," Jo said as I parked beside Alek's ATV, nodding at the men, who nodded back.

I didn't expect less.

I grabbed my pack from the back, and before I could exit the ATV and walk around to help, Jo was already up, leaning on her crutches, a steely look in her eyes.

"God, you're a fucking badass."

"Yes, I think I am."

I smirked. "There's that self-esteem."

"Thank you."

"Ready?"

"Ready."

Though Jo refused help, I kept my hand on her lower back as we approached the scene.

"He's in the woods, looking for something," Jessie said, speaking of Alek. "Told us not to move."

"Thanks."

I didn't have to ask where the woman was. The younger trucker was staring at a spot just behind the hood of the car, with a sickened, trancelike expression.

"Are you sure you want to see this?" I quietly asked Jo.

"Yes."

The body revealed itself to us in slow motion as we stepped around the back of the car.

A pair of snow-white bare feet with toenails painted in chipped pink polish. Long, skinny, bloodied legs, slashed along the veins of each calf. And a torso, lying in a pool of blood, the skin so white, it was almost luminescent underneath the pattern the killer had painted on her body.

The first wave of blood connected both nipples, then wave after wave stacked down her stomach, stopping just below her belly button. The woman's eyes were closed, her mouth barely open. Blonde hair and dirty gray roots splayed over the icy gravel rocks. Her arms were open, like Jesus on the cross, slashed vertically, against the veins. A horrific scene, just like all the others.

Jo exhaled, covering her heart with her hand. "I don't know her. Do you?"

"No."

"It's another message, Beckett. This location is no accident, and neither is the timing. His first attempt to kill me failed; she was my substitute. He knew we'd find her . . . it's a message. He's not stopping until I'm dead."

She was right.

"Let's get you back to the ATV," I said.

"No," she said, still focused on the body. "Wait. Hang on."

She pulled her cell phone from her coat pocket. At first, I thought she was going to take photographs of the body—and I almost stopped her, but instead, Jo opened the picture app and began frantically swiping through the files. When she found the picture she was looking for, she double tapped, maximized it on the screen, and turned it toward me.

"Look." One of Aria's paintings illuminated the screen. "This is her last painting. The one I was talking about earlier."

I scanned between the dead woman on the ground and the red waves painted over the canvas. The painting was an exact replica of the pattern on the woman's body.

"Beckett," Jo whispered, a hint of fear fueling the sharpness in her tone. "Aria painted this exact pattern in her last painting. She didn't see this victim on the news—because it *just* happened. But *she* knew. How? *Shit*, Beckett. It's Aria. If it's not her, then she's the key to all this. It's Aria. It's her, Beckett. She *knows*."

I recalled the way Aria had stared at me when we'd first met, the way she'd watched my every move as if trying to tell me something . . . or waiting for me to figure something out.

I pulled my phone from my pocket and called the office. Loren picked up on the second ring.

"Loren, I need you to figure out where Aria Ledger is right now. I need you to pin her location and send it to me. Call her house, call her mother, her father, call her cell phone, whatever. I need you to find out where she is right now and where she's been the last few hours."

"Will do, boss."

I hung up and looked at Jo, who was staring down at the dead body.

My gut twisted with a premonition, a strong feeling that we'd reached the final act in this horrific play. That we were on the cusp of the Pollock Butcher's final masterpiece.

Chapter Forty-Three

I began to salivate like a dog, watching her from behind a tree. I was ten feet away—ten feet—from Jo Bellerose, my final target. She stood shivering, despite the many layers she had on, mournfully staring down at the body I'd painted hours earlier.

Darla Thompson was her name. A middle-aged waitress, stuck on the side of the road, eager to accept help from a total stranger. The woman had been so scared and so grateful when I walked up that she blurted out her entire life story to me, a man she didn't know a thing about, as I pretended to get her unstuck. She told me her name, where she lived, where she worked, how many kids she had, and exactly how she'd slid off the road.

Idiot. The woman deserved to die.

As I watched the scene unfold around me, my final plan slowly began to reveal itself to me with such clarity that I began to shake.

Finally, I knew how I was going to create my last masterpiece.

It is called lino cutting. A form of art where the artist cuts a design into a hard surface using a knife, chisel, or gouge, creating an image in the uncut, raised areas. It's the opposite of painting, really. Instead of creating a picture by putting paint onto a surface, it is cutting a design out of the surface. It requires a completely different mindset, perception, and skill from canvas work.

Instead of painting Jo's torso, I will carve out pieces of her flesh, remove the long, thin strands of skin, allowing the oozing red contusions to create an image. A den of snakes slithering up her legs, her arms, her neck. Swirling inside her stomach.

It would be beautiful, a perfect representation of the intrusive, conniving menace she is.

A snake in the grass, soon to take her last breath.

Chapter Forty-Four

Jo

I'm ashamed to admit how relieved I was that the dead body did not belong to my mother, that it was another innocent woman caught in the wrong place at the wrong time. It was the first time—ever—that I considered my mother's mortality and that she will, one day, die. It felt like a turning point, emotionally. My time with Melinda was limited. Why would I make anything but the best of it?

Effort, Jo.

Put effort into creating quality time with her.

I made a promise to myself that once this mess was over, I would find a way to reconnect with my mother, find a common ground, and plant a seed for a new relationship to blossom between us.

For now, I needed to focus on the poor woman who'd been killed for no other purpose than to serve as a message for me.

Sergeant Rosa was the only responding officer to the scene because of the impassable roads. She had been staying a few miles away with her elderly grandmother, who was in no condition to survive the subzero temperatures, possible power outages, and food shortages.

Interviews were conducted, albeit slowly, copious numbers of pictures taken, and the area was searched using flashlights. I didn't have to ask Beckett if he'd found anything useful; his vile mood said enough.

Because the coroner couldn't reach the scene, Rosa had made the difficult decision to go against traditional protocol and wrap the body in a tarp and secure it in the trunk of the victim's car. It was the only option. Following protocol would have meant leaving the body untouched, which would have allowed the starving animals to ravage it and destroy any chance of a successful autopsy.

Once the body was locked away, the decision on what to do next was discussed at length.

Leave the scene and the body as is until the roads were safe enough for the medical examiner to arrive? If so, who would stay with it? Was it even safe to stay with the body? Forget hypothermia—what about the Butcher lurking in the shadows? In the end, the decision was made to pull the car—with the body in the trunk—from the ditch and tow it into town, with Rosa as an official escort.

It had taken over an hour to get the car out of the ditch. One by one, people cleared the scene, leaving nothing but a frozen pool of blood on the ground.

It was four o'clock in the morning by the time Beckett and I arrived back at the cabin. We were cold and exhausted, both mentally and physically. My ankle had swelled to double the normal size, and the pain tripled. I could feel my pulse throbbing underneath the brace.

"You need to try to sleep," Beckett said, pulling the covers over me after he'd helped me undress and laid me in the bed.

"*You* need to try to sleep, Beckett."

He didn't respond. I could tell he was doing his best to act calm so that I would relax, but his icy intensity gave him away.

"Seriously, Beckett, please," I said. "I have no doubt today is going to be another crazy day. Just try to get a bit of sleep—please."

"I will," he said. "I just have a few emails I need to respond to first."

"Okay," I whispered, squeezing his hand.

He leaned forward and stroked my hair, looking deeply into me. Butterflies fluttered in my stomach.

"Go to sleep," he whispered, and I nodded.

But I didn't sleep. Instead, I watched Beckett sitting next to the fire in silence, his gaze flicking between the cell phone in his hand and the window. The fire popped and hissed, the crackling flames the only sound in the cabin.

Eventually, my eyes began to get heavy, and my vision started to blur. I rolled over, tucking my arm under the pillow, and pulled my legs to my chest. I stared out the window, images of the dead woman flashing in my memory. Her pale, bloodless skin, her lifeless eyes, the gaping wounds running up her arms and legs. The blood painted across her torso.

Wave after wave flashed through my head as I slipped into the blurred moments before sleep. Dark red slashes on skin, on canvas.

Aria . . . everything was linked to Aria.

I blinked, trying to stay awake.

Movement outside the kitchen window pulled my attention.

Did I see something? Or had I fallen asleep, on the fringes of a dream?

Frowning, I squinted, staring at the black night outside the window. Something had moved—I was sure of it—just past the shadows.

My entire body jolted to life with an explosion of adrenaline. I shot up to a sitting position.

Beckett was on his feet and rounding the couch before I could even speak. "What's wrong?" he asked, filled with concern.

"I—I swear, I just saw something move outside the window."

His gaze snapping toward the window, Beckett crossed the cabin in what seemed like two steps and looked outside.

I continued, "I could be crazy—I could be seeing things. But I swear I just—"

"Get off the bed." The sudden shift in his tone sent a chill racing up my spine. "Get into a ball on the floor between the wall and the bed."

I did what he asked without hesitation, squeezing myself into the small space between the wall and the bed.

My heart roared as I listened to his footsteps, the opening and closing of a cabinet door. The unmistakable click of a magazine being slipped into a handgun. A smooth pop as he pulled back the slide, chambering a bullet into place.

My mouth went dry with fear.

"There's a gun under the bed, right next to you," he said from somewhere across the room. "I want you to find it right now."

I could tell he was speaking with his back to me. Because he was worried that somebody was watching us? He didn't want to draw attention to where I was?

I shifted, reaching under the bed with my left arm, my fingertips searching the cold hardwood until finally feeling something even colder.

"I've got it," I whispered.

"Remove the safety. It's cocked, and there's a bullet in the chamber. All you have to do is unlock the safety."

My hand trembled as I clicked the small button on the side. "Okay."

"If anyone enters this house, I want you to shoot them, no questions asked. Point and shoot. You have eight shots."

"Beckett . . ."

"You can do it, Jo. *Anyone.* If *any* person sets foot in here, I want you to shoot them."

"Where are you going?" I whisper-hissed.

"To get this motherfucker once and for all."

Chapter Forty-Five

Beckett

I slipped out the door.

Double fisting my gun, I hunched over and sprinted into the tree line, flying over the ice-packed ground. I pressed my back against a tree and stilled.

My breath came out in heavy puffs, the steam disappearing into the cold, still air.

The clouds had moved on, the full moon shining overhead, a million little stars twinkling around it. The moonlight reflected everywhere, bouncing off the layers of ice that covered the trees, the bushes, the ground. The night was lit in a shadowless silver glow, almost as bright as early morning.

I mentally slipped into the hunt, pulling my focus inward, heightening my senses and awareness of the world around me. I listened, cataloging every sound in the vicinity, calculated the direction of even the slightest movement of air. I felt the support of the ground beneath my feet. I shifted my weight onto my heels, assessing the thickness of the ice, and therefore, how light and quick I would need to move to make as little noise as possible. I squeezed the cold steel of the gun in my palm.

My entire focus shifted to my prey. The Pollock Butcher.

Then, as if the universe were presenting him to me on a silver platter, I picked up his first track, an almost-perfect impression of a boot tread on a layer of cracked ice, laid within the last minute.

And with that, the hunt began.

Shoulders down, head up, I silently followed the tracks, jumping from rock to rock or fallen limb to limb to keep my boots from cracking against the ice and potentially tipping off my prey.

The space between the boot prints widened, suggesting he'd broken out into a jog. Had something spooked him? Had he seen me exit the cabin?

I picked up my pace.

The tracks took a turn, circling toward the lake. What the hell was he up to? The tracks were erratic, a few places indicating that he'd stumbled.

Something wasn't right.

One thing the authorities were certain of was that the Pollock Butcher was an avid outdoorsman. That he was cunning, smart, ruthless. Not someone who'd be stumbling his way through the woods on an incoherent path.

Was he possibly injured?

The sound of rushing water and the musty scent of a riverbank filled the air. We were getting close to the river that ran through the woods, feeding into Skull Lake.

Had the Butcher used a canoe to throw us off? Had he parked miles away at the lake and sneaked into the area through the river?

My pulse rate picked up, the back of my neck tingling with adrenaline.

I followed the prints out of the trees and onto the small shoreline. The reflection of the full moon rippled over the rushing water, the shimmering waves reminding me of the pattern painted on the victims.

I frowned, studying the prints. Something wasn't right.

The boot prints seemed to disappear into the water, but there was no sign of a canoe or kayak. No drag marks on the shore and no deep indents where a vessel might have lain in wait.

I studied the icy ground, noting a few freshly overturned stones, which could have been from an animal. Where the fuck did he go?

Suddenly, a trio of birds shrilled against the night sky, exploding out of the canopy, wings flapping angrily.

Bingo.

I took off in the direction of the fleeing birds, slipping my first few steps, then adjusting my gait so that my heel strikes cracked the layer of ice, allowing for traction on the dirt. I burst through the tree line, tree limbs and bushes tearing at my clothes. Stealth was no longer a concern. I double gripped my gun as I neared a thicket of trees.

A silhouette darted out of the shadows.

I pivoted, pushing to a full sprint, chasing the man who was now running for his life. A branch sliced my cheek, sending a trail of blood down my face.

He was faster than expected, especially considering the conditions.

Holding the gun was slowing me down, affecting my balance more than the ice. I shoved my gun into my waistband and surged forward.

I could smell him, his sweat, his fear.

Closer, closer, I was almost close enough to grab the black coat that was flapping behind him.

We came to a rocky patch of terrain where massive boulders speared up from the ground. He scrambled over the first. I took two leaps, jumped, caught a limb, and propelled my body forward, releasing and flying through the air.

The man didn't know what hit him.

We slammed into the top of a boulder, tumbled down the rock and down a short hill, hitting with a thud at the base of a small valley.

His attempt to fight back was futile, at best. We wrestled on the ground. I caught a lucky kidney shot and answered back with a right hook, momentarily stunning my prey. The man, wearing a black bala-clava, groaned. But still, he fought.

Another pop in the face, another, and another.

Finally, his body went limp beneath me.

My chest heaving, I used one hand to pin his wrist above his head, and with my other, ripped off the black ski mask. Blood spattered his face, pouring like a river from his nose and mouth.

I recognized him instantly. Leif Ellis.

Rage flew through me.

"Fucking son of a fucking b—" I reared back to punch him again.

"No," he mumbled, spitting up the blood that was running down his throat. "No . . ." He blinked wildly, coming to. "I didn't do it."

He struggled against my hold, and I sent my knee into his groin. *"Fuck."*

"Don't fucking move," I said. "What the fuck are you talking about?"

"I'm not the Butcher. I didn't kill Marissa, and I didn't attack Jo. I promise it wasn't me. I'd never hurt her."

He turned his head and vomited. The smell was rancid, and rage overtook me.

I wrapped my hand around his skull and bashed it against a rock. He screamed out in pain.

"I fucking swear to God, I'll kill you right now if you don't tell me this second why I should believe you aren't the Butcher."

Leif spat out a tooth. "I—I was hired . . ."

"Hired to do what?"

"Clean up messes."

"What kind of messes?"

Leif closed his eyes. "I didn't know, I promise. The money was good—really good. I paid off gambling debts and quit dealing."

"What kind of messes, Leif?"

"Whatever he told me to do, I did. I didn't realize until . . ."

"What did he have you do?"

"Take care of evidence, tracks, throw off the police, whatever."

I ground my teeth. "So, you were the Pollock Butcher's cleanup man?"

"Yeah, but I swear, I didn't realize it at first. I—"

"Fucking *Christ*," I bellowed.

"I promise," he screamed back.

"What the hell are you doing with Jo's mom, you sick fuck?"

"She's—we're together. We don't talk about Jo, I promise. Melinda keeps her separate from . . . us."

"Did she know you were partners with the Butcher?"

"No—God, no."

A wave of relief washed over me. Jo couldn't handle any more betrayal from her mother.

"Were you the person Jo saw around Lookout Point a few nights ago?"

"What? No? Ah . . ." His eyes flashed with an epiphany of sorts. "The keys . . . Marissa's keys . . . he'd dropped them somewhere after dumping her vehicle. After he'd searched, he asked me to go back and look."

"Did you paint her house with blood?"

"No, man. No. He did."

"Who's *he*? Who hired you? Give me a fucking name!"

"He'll kill me, dude."

"A name!"

The former badass biker began weeping like a child.

My patience ran out.

"Tell me!" I screamed, a rush of anger blowing through my veins.

"He'll kill me—"

"Tell me!" I shouted again.

Leif's eyes fluttered.

He opened his mouth, inhaled, then mumbled something inaudible a split second before he drifted away and his head lolled to the side.

Chapter Forty-Six

Jo

The silence wrapped around me like a straitjacket, slowly squeezing me to death, as if hiding between a bed and a rock wall weren't suffocating enough.

Minutes ticked by.

Five . . .

Ten . . .

Twenty . . .

The hilt of the pistol was sweaty under my viselike grip.

If anyone walks into this cabin, shoot them.

When Beckett had said these words to me, I'd nodded feverishly. Yes, yes, of course I would, I'd thought at the time. But as the minutes ticked by, I began to wonder if I could actually shoot another human being. If I could intentionally kill another person.

The thought seemed almost inconceivable to me. After all, I'd made a career out of doing the exact opposite. Saving those who didn't want to live.

I thought about a client I had once; his name was Bruce Wellington. He was a forty-six-year-old account manager for the local electric company. Bruce wanted to kill himself. Not because he'd committed some sort of unforgivable sin, but because his wife had left him for another man, leaving him a mountain of debt, an empty house, and a hole in his heart, which had recently undergone a valve-replacement surgery.

In all my years of meeting humans in their darkest times, I'd never met one more determined to kill himself than Bruce.

Twenty-five minutes . . .

Bruce and I went through the torment of medication trial and error for what Mia had diagnosed as PTSD and severe depression. During those six months, Bruce called my cell phone ninety-six times. Ninety-six times, I answered, excused myself from whatever it was that I was doing and disappeared into a corner, where I proceeded to talk the man off the ledge.

I'm ashamed to say that there were times I secretly wanted him to do it. Get it over with. And it was in those times that my weakness was revealed. I was someone who would give up when things got too rough.

Bruce taught me the greatest lesson someone could learn in my position: if a psychiatrist is willing to give up on his or her patients in moments of frustration, then he or she isn't fit for the job.

I made a decision not to give up on Bruce. To not give up on any of my clients. Because they deserved better from me.

Could I really pull the trigger? Could I really kill someone?

Thirty minutes . . .

The world outside the cabin was eerily still. Inside, you could hear a pin drop. Even the fire in the fireplace was waning, the pops and hisses more like pitiful exhales of breath. I could feel the air, like a weight slowly pressing around my body.

My attention drifted to the stack of inkblot cards on the floor a few feet in front of me. I thought of Aria.

I studied her paintings taped to the walls. Dark red waves of paint, each resembling the pattern on each of the victims.

I pictured the woman I'd seen, dead on the side of the road, hours earlier. Aria's last painting was an exact replica of this woman's bloody pattern.

How did she know the pattern before the next victim was even painted?

How was she involved in all this?

Was it her? Was *she* the Pollock Butcher? Or was it her mother, Jamie? A jealous woman on the edge?

I stared at the death card, the large imposing blot of ink that represented an authoritative figure. The one Aria had said reminded her of death.

Death . . .

An authoritative figure . . .

I focused my thoughts, feeling like I was onto something.

An authoritative figure . . .

I studied the canvas, the cards, the stack of news articles, then back to the canvas.

An authoritative figure . . .

As if pulled by some unseen force, I pushed to my knees and slowly crawled across the room, focused on Aria's last painting.

Using the crutches that were leaning against the wall, I knocked the canvas off the wall and centered it on the floor in front of me. Squinting, I studied the strokes, the smooth ebbs and flows of the waves, and how eventually, each wave faded into nothing, disappearing against the white canvas.

Wave over wave on top of each other, fading into nothing.

An authoritative figure . . .

My gut tingled more intensely. Like I was staring at the answer, but I couldn't see it.

Apophenia: The ability to spot and recognize patterns. Patterns that meant something. Pattern recognition that was essential for identifying both food and predators.

Predators.

Authoritative figures . . .

I picked up the canvas and shifted my weight on the floor, kicking out my bad ankle in front of me, and studied the art. The canvas began to blur as I slipped into a weird daze that reminded me of staring at one of those pictures that eventually turns into a 3D image.

Red lines.

Stacked red lines.

But they weren't lines, really. More like wax . . . like melting wax.

Melting red . . . blood . . .

Predators . . . authoritative figures . . .

I gasped.

Slowly, I covered my hand over my mouth. My heart began to race as I stared at the streaks of red that Aria had said were blood. Except it wasn't blood.

It was a scar. A scar of burned skin—of melted skin.

Aria's final painting was of the upper part of the scar that marred the side of her stepfather's face, the part that ran along his jawline. Just a tiny piece of the large scar he'd gotten while becoming the hero of Skull Hollow.

Each of Aria's paintings represented a section of the large scar. Each pattern on each victim also represented the same thing.

Cyrus Ledger had painted pieces of his scar on each of his victims.

And Aria had put it all together, right there on canvas for us to figure out.

Cyrus Ledger was the Pollock Butcher.

Chapter Forty-Seven

Beckett

I smacked Leif's cheeks, shook his body, and yelled in his face, trying to bring him back to consciousness. It was no use.

I felt for a pulse. Slow, but there. I shouldn't have punched him. I shouldn't have lost my damn temper.

"Goddammit," I yelled, staring down at Leif's body between my legs.

If Leif wasn't the Pollock Butcher, who was? Who hired him to clean up their messes?

My mind racing, I took in the old biker before me. The long gray hair, the piercings in his ears, the tattoos. The black sweatshirt, jogging pants, worn leather boots.

I shifted my weight, pushing off him, and began searching his pockets. A pair of keys, an expertly rolled joint, a few sticks of gum. A handful of change. In his back pocket was a wallet, secured by a chain that hooked into the inner tag at the bottom of his sweatshirt.

I popped loose the chain.

Squinting through the darkness, I opened the wallet and began going through the contents. Credit cards, appointment reminders, a condom, receipts, his driver's license, a random seashell. Buried deep in the back pocket was a small folded piece of paper. A telephone number was scribbled across the top, and written below that was one single word. *Delta.*

Delta?

I frowned, staring down at the paper. The number was a local number. However, I didn't recognize the name Delta. An uncommon name—first or last. Unfortunately, I didn't have my cell phone, so there was no immediate way to know who was on the other end of this number.

I desperately searched my memory, unable to recall anyone with that name—and definitely no one associated with Jo, Marissa, Aria, or anyone involved with the Pollock Butcher.

Delta, delta, delta . . . did it mean something?

The memory of my first meeting with Jo popped into my head, her pouring out her beer and asking what I saw in the puddle of fizz.

"Apophenia," she'd said. "Finding hidden meanings in images and/or symbols."

I began thinking of what the word delta meant—the meaning of it.

A flat landscape.

A code word used in radio communication that represented the letter *D*.

The fourth star in a constellation.

The fourth in a series of items or categories.

None of these fit.

Delta . . .

"What is delta?"

I surged to my feet and began pacing. Something tapped at the fringes of my subconscious. A distant memory of something. Something was there; I just had to find it.

"Delta . . ." I turned and stared down at Leif's body.

I thought of Marissa, a victim of the Pollock Butcher. I thought of Aria, finding Marissa in the middle of nowhere. How? How had she found her?

Why had Aria gone into the woods that day? What had drawn her to Skull Lake?

I thought of Aria's paintings . . .

I thought of her mother, Jamie.

I thought of her stepfather.

The memory that had been tickling my senses suddenly firmed, like smoke merging together.

I remembered the key chain that had fallen out of her stepfather's, Cyrus Ledger's, backpack while I was digging into it. The one that had a triangle etched into it.

A triangle . . .

A chill flew up my back.

The triangle—otherwise known as a delta symbol, a representation of heat and fire. Delta was a symbol of a firefighter.

Holy *shit*. Delta was Cyrus Ledger.

Cyrus Ledger was the Pollock Butcher. *He* was who Jo saw in the woods that night.

He was the one hunting Jo.

Suddenly, everything made sense.

Cyrus was an avid outdoorsman. He'd been trained in survival by not only his job as a firefighter but also by experience. A man like that would know how to survive in an ice storm overnight. Hell, the man had survived getting half his face melted off while saving three children from a burning house. A night in the ice was surely nothing compared to that.

Cyrus was good looking—despite the scar—charismatic, with a huge ego. And likely, huge insecurities as well. He was a man who surely could lure any woman into his path. A modern-day Ted Bundy.

Cyrus was also an avid fisherman, who'd even admitted to fishing on Skull Lake several times before. He was wholly familiar with the area. His intense need to find his stepdaughter that night now made sense. It wasn't that he was worried about her safety . . . he was worried that she was going to find Marissa's body. And she did.

And the next night, Jo saw him sneaking through the woods.

I thought of Aria's paintings and our conversation. Had she known? Was this her way of trying to tell us? Had she suspected her stepfather was a serial killer?

I thought of the bruises on Jamie Ledger's neck. The marks weren't from her lover, Grady. They were from her husband, Cyrus.

Cyrus fucking Ledger.

I stilled . . . suddenly recalling what Leif had told me just minutes earlier. Cyrus had paid him to throw off the police.

A chill rolled up my spine.

Was that what Leif was doing tonight? Was he serving as a decoy to pull me out of the cottage?

I pocketed the wallet, lifted Leif's limp body from the ground, and with his body slung over my shoulder, took off toward the cabin.

To Jo.

Chapter Forty-Eight

Jo

I scrambled across the floor to the nightstand, where I'd plugged my phone in hours earlier. My stomach was churning, visions of Cyrus's scarred cheek and neck filling my vision.

I should have seen it.

The arrogant, sick fuck had painted *his* scar on his victims.

Aria had painted *his* scar in her own form of communication.

My cell phone wasn't on the nightstand. I turned, peeking over the bed, scanning the room until I spotted it on the couch in front of the fireplace.

But it was too late.

A window shattered, but the explosion of glass wasn't what stole my attention—it was the *whoosh* of air, followed by a heavy thud on the floor.

The object detonated, sending a wave of blazing yellow flames across the floor.

A Molotov cocktail had been thrown through the window.

The rug ignited instantly, turning into an ocean of fire. The drapes caught, the couch. The single-room cabin went up in flames so quickly I didn't have time to react.

A series of gunshots rang out, one deafening pop after another. The remaining window shattered. Rock and wood and glass exploded over my head as I curled into a ball on the floor, tucking my head into my arms.

I could already feel the heat, a thick cloying smoke wrapping around me like a straitjacket.

I heard the door burst open, popping on the hinges.

"If anyone comes into this cabin, shoot them."

My pulse spiked as I surged forward, pulling myself across the floor that hadn't caught yet, reaching for the gun Beckett had left for me. Just inches from my grasp, the gun was kicked away.

Two black boots appeared before my face. I recoiled, lifting my chin upward. Like the devil emerging from hell, he strutted in front of the dancing flames, which backlit his black pants and a black sweatshirt. It was the same man I'd seen in the woods; I knew it with every fiber of my being.

I pulled myself into a seated position, dragging my injured ankle to the side.

Cyrus Ledger stared down at me, but instead of meeting his gaze, I focused on the wavy scar that mottled his jaw and neck. Grotesque stacked layers of melted skin. Cyrus raised the gun, aiming directly between my eyes.

My world, and everything in it, stopped. The sounds, my breath, my heart, my thoughts, even my fear.

I now know how someone feels—or rather, doesn't—the split second before they die.

Chapter Forty-Nine

Beckett

There are many stories of heroic displays of superhuman strength in the military. In moments of life or death, our bodies answer the call for survival. It's called hysterical strength. A seemingly normal person exuding extraordinary strength during a time of crisis, such as lifting a car off a trapped child.

I'd never experienced it before that night.

Hysterical strength is one way to explain how I was able to make it back to the cabin as quickly as I did with the weight of a man on my shoulders and the instability of ice below my feet. The other? Love. *True* love—the all-consuming feral need to protect my woman.

I smelled the smoke before I saw the fire. Angry tongues of flames licked out of the cabin windows, followed by a thick billowing smoke that blackened the virgin snow around it.

I lowered Leif's body onto the ground and sprinted to the cabin, screaming her name, pitched shrills of panic exploding out of me.

Using my shoulder, I burst through the door.

Cyrus stood over Jo, a pistol pointed between her eyes.

Jo lay on the floor, paralyzed in fear.

Six inches from my boot lay the gun I'd left her for protection.

Chapter Fifty

Jo

My eyes drifted closed, and I braced for the shot.

Bam!

My body jerked violently. I waited for the rush of heat, the searing pain, the blackness to take me under. But there was none of that.

Instead, another body had entered the room. A large, menacing figure that I knew very well. Using the gun that Cyrus had kicked out of my reach, Beckett had shot Cyrus in the thigh a split second before he would have killed me.

I was yanked off the floor, into the air. I began choking as I was carried through the smoke. Sweat poured off my face; my vision began to waver. My body was laid on the frozen ground, and relief washed over me.

The next few seconds were a blur.

Shouts. Screams. Lots of running back and forth.

When I opened my eyes, I saw Beckett, gun in hand, standing over Cyrus's writhing body on the ice, next to me. Leif Ellis lay under a sagging pine tree, with tears and blood streaming down his face.

Chapter Fifty-One

Interview Transcript #3.
Interviewee: Jamie Ledger
Interviewer: Special Agent Martin Lance, FBI

༄

MARTIN: Mrs. Ledger, can you state your full name and date of birth for the record, please.

JAMIE: Jamie Sharon Ledger, April 7, 1979.

MARTIN: Thank you. Can I call you Jamie? Or would you prefer Mrs. Ledger?

JAMIE: Jamie's fine.

MARTIN: Thanks. Now, forgive me for the repetition here, but at the beginning of each interview, for the record, I need to state that I presented you and your attorney with what's called a criminal investigation warning form, which you have confirmed that you and your attorney have gone over. Is that correct?

JAMIE: Yes.

MARTIN: Great. So, to reiterate, you're here voluntarily, on your own accord. You're not under arrest. You're not going to be arrested. We're here to take a voluntary statement from you. Do you understand this?

JAMIE: Yes, sir.

MARTIN: Thank you. I'm going to start today's interview by asking you a series of questions that might be a bit uncomfortable for you. Is that okay?

JAMIE: Yes.

MARTIN: These questions have been derived from our first two interviews, the first on January 9, the day your husband was shot, and the second, the following day, on January 10. Do you remember these two interviews?

JAMIE: Yes.

MARTIN: Good. Are you ready to begin?

JAMIE: Yes.

MARTIN: Can you please tell us again, perhaps in more detail, how you and Cyrus Ledger met?

JAMIE: I met Cyrus at a barbecue at a friend's house.

MARTIN: How long ago was this?

JAMIE: About three years ago.

MARTIN: And you two began dating immediately?

JAMIE: Yes. He asked me out that day, and we went on a date the following weekend.

MARTIN: Where did he take you on your first date?

JAMIE: To an Italian restaurant in Searcy. After that, we came back to Skull Hollow and watched a band over at Jolene's.

MARTIN: Can you describe his behavior on the date?

JAMIE: He was nervous, I think. But normal . . . nothing out of the ordinary, I guess.

MARTIN: Did Cyrus show any signs of aggression toward you on that date?

JAMIE: No.

MARTIN: Did he show any signs of aggression on the night of the barbecue at your friend's house?

JAMIE: No.

MARTIN: Was there anything that stuck out to you at that point? Any odd behavior that you may have noticed?

JAMIE: No.

MARTIN: Tell me about your courtship with him.

JAMIE: It was short. We only dated a few months before he asked me to marry him. The next week, we went to the courthouse and got married. It was a very, very short courtship.

MARTIN: Had he met your daughter, Aria, at this point?

JAMIE: Yes. He was very good with her.

MARTIN: In what way?

JAMIE: I don't know, patient, I guess. He made an effort to get to know her but backed off when she needed some space—which is what Aria needs sometimes.

MARTIN: What did Aria think of Cyrus?

JAMIE: She never said.

MARTIN: Did you ever straight-out ask her?

JAMIE: Yes.

MARTIN: And she didn't respond?

JAMIE: No.

MARTIN: Did Cyrus ever open up to you about his childhood?

JAMIE: No.

MARTIN: So, he never told you that his father physically abused him as a child?

JAMIE: No—like I said yesterday, I didn't know until I spoke with his cousin a few days ago, after you guys did. I had no idea.

MARTIN: And during this courtship, you saw no signs that Cyrus had an aggressive personality?

JAMIE: No, not at all.

MARTIN: When was the first time Cyrus hit you?

JAMIE: On April 7 the following year.

MARTIN: That's a pretty exact recollection.

JAMIE: I'll never forget it. It was my birthday.

MARTIN: Can you tell us about that day?

JAMIE: We got into an argument.

MARTIN: About what?

JAMIE: It was something stupid. Over money. I bought myself a new jacket and hadn't told him about it, and he just . . . snapped. Like, lost his mind about it. Screaming . . . grabbing his head.

MARTIN: And this was an abnormal reaction for him?

JAMIE: Before the incident, yes. After the incident, no.

MARTIN: Okay, let's talk about the incident. Can you confirm, for the recording, what you are referring to when you say "the incident"?

JAMIE: It was just a few months after we got married. The day Cyrus responded to a house fire and almost died. The day he got the scars.

MARTIN: What else do you know about that day?

JAMIE: I know that he ignored orders and went into the house to save those children, and . . . and the room collapsed, and something landed on his face and neck, catching him on fire.

MARTIN: Kerosene from an upstairs lamp.

JAMIE: Right. He got third-degree burns. It was so—so awful.

MARTIN: Your husband was in the hospital for how long after that? Do you remember exactly?

JAMIE: A couple of weeks, I think—I'm sure you can get the exact time frame from the hospital.

MARTIN: Yes, I have it. I understand that at the hospital, they talked to him about getting a skin graft to help with the scars. Can you tell me about that? What he said about it?

JAMIE: Yes, he was adamant that he didn't want to do that.

MARTIN: That seems odd for someone who was so notoriously confident and handsome. Why do you think that was?

JAMIE: I don't know . . . I don't know much about why he did the things he did from that day forward. He was never the same after that day.

MARTIN: Explain this to me.

JAMIE: Cyrus was depressed for a few weeks after the incident. Extremely depressed. Weirdly so. I'd catch him just staring at himself in the mirror, at his scars, I guessed. One day, I walked in, and the mirror was busted. He was a completely different person after that incident.

MARTIN: Angry?

JAMIE: Yes. Short tempered, mad. When he wasn't mad, he was sad. He had bad PTSD, I guess—I mean, that's what I've overheard from the doctors over the last few days.

MARTIN: And aside from being angry, how else did he deal with these emotions?

JAMIE: Started going out with his friends. To the bars. He took every volunteer shift at work he could. It was like he never wanted to be home. He began completely distancing himself from Aria and me.

MARTIN: So, he was withdrawing?

JAMIE: Yes.

MARTIN: And is this why you cheated on him?

JAMIE: Yes . . . I think so . . . yes. He . . . I . . . . nothing was the same anymore. I actually thought he was cheating on me.

MARTIN: Was he?

JAMIE: No, I don't think so.

MARTIN: So, you sought solace from another man, Grady Humphries, and you also sought solace a different way. Is that right?

JAMIE: Yes.

MARTIN: Can you talk about that?

JAMIE: I started . . . doing drugs. Xanax and pot every now and then.

MARTIN: And where did you get these drugs?

JAMIE: Leif Ellis.

MARTIN: Jamie, did you know that Cyrus and Leif were gambling buddies?

JAMIE: No, I had no idea.

MARTIN: Did you know that Cyrus asked him to help cover up his crimes? That he used your daughter's college fund to pay him?

JAMIE: No. Of course not. I would have—no.

MARTIN: Sorry, Jamie, I know this is a lot.

JAMIE: Just keep going. I want to get this done and move on with my life.

MARTIN: Okay, just a few more questions. To confirm, it wasn't until after Cyrus almost lost his life that he began getting physical with you, correct? Meaning, that appeared to be his trigger. The trauma both emotionally and physically that he went through.

JAMIE: Right, and I think so, yes.

MARTIN: That was the beginning of April, last year.

JAMIE: Right.

MARTIN: Can you tell us again where Cyrus had said he'd been in the few days leading up to April 18?

JAMIE: He'd gone to Houston for work training—something like that.

[*Insert Interviewer Note: Pollock Butcher victim #1 found on April 19 in Hennessy Park in Houston, Texas.]

MARTIN: Can you talk about when he got home that night?

JAMIE: He came home really late that night. He was acting really weird.

MARTIN: How so?

JAMIE: Just really hyper—oddly so. And I remember he just had this weird, hyper look in his eyes. I actually thought maybe he was doing drugs. Meth or something.

MARTIN: Like he was on an adrenaline high.

JAMIE: Yes, I confronted him about it.

MARTIN: About what, exactly?

JAMIE: I asked him if he was on drugs and also if he was cheating on me. He exploded, and we got in a fight. He threw me against the wall and slapped me across the face. Told me to never question him again . . . I should've left him. I know that now. I stayed because I felt like he needed somebody. I felt like he was going through something from the incident still, and that I'd be wrong to leave him. I thought he wouldn't hit me again.

MARTIN: But he did?

JAMIE: Yes.

MARTIN: Can you tell me about the third time?

JAMIE: Yes. Only about a month after he went to Houston, he said he had another trip for work. I thought this was weird because he never traveled, really. Firefighters don't take work trips.

MARTIN: Can you confirm the location of this trip? Or where he told you he was going?

JAMIE: Yes, Waco for two nights.

[*Insert Interviewer Note: Pollock Butcher victim #2 found on May 13 on Highway 19 in Waco, Texas.]

JAMIE: He was weird again when he got back. Again, I thought he was using. I'd had some wine—I shouldn't have, but I did—and we got into an argument, and this time, he punched me in the face. He dragged me by my hair through the house and shut me in the bedroom and told me if I came out again that he would kill me. He gave me a black eye that night.

MARTIN: And where was Aria when this happened?

JAMIE: In her room.

MARTIN: So, she didn't see this?

JAMIE: No.

MARTIN: Did she hear it?

JAMIE: No . . . I don't think so . . . I mean, I guess she could've.

MARTIN: And then what?

JAMIE: And then it became kind of a regular thing, you know. I don't know . . . it just slowly became a regular thing.

MARTIN: What did?

JAMIE: Him hitting me.

MARTIN: Were there times that were worse than others?

JAMIE: Every time was bad.

MARTIN: Jamie, yesterday we provided you with a list of three dates, and we asked you if you remembered if your husband was out of town on those dates.

JAMIE: Yes, the two we just talked about and one more, about six months ago, but you said that you already confirmed that he was gone on those dates and where he was.

MARTIN: Right, yes, the phone company verified his cell phone location on each of the dates. But I wanted to know a little bit more. I wanted to know his behavior leading up to those days. If you remembered how he was acting.

JAMIE: I don't remember, or nothing sticks out, about how he was acting before the Houston, Waco, and Tyler trips. But the last two dates . . . the night that Marissa Currie was killed and, most recently, Darla . . .

MARTIN: Thompson.

JAMIE: That's right. Anyway, I do remember he wasn't sleeping well. He went out the night after Marissa was killed. He seemed more tired and agitated than usual. Before Marissa was killed, he . . . well—he strangled me.

[*Insert Interviewer Note: Pollock Butcher victim #4, Marissa Currie, found on January 12*

*at Lookout Point, Skull Lake, Skull Hollow,
Texas. Pollock Butcher victim #5, found on
January 16 on County Road 530, Skull Hol-
low, Texas.]*

MARTIN: It was the first time he'd done that?
Strangled you?

JAMIE: Yes.

MARTIN: Do you feel like his mental health was
deteriorating?

JAMIE: Yes, I think so.

MARTIN: Did you ever try to seek treatment for
him?

JAMIE: You mean, like, therapy?

MARTIN: Yes.

JAMIE: Yes, I suggested it. But he wouldn't do
it.

MARTIN: I'd like to revisit the days leading up
to his arrest. When exactly did you start
to suspect something was going on?

JAMIE: Two nights after Aria went missing and
Marissa's body was found.

MARTIN: And what did you find that made you suspicious of him?

JAMIE: I found . . .

MARTIN: It's okay, Jamie. We know you didn't
know.

JAMIE: I found a black trash bag of what appeared
to be remains of pigs in the back of his
truck. Blood . . . all on the inside. I know
now he'd stolen them from a farm a few miles
away and desecrated Dr. Bellerose's house

with their blood. I guess he thought she saw him at some point.

MARTIN: That's right. Jamie, you said in the interview yesterday that Cyrus had always been interested in art. And that you think this is what got Aria interested in it as well, correct?

JAMIE: Yes. Cyrus liked to draw. He had multiple sketchbooks. I found a bunch of drawings from when he was a kid in his old boxes in the garage. I remember when we were dating, he drew me once. I still have that picture.

MARTIN: And what did he like to draw? People?

JAMIE: No, landscape stuff mostly. Like mountains and stuff.

MARTIN: Thank you, Jamie.

Chapter Fifty-Two

Interview Transcript #2.
Interviewee: Aria Ledger
Interviewer: Special Agent Martin Lance, FBI

࿐

MARTIN: Aria, can you confirm for me, Did you
    ever see your stepfather hit your mother?
ARIA: Yes.
MARTIN: How often did this happen?
No response.
MARTIN: Can you talk to me about the incidents?
No response.
MARTIN: Can you talk to me about how this made
    you feel?
No response.
MARTIN: Aria, do you remember the day before you
    found Marissa Currie's body in the woods,
    at Lookout Point?
ARIA: Yes.

MARTIN: Can you tell me what you did? What were
   you doing?
No response.
MARTIN: I understand that you took your mother's
   car without permission. Is that correct?
ARIA: Yes.
MARTIN: Why did you do this?
No response.
MARTIN: I understand you had taken your camera
   with you too. Is that correct?
No response.
MARTIN: There are pictures on your camera, taken
   that day, of the back of your stepfather's
   car at stoplights. Can you confirm you took
   those pictures?
No response.
MARTIN: Aria, were you following your stepfa-
   ther, Cyrus, on that day?
ARIA: Yes.
MARTIN: Why?
No response.
MARTIN: Aria, you didn't like your stepfather,
   did you?
ARIA: No.
MARTIN: Because he was mean to your mom?
No response.
MARTIN: Aria, I understand you seemed upset,
   according to your parents, in the days lead-
   ing up to you getting lost in the woods.
   Is this because you saw your stepdad phys-
   ically hurt your mom?
ARIA: Yes.

MARTIN: Did he ever hurt you?

ARIA: No.

MARTIN: Okay, back to the day you followed him. Did you follow him that day because you thought he was cheating on your mom? Because you'd heard her accuse him of that over and over?

ARIA: Yes.

MARTIN: You wanted to catch him. Give your mom proof so that, hopefully, she would break up with him.

ARIA: Yes.

MARTIN: So, that day, you followed your stepfather to Skull Lake?

ARIA: Yes.

MARTIN: Did he park his truck outside of Camper's Hollow?

ARIA: Yes.

MARTIN: Do you know if he saw you?

ARIA: No.

MARTIN: No, you don't know, or no, he didn't see you?

ARIA: Didn't see.

MARTIN: Did you get out of your mother's car?

No response.

MARTIN: Did you follow him into the woods?

No response.

MARTIN: Did he see you follow him?

ARIA: No.

MARTIN: Aria, did you see your stepfather talking to Marissa Currie?

ARIA: Yes.

MARTIN: Did you see your stepfather hurt Marissa
  Currie?
ARIA: Yes.
MARTIN: What did you do?
No response.
MARTIN: I understand you moved your mother's car?
  Maybe because you were scared? Panicked?
ARIA: Yes.
MARTIN: Did you go back to Lookout Point? Maybe
  to check on Marissa Currie, see if she was
  okay?
ARIA: Yes.
MARTIN: And you stayed with her, with Marissa
  Currie's body, until you were found later
  that day.
No response.
MARTIN: Why?
No response.
MARTIN: Because you were too scared to go home?
ARIA: Yes.
MARTIN: Because you thought your stepfather
  might do the same thing to you?
ARIA: Yes.
MARTIN: Aria, I can assure you now that your
  stepfather will never be able to hurt your
  mother or any other woman ever again. Now,
  if it's okay with you, I'd like to dis-
  cuss the paintings you did at the Dragonfly
  Clinic. Considering this new information,
  the red waves you painted didn't represent
  blood. Is that correct?
No response.

MARTIN: They represented your stepfather's scar, correct? Something that could easily identify him.

No response.

MARTIN: And this, Aria, was your way of telling someone what he did. A safe way, so that you might not be caught. Right?

ARIA: Yes.

MARTIN: Thank you, Aria.

ARIA: Thank you.

Chapter Fifty-Three

Beckett

Five days later . . .

The parking lot was empty, the building completely silent when I walked inside.

The reception area of the Dragonfly Clinic was dimly lit by a table lamp in the corner, a light that Stella insisted on leaving on at all times to ward off potential intruders. I laughed at this, assuming that a mental health clinic would be the last place an intruder would want to find themselves in.

Upstairs was completely dark, save for a dim glow in the corner office. It was just past six thirty in evening.

I closed the door behind myself, slipped the key that Jo had given me back into my pocket. With a handful of roses wrapped in brown kraft paper, I slowly ascended the staircase to the second floor.

Jo didn't see me at first. I paused, taking a second to soak in her sultry silhouette.

I felt my heart stutter as I watched her, the woman who I was totally and completely head over heels in love with. The woman I knew, without question, I would spend the rest of my life with.

There is a famous saying I've heard many times in my life: you never know how important something is to you until you've almost lost it.

Almost losing Jo had altered every fiber of my being, right down to my soul. It went deeper than realizing how important she was to me. It made me realize how important what we have *together* is.

The night I almost lost her reminded me of how unpredictable, precious, and fragile life is. I had experienced a lot of death while serving my country. But that was different. As a soldier, loss is expected. It is part of the job. We are trained and coached on how to deal with it.

Losing Jo is something I will never allow to happen.

Jo is my soulmate. She will be the mother of my children. She will be the woman that I will grow old with. I looked at her differently, not just as this exquisite, beautiful woman who I was falling in love with but as something to cherish. Something to grip onto, take the time to appreciate every single word that escapes from her lips, every inhale into her lungs.

She was sitting behind her desk, her face glowing in the light of the monitor. Her eyes were heavily shaded, brows squeezed together, mouth drawn downward. She wasn't staring at her computer screen but staring through it, obviously in deep thought. It is a look I've come to know very well. It is a time for me to offer an ear to listen and allow her to untangle the jumbled thoughts tumbling through her beautiful little head.

She saw me as I crossed that hallway to her office. I opened the door. She smiled before she even saw the roses.

"Hi," I said.

"Hi."

I lifted the flowers, and life sparked back into her tired eyes. I love to know I can do that.

She pushed back from her desk and crossed the room. Instead of taking the flowers, Jo stepped into my arms, rested her cheek against my chest, exhaled, and stilled. After slipping the roses on a chair next to the door, I wrapped my arms around her. For two solid minutes, we simply stood there, in silence, and just breathed together. Savored the solace only found in each other.

"You okay?" I whispered.

Jo took a deep inhale, then stepped back. "Yeah, I'm okay."

"How did it go?"

She blew out a dramatic exhale. "It went well—really well, actually. A lot better than I had anticipated."

"Do you want to talk about it?"

"Actually"—she looked at me—"yeah, I do."

I smiled. "All right, then, Dr. Bellerose where would you like me to sit?" I mocked, playing the part of a new patient.

She grinned and played along, gesturing professionally to the couch.

I sank onto the soft leather. Jo settled behind her desk and slid on her glasses.

I could smell the presence of another woman mingling with the leather. I pictured Jamie Ledger's face.

The days following the incident at the cabin were a whirlwind of interviews, sleepless nights, multiple retellings of the horrific story to friends and family—not to mention the arduous task of dealing with what remained of my cabin after it burned down. It had been a hell of a few days. Yet, in the midst of this chaos, Jo reached out to both Jamie and Aria, offering anything her clinic could do to help them weather the storm.

Aria was quick to accept the offer, spending a total of seven hours painting in the days following the incident. The first paintings were angry red slashes like the ones before, obviously a reflection of her anger at her stepfather. But gradually, as art therapy is meant to do, the paintings began to reflect more of an inward focus. Less anger, more exploration of emotions. According to Jo, it was a wonderful sign.

And to both my and Jo's surprise, Jamie was also open to receiving treatment. She began with therapy, meeting for an hour with both Mia and Jo. After, she requested to only meet with Jo, feeling a kindred spirit with the woman who had helped bring her evil husband to justice.

They had just completed their third session together, meeting after hours so Jamie didn't have to deal with the public.

"Give me the highlights?" I asked when Jo seemed to be struggling with how to regurgitate the last hour of her life. Understandably so. It was not only a challenge to get Jamie to open up but also for Jo to listen to behind-the-scenes details of the man who had tried to kill her.

Jo threaded her hands behind the back of her head, leaned back, and stared up at the ceiling.

Then, she began.

"As you know, Cyrus Ledger is currently going through an extensive psychiatric evaluation. He is still on a 5150 hold in the hospital. Apparently, his abuse as a child was way worse than anyone realized. Jamie said he's just sputtering out random horrific stories of his father abusing him. He appears to be totally disconnected from reality."

"Did she give details?"

A hint of sympathy sparked in Jo's eyes. "She said that someone on his medical team told her that Cyrus told them that when he was a kid, his father used to put his cigarettes out on the underside of his arm and also down his torso, along his rib cage. He's riddled with tiny, little scars, though most have faded over the years. He'd lied to Jamie about them when they'd first gotten together, saying they were scars from an old four-wheeler accident."

"No one at Cyrus's school saw this?"

"The scars were hidden under his clothes."

I shook my head. "I just don't get it, though. All that happened when he was a kid. What triggered it now? The man has worked at the fire station for how many years? A normal job, seemingly normal life. I mean, he literally saved lives for a living."

"Yeah, until he almost died—until he got third-degree burns over half his body." She took a deep breath. "You don't—not many do, really— understand what it does to someone's psyche to go through such a painful, traumatic event. One where they truly believe that they are going to die."

Amanda McKinney

"You know, Jo. You had a moment where you thought you were going to die."

"It's different. Cyrus's body was *literally* on fire. He was *literally* burning alive. I can't imagine . . . Mia spoke confidentially with one of the doctors who is evaluating him and was told that the working assumption is that this horrific event triggered the pain from his childhood, reignited his hatred for his father. Combining that with becoming disfigured is what sent him over the edge. There are a lot of studies on the lasting effects of childhood trauma, like being beaten daily. It literally changes the physiology of the brain. There is a lot left to learn."

"What about the victims, the women he targeted? Did he target those women specifically?"

"Jamie doesn't think so. And neither do I. We think he planned on doing something violent, simple as that. It could be that he just picked a town close enough to drive to at random and drove around looking for his victim. And that was that. It's not uncommon. If somebody decides they want to kill, they're going to kill. There doesn't have to be a deep-rooted 'she reminded me of my mom' scenario. He probably saw the opportunity of the woman alone with her baby and took it. And then did it again and again and again."

"So, they're considering the killings as premeditated."

"Absolutely."

"God that's fucked up."

"Yeah, it is. But that's not the focus now. Cyrus Ledger is in custody, and now we have to focus on the people he emotionally destroyed in the process. His wife and his stepdaughter. That's where my focus will be. Both Mia and I agree that we will do whatever we can, no fee, to help carry them through this."

"You're forgetting about someone in that scenario, Jo."

She frowned.

"You."

Jo looked down, her jaw clenched. She hated being the victim. And I hated seeing her like this.

I rose from the couch, walked around her desk, and knelt at her feet. I took her hands in mine.

"Jo, you are just as worthy as Jamie and Aria to receive therapy, time, and to allow yourself to cry, to hide under the covers for days or weeks. You are worthy enough to grieve and go through all the stages that they are going through."

Tears filled her eyes.

I squeezed her hands. "Baby, you are an amazing woman for being so driven to help these other two women, but you have to remember that you need time too. And that's what I'm here for. I am here to be your partner, to be your pillow when you need to rest, to be your sounding board when you need to speak, to be an ear when you need to just talk or just cry."

Jo burst into tears, crumbling into my arms. "Thank you," she sobbed. "I love you, Beckett. I do."

My heart skipped a beat. She said it back, finally.

Jo loves me.

Her tears came hard and fast. "I do love you, Beckett. I love you so much—but I am so terrified you're going to leave me."

"Let it go. Trust me. I'm not going to hurt you." I squeezed her tightly against my chest. "*Let me in*, Jo . . . let me in."

Together, we sat on the floor behind her desk, Jo curled into a ball in my lap, while I held her until she stopped crying. And in that moment, I vowed that I would do this, every day, for the rest of my life if I had to. I would never leave her. Because she is worth it.

Because love is worth it.

Chapter Fifty-Four

Jo

Unwrapping my scarf, I pushed through the doors of Mocha Mondays, a new coffee shop that had recently opened on the square.

A bubble of nerves crept up as I scanned the crowd. Melinda's hand shot up excitedly, her long porcelain fingers waving in the air. I smiled as I walked over.

"Mom, is that you?"

Melinda smiled and winked.

I slid into the booth, studying my mother's somewhat startling appearance.

Melinda Bellerose's hair wasn't curled to its usual perfection; her eyebrows were not painted on; her nail polish was chipped; and there was a ketchup stain—or was it barbecue sauce?—on her white sweater. She wore jeans instead of a tennis skirt and boots instead of heels.

Her eyes, however, were as clear as the blue sky outside, reflecting a mixture of both love and worry.

The waitress, a young twenty-something with bright-red lipstick and a massive nose ring, approached the table. "What can I get for you lovely ladies?"

I nodded for Mom to go ahead.

"I'll take a green tea with honey."

"Creamer?"

"No, thanks, dear."

The waitress turned to me.

"Do you have whiskey-barrel-cask coffee?"

"Sure do."

"That please, with cream and sugar."

The waitress scribbled down our order and disappeared behind the wooden counter.

"Thanks for meeting me," I said.

"Thanks for finally inviting me. I wasn't sure how long I was going to have to stick around until you did."

"Mom, I told you that you didn't need to stay, and you know you could have stayed at my house."

"Like usual?"

"Right."

"Well then, usual would have been me barging in without an invite."

An awkward moment passed.

"Have you talked to Leif?" I asked.

"He's in jail . . . I thought you knew—"

"Yeah, I know. I mean, have you visited him?"

"Yeah." Melinda looked down, genuine sadness washing over her face. "He's doing okay."

"He struck a deal, you know. Made a full confession, provided everything the Feds needed to basically ensure a slam-dunk case against Cyrus Ledger. He'll be out soon."

"I know."

"Do you really believe he didn't know what he was doing? That he really didn't know Cyrus was the Pollock Butcher, and that he was single-handedly helping cover up a local murder?"

"I think he was blinded by the money. I think he looked the other way and believed what he wanted to. I knew he had secrets—he always carried around this bag with him. I know now, it was filled with whatever drugs he was selling that day. But no, I never suspected he was involved in anything regarding the murders."

Another beat passed between us.

"Are you going to see him again?" I asked. "After he gets out?"

"No. We both agreed we need to go down our own paths."

I swallowed back an exhale of relief.

"Jo, I—"

"No, Mom. I'm sorry—"

"No, baby, please. Let me talk. I want to explain everything to you."

The waitress delivered our drinks, picked up on the tension, and hurried away.

"Six months ago," Melinda said, "I found a stash of pills."

My stomach rolled. "W—where?"

"Under your vanity, in the bathroom. I was looking for a face exfoliator and found six bottles of Xanax instead."

Heat rose to my cheeks, and I looked down.

"That's why I started visiting more and more and demanded to stay at your house instead of getting a hotel. I was worried about you, Jo."

"I didn't take them, Mom."

"I know. I realized that quickly because none were ever gone on my subsequent visits. The bottle would always be just as full as when I'd left. Regardless, I knew something was going on . . . it's my fault—I should have asked you directly. But, you know, you and I don't have the best or most open relationship."

She sighed, then continued.

"Listen. There's nothing I can say or do to show you how truly sorry I am for not being the mother you needed me to be—that every child needs and deserves. I . . . I always felt like I owed your father something for the way he swept me out of poverty, and because of that, my focus was always on him. He was my priority. I guess I felt like that was how I could pay him back. That was what he deserved."

"That's pretty fucked up, Mom."

She swallowed hard. "I know. Trust me, I know now. Compared to him, you were kind of an afterthought. And if I'm being totally honest, anytime you weren't being"—she used air quotes—"the perfect daughter, I felt like it was a reflection of me in you. And I didn't want to disappoint your father. So, I pushed you to be better so he would be proud of me."

I blinked, the gut-wrenching, honest admission jarring me.

"Anyway . . ." She sniffed back tears before taking a long sip of tea. A minute passed in silence.

"Mom, can I ask you something?"

"Of course."

"Why Leif? Why him? I mean, what was it about him that you liked?"

Melinda took a minute to consider her answer.

"He made me relax, or maybe I should say I felt relaxed around him. He complimented me often—I could tell he really liked me. And he's just . . ." She laughed. "He's sooo cool, you know. Like nothing is a big deal to him. He just goes with the flow. I just felt lighter because of him, his free-spirited personality."

"Can I respectfully tell you that I think you're wrong?"

Her brow cocked. "I think you just did."

I smiled. "Sorry." After a deep inhale, I began the assessment I'd spent the last few days putting together in my head. Thing was, thanks to Beckett, I realized how similar my mother and I were. How my faults mirrored hers and vice versa. "Here's where I'm going with this. I don't think you liked Leif because of his personality. I think you liked him because you knew you were better than him."

"That's rude."

"Well, by society's standards, I mean. He was a drug dealer who gambled on the weekends and paid for his groceries with food stamps. No education, no real job, nothing really to look up to."

Melinda stared at me, her wheels turning, and I continued.

"Leif was a confidence boost for you—that's all. Think about it, Mom. The issue, deep down to the core of it, is your insecurity. Low self-esteem. You grew up being ashamed of being poor, then spent your entire adult life feeling like you owed Dad for *allowing* you into his world of wealth. You felt like you had to repay him, which means you didn't feel like you alone—*you*—were a worthy enough payment, so to speak. And think about this with me—you were so insecure that you looked at my mistakes as a reflection of your younger self. It all boils down to a lack of confidence and self-worth. It's my issue, too, you know." I looked to the floor in a moment of vulnerability. "Beckett—"

"Oh my God, I love him so much for you, Jo."

"I know, Mom. Hang on, I'm not done." I smiled. "Beckett has really made me aware of this fact. That all my issues are rooted in a deep-seated feeling of inadequacy. A lack of self-confidence. I, Mom, have confidence issues—and so do you. And this is where we need to start. We need to totally reset, learn to love ourselves."

"How the hell do you learn to love yourself?"

I shrugged. "I assume this is the first step."

She smiled. "God, I love you. I really do, Jo."

"I love you, too, Mom."

We simultaneously sniffed away an onslaught of tears.

"Anyway," I said, wiping away a tear. "So, I was thinking. We should do something together, like a hobby."

"I love it. I was thinking about getting into sailing—"

"No. No, Mom, good Lord. I'm not talking about totally useless pursuits of leisure. I'm talking something meaningful. I thought we could volunteer together."

"Volunteer?"

"Yeah. There's a soup kitchen next to the grocery store. I know they're looking for people to deliver meals to people who need them. It sounds selfish, but it feels good to help people, right? We should start there. It makes us feel good about ourselves, and others feel good too."

"A win-win for confidence all the way around."

"Exactly. And you like decorating, right? Maybe you could offer your services for free to single moms and help them make the most of their space."

Melinda lit up. "That's a good idea. I know how hard it is to be a single mom. I could help get them clothes and stuff, too, like nice things for their jobs."

"Yeah, Mom, that sounds awesome." I smiled, and Mom matched it. "And the other thing, I thought we could get into tai chi. I've read a few articles about it. It's apparently huge for reducing stress and depression and for increasing your stamina, mood, and energy." I took a deep breath. "I think this could help us, too, our relationship. Learning it together, this peaceful, intentional de-stressor."

"What a wonderful thing to share."

"Yeah, that's what I was thinking too."

"I'm sorry, Jo."

"I'm sorry too."

"Can we just start over?"

"I think we just did."

∽

An hour later, I pulled up the driveway.

The yard looked beautiful under the late-afternoon sunlight, long shadows stretching next to spears of golden light. The ice from the record-breaking storm had melted, and soon spring would be on the horizon.

Beckett's truck was parked under the massive pine tree that hugged the garage. The spot had become *his* spot—just as the right side of my sink and the left side of my closet had also become *his* spots.

It happened slowly, really. Organically. Beckett didn't leave my side in the days following Cyrus's arrest, including during the night. Eventually, however—as the saying goes—life must go on. Beckett had meetings he couldn't miss, and I had a commitment to clients. But at the end of every day, Beckett was there, by my side, offering me a smile and the embrace of two big muscular arms. Some evenings we would laugh, some I would cry, and others we would just sit in comfortable silence watching cheesy '80s movies and eating oversalted popcorn.

I learned that my comfort in Beckett—in *us*—came in the form of action. Not in continuous verbal reminders by him that he will never leave me or hurt me. Beckett never pressed me to open up; instead, he was simply *there*. And in simply being there, trust began to form.

Through this crazy experience, I have learned that my personal growth cannot be dependent on someone else. The power to change resides in me—and only me. I cannot fully trust someone else until I learn to trust myself. I have to trust myself to make good choices. I have to trust my judgment.

I do not need pills. I do not need reinforcement from my mother. I do not *need* Beckett.

Because I, alone, am enough.

A smile caught me as Beckett's silhouette passed by the window.

I rolled my truck into the garage, grabbed my to-go cup of coffee and my purse, and made my way into the house.

A fresh bouquet of flowers sat in the middle of the kitchen island, his cell phone and keys next to the mail basket. His scent lingered in the air as if he'd just passed by, clean soap tinged with the fresh leathery scent of his cologne. Beckett must have just gotten home from work.

Home . . .

Beckett emerged from the laundry room, a basket full of towels in his arms, a smile on his face. "How did it go?"

He set the laundry on the couch and met me in the center of the living room. I took his hands, and he smiled with a twinkle of suspicion.

"I love you, Beckett."

"I love you, baby."

I did love him, so very much. And while, yes, admitting this fact still, on occasion, sent a rush of nervous butterflies into my stomach, the thought of allowing him to walk out of my life was even worse.

Beckett was mine. My friend, my partner, my soulmate. There was no question. He and I.

It would be he and I.

Always, and forever.

I inhaled, and my heart skipped a beat before the words even escaped my lips. "It's time. Time to start over."

Beckett's hands squeezed mine. He leaned down and kissed my forehead, my cheek, and finally, my lips. "Are you sure?"

"Yes."

"Okay. I'm ready. I'm here to hold your hand through every second of it."

Together, Beckett and I gathered every single prescription pill bottle in my house, in my car, and from my hiding spot under the floorboards in the kitchen.

Together, we drove to my office and emptied the safe I kept filled under my desk, then to the gym, where I kept a bottle stashed in my locker.

Together, we bagged up the pill bottles and dropped them off at the police station for proper disposal.

I'll never forget the feeling the moment the bag dropped from my fingertips, the same moment Beckett's hand squeezed my other.

"And the cigars?" he asked with a smirk.

"I like my cigars, Beckett. I do."

He nodded. "I thought you might say that."

To my complete shock, he pulled one of my coveted cigarillos from his pocket, lifted it to his lips, and fired up the tip, right there in the Skull Hollow Police Department parking lot. He inhaled, and while rolling the smoke around in his mouth, lifted his brows and canted his head to the side—*not bad*.

My mouth gaped open with a dopey, shocked smile.

He handed the cigarillo to me.

Still grinning, I inhaled, then smiled as I blew out the smoke. And it was glorious. Not just the taste or the buzz but the compromise. The—his—willing acceptance of *one* of my faults. Another validation that I was good enough for him, sharp edges and all.

Beckett pulled me to himself and kissed me, despite the hoots and whistles from the passing cars. With a sparkle in our eyes and a grin on our lips, we turned away from the station and took the first step into my new self, my new life.

The one where I am good enough. Where I choose which path I take.

And for the first time in my life, the path I chose was wide enough for two people, not just one.

CONNECT WITH AMANDA

Text AMANDABOOKS to 66866 or go to her website, www.amandamckinneyauthor.com, to sign up for Amanda's newsletter and get the latest on new releases, promos, and freebies.

ABOUT THE AUTHOR

Amanda McKinney is the author of more than twenty romantic-suspense, mystery, and action and adventure novels. Her books have received more than fifteen literary awards and nominations. She lives in Arkansas with her handsome husband, two beautiful boys, and three obnoxious dogs and enjoys hiking, daydreaming, and very dirty martinis (on occasion, all three at the same time).